HOLLY AND THE NOBODIES

Ben Pienaar

A HellBound Books Publishing LLC Book
Austin TX

Ben Pienaar

**A HellBound Books LLC
Publication**
Copyright © 2021 by HellBound Books Publishing LLC
All Rights Reserved

Cover and art design by
HellBound Books Publishing LLC

www.hellboundbookspublishing.com

Printed in the United States of America

Bibliography

Short Story Collection: Worlds Without Light (available on kindle)

'Screams for Stargirl' in Dark Moon Digest #35 and in Years Best Hardcore Horror Volume 5
'Fear' In Darkfuse Magazine
'Fair Trade' In Daylight Dims anthology
'Muse' in Death Throes Magazine
'Spider Men' in Great Old Ones: Bugs Anthology
'Halo' in What has two heads, four eyes and no table manners? Anthology
'Small World' in Horrified Press, Biohazard Anthology

Dedication

This book is dedicated to Lucy, Jay, and of course Mom and Dad. Thanks, guys.

HOLLY AND THE NOBODIES

Lonely Girl

1
Hollow Heart

The great house in which Holly Anderson lived had always been aligned with her soul. When she was happy, its halls were bright and spacious and the kitchen smelled of fresh baked bread, and sunlight shone even in rooms without windows. When she was angry, the floors were splintery, and glass was apt to break. Lately, though, it hadn't changed much, and when the first days of winter came, the whole place had been nothing but groaning wood and darkness for a whole season.

Even Mr. Stretch, dangling from the chandelier in the lounge on the second floor, couldn't cheer her up. He twisted around the bulbs and pulled his mouth with his fingers until it reached from one ear to the other, then did a clumsy flip and landed, hands outstretched, on the dining room table. 'Ta Da!' Ordinarily such acrobatics would have had her in uncontrollable giggling fits, but today she scowled at him until his loopy grin vanished. "What's wrong, puddin pie?"

"Don't call me that anymore. I'm too old for that stupid name."

"Okey doke." He slid off the table onto his gangly legs, but she brushed past him and went over to the window. It was the largest in the house, taking up half the wall and affording a panoramic view of the front gardens, the long gravel driveway, and the heavy iron gates. It was stormy and the rain fell hard, as it had since summer began. Holly wished she could step out of those gates and feel what the weather was like in the real world, but the thought terrified her as much as it enticed her. "Why don't you care about the weather?" she said.

Stretch leaned against the table and scratched his head. "Gee, I guess I don't know. Rain, hail, or shine doesn't bother me."

She sighed. "You don't care because you're not really alive, are you?" The last two words were more an accusation than a question, and Stretch recoiled, his eyes registering a hint of fear. "Well, sure I am, Holly bee. I'm as real as anyone." He rapped his knuckles on the window. "See?"

"I guess." She folded her arms, appraising him for a minute. She'd given him his name because of his disproportionately long limbs and digits, and the way his face moved when he spoke, his skin flexing and tightening as though each expression was a conscious effort. Everything about his body from his spider legs to his floppy neck said stretch, but she didn't like any of it one bit. Nothing she made ever seemed to come out right, somehow. Everything she created was an almost, a nearly, no matter how hard she tried.

Except out there. She turned back to the window and looked past the miserable rain and clouds that surrounded the house, and over to the street beyond, where sun shone on the asphalt and people drove and walked and talked. Real living people, with their own lives and thoughts and feelings. This house was only on the outskirts of the suburbs, but Twisty Lane was a pleasant route through the pines – and the view of Templeton was spectacular – so people often chose to walk it. An old man passed by and glanced her way, but he would see only what Holly wanted him to see; a stately well-kept mansion, home to a stately well-kept family, and nothing of note besides.

Stretch put a tentative hand on her shoulder. "You look lonely, Holly. Why don't ya let Miss Pinky out of the shed and we can all play? Or explore the gardens? Hey, you could even make a puppy dog if you wanted!"

"I don't want a puppy dog," she snapped. "And Miss Pinky has to stay in the shed three more days, you know that." Pinky had called her a Silly Girl when she told her about her dream to leave the house one day, so Holly had to put her in the shed with Greeny and his rusty tools. She didn't want to – she loved Pinky, but it had hurt her feelings, like spikes piercing her heart. It was only right that Pinky should have to feel the same pain.

Stretch seemed genuinely worried. "Well Gee, Holly, I just want to help. What's got ya down so bad?"

She shrugged, guilty for snapping at him before. "I'm just lonely, Stretch. Everything's so hollow here. Don't you ever get hollow inside?" He looked blank. Of course, he doesn't – he's not like you. He's not like 'them'. None of them are, not Greeny or Pinky or anyone.

As if to prove her thought, a boy and girl just a few years older than Holly reached the top of Twisty Lane and passed by the front gates, talking animatedly. Something about them struck Holly right to her aching heart. It was the girl – a dark haired, rosy cheeked beauty. It was in the way she smiled as she listened, and then said something that made the boy laugh. And it was in the way the boy looked at her, shy and eager at the same time. He was handsome, too – tall and healthy, like the pictures of the princes in the books she'd read in her library. Holly felt a twinge of jealousy.

"I want to meet them. I want friends like that, real friends."

Stretch looked wounded. "Well, I dunno, Holly – don't you think that's dangerous? There's no control out there, no way to stay safe. The house can't protect you if you go too far away."

She didn't reply. The couple had reached Holly's front gate and had stopped in front of it, the boy pointing at something he saw on the house – probably one of the gargoyle statues on the balcony. Holly watched them with narrowed eyes, frustration and desire boiling inside her, and then an idea entered her mind, so clear and simple she couldn't believe she hadn't thought of it immediately. In that instant, a smile that could rival one of Stretch's own lit up her face and she turned to pull him into an embrace.

Stretch laughed and wrapped his ropy arms around her, surprised. Whoa "Woah, there, what's with the sudden change?"

"I'm sorry about before, Stretch. I'm going to have friends after all – real living friends from outside!'"

"But… But, Hollster, what about leaving the house?"

"I'm not going to leave the house, silly," she said, slapping him on the arm. She turned to look back out the window in time to see the couple start back on down the lane. For the first time she noticed they were in school uniform, and the bags on their backs said Templeton High. She raised a finger and drew a heart in the misted glass so that it framed them.

"I'm going to bring them here."

For the first time in months, the rain slowed to a drizzle, and Stretch gave her his widest grin yet.

2
Strange Girl

James took Twisty Lane to school for the second time, even though it meant he had to wake up twenty minutes earlier for the longer route. He had a feeling it would lift his mood for the day ahead, and he was right; the morning sun lit up all of Templeton, green gardens and fields flooded with mist, and the air up here was a hundred times fresher – each breath filling him up like a drink of iced water.

And there was the house.

He wasn't sure what it was that had caught his attention when he and Alex had passed by yesterday, but something had. Maybe it was the stone gargoyles that Alex had loved so much with their oversized jaws and long tongues, or maybe it was the house itself, its vine curtained walls and gothic structure appealing to the artistic side of him. Alex had laughed when he'd said it reminded him of Hogwarts, but it did, and when he came to it again it still did; now he found himself at the gate once again, admiring the place, wondering what kind of people might live there.

He wasn't sure how long he'd been standing there when a girl appeared at the side of the gate. "Hello," she said brightly.

It took him a second to work out where she'd come from, but then he saw the fountain to the left of the driveway and figured she must have been playing around there. "Um. Hi," he said. She was pretty enough – although a few years younger than him – but her appearance was so strange that it jarred him: prim and proper with a neat white dress, sunhat, and knee-high socks. She reminded him of an English schoolgirl from an Enid Blyton book.

"My name's Holly," she said. "What's yours?"

"James." He half extended one hand and then changed his mind and stuck it in his pocket instead. "Do you live here?"

She rolled her eyes. "Duh. What about you?" She had a high, strong voice, and he immediately picked her as a girl used to getting her way. It made sense, given where she was being brought up. She was probably spoilt rotten. He waved his hand in the vague direction of the valley. "Down in Templeton. Dove Street. I'm just going to school now."

"Oh." She took a sharp breath and looked down at her feet, her face falling. "Don't you want to talk to me?"

"No! I mean, it's not you or anything. It's just that I'll get in trouble if I don't turn up."

"Yes, that makes sense. They'd miss you if you didn't go." And then, as an afterthought, "And your parents too, I imagine."

"Right. So, I should…"

"Can't you come in just for a minute?" she said, leaning up against the bars of the enormous front gates and making them rattle. "I'm never allowed out, you know. I never have anyone to talk to."

"Oh. You're home schooled?"

She paused, then nodded.

"Uh, I kind of have to go, or I'll be late. Sorry?"

She pouted comically, then brightened when he added, "maybe next time?"

"Yes, please. Nice to meet you, James." This time it was she who extended a small pale hand. She left it limp in his grasp, so that it was like shaking a dead fish.

"You too, Holly. I guess I'll see you around." And then, feeling painfully awkward, he pulled his pack over his shoulders and headed on down the road at a fair clip, determined not to look back. He did, of course, and she was still there a minute later, face pressed against the bars and a dreamy look on her face, watching him go.

When he related the episode to Alex Miller in Health Class an hour later, she stared at him with an expression of comical disgust. "You're such an asshole!"

"What? Why?"

"All she wanted was someone to talk to for five minutes! Can you imagine being stuck in the same house all day for your whole life?"

"Yeah, but have you seen that house?"

She sighed. "And you just walked away. She probably had a crush on you too, and you killed her dreams."

"Ha ha."

No one overheard their conversation. The whole class was chattering. Paper planes were flying, and phones were out, but Mr. Davidson stood resolutely in front of the chalkboard, thick glasses mirroring the chaos before him, and continued his lecture unperturbed. "At this point the male sperm will enter the egg, which is many, many times larger, and the process begins."

James hunched over his latest artwork, a full-page project in the middle of his exercise book. He was a compulsive sketcher, outlining and doodling at school and then filling up his bedroom walls with his own pictures in pastel, watercolours, and anything else he could get his hands on. When people asked him (unless it was his father) what he wanted to do "when he grew up" he told them an animator or a cartoonist, but the truth was he only wanted to draw these things for himself – these surreal images that always seemed to emerge from inside him like blood from a blister. This one was of an eyeless Alien busting out of a pregnant woman's belly while she screamed in agony. He'd written a caption at the bottom: Still better than school.

"I just got a weird vibe from her," he said.

"Of course, you did, you're probably the first person she's spoken to besides her parents all her life. God, who knows? Maybe she's been abused, you know? Like they whip her with sticks and make her clean the house and stuff. She probably wanders the garden all the time just to get away from them." Alex pondered this for a minute, frowning. It was one of the things James liked about her, the way she could get a sense of someone. The stories she made up about them were never true, but they always made him see people in a different light.

She gave him a nudge, making his pencil tear the paper. "She's a damsel in distress, James. She's looking for her knight in shining armour to come rescue her. Was she hot?"

"Jesus, she was like, twelve." He searched his pencil case for a red so he could bring life to the blood in his picture. Davidson went on. "It is especially important to wear protection, as diseases can be passed on very easily. Some diseases you can obtain through sexual intercourse are AIDS, syphilis, gonorrhoea…"

"Anyway, you could have talked to her for a few minutes."

"Yeah, I guess."

"She's probably gonna cry herself to sleep. Maybe you were her last desperate attempt for escape. Oh, God, what if she kills herself? Could you live with that?"

"Alright, alright, I'll say hi next time. If you're so concerned, why don't you go up there?"

"Yeah, well, maybe I will. I got two free periods at the end of the day, maybe I'll take a walk up. I'll bet she's lonely."

"Or I could skip my last two as well, and we could do something after school?"

She brushed a strand of hair out of her face, a habit so ingrained that he'd seen her do it even when her hair had been too short to brush back. "I can't," she said. "If I don't study tonight, I'm going to fail Bio."

"Come on. Just wing it. You know Grey Tide just came out the other day." Grey Tide was a movie about a blood borne parasite that turned people insane. Horror movies had always been irresistible bait for Alex, but not today. She shook her head. "We can't all be like you, James. I actually have to try to get good grades. My parents threatened to ground me if I get worse than a B."

"I can help you study."

She gave him a look. They both knew that if he went to her house to help her study, they would both end up playing Plants vs. Zombies on her computer, or going out and watching Grey Tide, or talking, or doing anything except what he really wanted to do. Stop playing games, man. Just say something real. Ask her out. Tell her you love her.

But he didn't, and their conversation was interrupted by Mr. Davidson a minute later, when he pulled a string of condoms and a bundle of bananas from his desk, his face completely deadpan, and told them it was time for the practical part of the lesson.

"Hey, Davidson," Danny Trio yelled from the back, "Can I have some spares?" The class erupted with laughter, and any remaining semblance of order went out the window.

Later, when they parted ways – James to his dreaded Chemistry and Alex to English- she promised to catch the movie with him on the weekend, and his spirits lifted a little. That would be the place, he thought. That would be the time.

But by then, she'd already be gone.

3
Threshold

Alex was aware of being followed almost as soon as she left school.

It was something not so much seen as felt: a prickling pressure on the back of her neck. She looked over her shoulder several times as she made her way up Dryden street and then turned onto Twisty Lane, seeing nothing each time but still feeling it, as impossible to ignore as a mosquito's persistent whine.

You're being ridiculous. It's the middle of the day. You shouldn't have watched The Shining last night. One of the scenes – when the groundskeeper showed up just in time to have Jack Nicholson bury an axe in his back – still haunted her. That was how she felt now, as if the next tree or bush lining the sidewalk concealed a crazed murderer, and she would only have time to hear a foot land on the asphalt before a heavy blade divided her spine in two.

She pushed the thought away and hurried on, determined to see the strange house on her way home. Since James had told her about his encounter that morning,

Alex had been dreaming up all kinds of horrible possibilities concerning the strange girl. She imagined being trapped in an isolated mansion with only her parents for company. The idea was a kind of horror all on its own. God, she wouldn't be able to take a breath without someone judging its quality.

A tree branch creaked loudly just behind her and she spun on the spot, air catching in her lungs. Had something moved there, behind that letterbox? No, it was just the chill wind that had picked up as the sun went behind a thick cloud. Okay, tonight, the scariest thing you get to watch is The Little Mermaid.

By the time she reached the top of the hill the sun had returned, accompanied by a light drizzle. She stopped and looked out over Templeton, where long shadows passed across the sunlit streets so far below. Everything smelled like rain and pine needles, and she closed her eyes, savouring it.

There wasn't a soul on the lane with her, and the wind lulled, so when she heard the scrape of shoes on asphalt directly behind her, there was no mistaking it; the axeman coming for her neck.

This time she saw the culprit – a little girl – scrambling up the high brick wall across the road. A white skirt billowing in the wind revealed skinny pale legs. The girl toppled over the wall, but she glanced over her shoulder at the last instant and Alex caught sight of a face that didn't make sense: black eyes with no lids, a flat lipless mouth, and no nose at all; porcelain skin like a doll. Then she was gone.

What the hell? Alex stared at the top of the wall for a long time, trying to decide whether she'd really seen what she thought she had, before she realised where she was. The big black gate was a bit further down the lane, and when she looked over, she noticed that it wasn't locked, as it had been when she'd come past with James. It was, in fact, cranked open just wide enough for someone to slip through.

Forget this, just get out of here and go read about mitochondria or the endocrine system or something. Alex hurried past the gate, not intending to break stride for a moment until she was at her front door, when a small voice called after her. "Please don't go, Miss. She's sorry she scared you."

When Alex turned, she was relieved to find that this girl did not have a porcelain face. Judging by her straw sunhat and neat dress, it had to be the same one James had seen. Her expression was every bit as pitiful as Alex had imagined. She stopped. "I'm sorry… what did you say?"

"My little sister. She was playing spy games, that's all. She didn't mean to scare you. She's very shy."

And very nimble, Alex thought, considering the speed at which the tiny girl had scaled the steep wall. The girl watched her, head cocked to one side, half hanging from the gate. "My name's Holly," she said, and then before Alex could reply – "You're very pretty."

"Oh, thanks. So are you. I like your dress."

The girl smiled, and this expression was somehow more pitiable than the frown she'd had a moment ago. Alex approached the gate across the quiet road, scolding herself for overreacting. She looked up at the looming house, its windows dark and empty, and wondered what kind of people would raise two girls in that lonely place.

"How come you're out of school?" Holly asked. "It's still three hours before the last bell rings," and then, again before Alex could answer: "Are you James's girlfriend?"

Alex laughed. "No. We just kind of hang out together." She brushed her hair back and craned her neck, trying to see if the sister was hiding somewhere behind Holly. The garden was empty except for a well-kept vegetable patch and a line of oaks along the far wall. "He said you seemed lonely, though. I thought I'd come up and make sure you were okay."

"Oh, that's nice. I suppose you've got somewhere to go, too."

Alex was tempted to agree – she did have to study, after all. But she knew she'd never live it down if James found out, after all her scolding, that she'd left the poor girl alone because she'd got the creeps. You're the horror buff, aren't you? Creepy girls and big old houses are supposed to be your bread and butter. "No, that's alright. We can talk, if you want."

Holly brightened, her pout vanishing like a magic trick. "Really?"

Alex couldn't shake the feeling she was being manipulated but found herself nodding all the same. "Sure. What do you want to talk about?"

"Do you want to play spies with us?" Then, frowning, "No, my sister will be too shy."

"Oh? What's her name?"

A blank look passed across Holly's face. "It's… Sister. Sis for short."

"Your sister's name is Sister?"

"Yup."

"Huh. What are the odds of that?"

Holly stepped back, pulling the heavy gate open with an ear-splitting squeal. "Never mind her, she was calling me names anyway. She can hide in the bushes if she wants. Why don't I show you all around my house!"

"Will your parents mind?"

She shook her head, but said nothing, waiting expectantly in her driveway for Alex to enter the grounds. Alex looked back at the pretty view behind her and felt the slightest tug of unease; a desire to turn and hurry on down the street and forget all about the house on Twisty Lane, until perhaps she saw it on the news a month from now in the headlines: Two Young Girls Murdered by Evil Parents. Or her over-active imagination prompted: Parents Horribly Slaughtered by Devil Daughters.

But then she turned and saw Holly's hopeful gaze, the poor girl so desperate for attention and someone to play with, and she knew her fears were unfounded. She smiled. "Okay, I'll come in. And if your sister comes out of the bushes, we can even play spies."

And, chuckling at the look of unbridled joy on Holly's face, she stepped through the large gates and started down the long driveway.

A small white blur shot through Alex's peripheral vision, and a moment later the gates screamed shut behind her. She turned, but the world was swirling beneath her feet of its own accord. She slipped in the gravel and came down hard on her side. *What the hell is…* She rolled onto all fours and vomited, gripping the grass in a vain effort to stop the earth moving. It was like being on the world's worst roller coaster. There was a howling sound in her ears, and tears flowed down her cheeks unbidden. *Am I dying?*

Then, just when she thought she was about to black out, the hellish ride slowed to a stop and her senses returned. She sucked in a shaky breath and wiped her eyes with one hand. Holly took hold of her elbow and pulled her onto wobbly legs. "Are you okay? Do you need some water?"

"No, no, I'll be –" she swallowed. "I'll be fine. Just had a – a really bad head rush or something. Maybe…" She'd been about to say *maybe I didn't get enough to eat today* when she looked up, blinking, and saw where she was. Or rather, where she wasn't.

Holly smiled proudly and stood back as if admiring an artwork. "It's beautiful, isn't it?" She said. "It's all mine, you know. Everything belongs to me, even the house and everyone who lives in it." She paused, cocking her head to one side as she'd done earlier.

"Just like you."

4
The Monster Game

The house was not the house: it was a gothic ruin of stone and wood with moss growing in the cracks and windows like shining black eyes, watching her. The garden was not the garden: it was an ocean of flowers, from roses to tulips to thorny weeds, stretching all the way to the oaks that lined the perimeters. In the space of a minute, even the sky had changed from overcast to clear and sunny, with the softest breeze. In an instant, nothing about the house looked the way it had before Alex had stepped through the front gates.

Alex's gaze settled last on Holly, who was standing back and watching her carefully. "Are you okay?" she said.

I'm in another world. I'm losing my mind. I'm dreaming… I'm dreaming. She had fallen and hit her head, after all. It had to be one of those intense visions people reported sometimes after being knocked out or going into a coma.

She took a deep breath, and the smell of daffodils filled her nostrils. Grassy pathways wound through the flowers, one of which led to the front door – though at the moment Alex would much rather have headed the other way. Nothing felt right. "Am I awake?" she said.

"You'll be okay. It just takes some getting used to, that's all." Still smiling, Holly took Alex's wrist in her soft hand and pulled her along one of the pathways. Alex went in a daze, waiting to see something so ridiculous she'd be forced to accept it was a dream. Instead, she was struck by the realness of the sensations all around her. As Holly chatted away, she allowed herself, as James so often advised her, to chill. Whatever was happening, she'd just have to ride it out and wake up in the ER or bed or whatever.

"I'll show you round the back garden. I've got lots of interesting things there. We can play with whatever you want, but I think you'll want to play the Monster Game most, once you try it. Do you like hunting? Never mind. We could fish in the pond instead – I swear I saw a shark in there the other day!" She laughed brightly, and Alex smiled, relaxing a little more. Whatever dream this was, it wasn't so bad.

As they rounded the vine-draped west corner of the house, the flowers gave way to a grassy clearing at the side of the house. A crystal blue pond lay at the far end, with a rock formation and a waterfall surrounded by elms. A forest of ashes and elephant-ear plants blocked her view of the west wall, and a dirt path at the far end of the clearing led through thicker undergrowth to an old shed.

Holly stopped in the middle of the clearing and Alex spun in a slow circle, looking from the magnificent vine and stone-walled house to the lush greens and browns all around her. "It's beautiful," she said. Holly made a curtsey, touching the hem of her dress to the ground. Alex noticed that she wasn't doing it ironically – she'd actually been taught to do that, like some fairy-tale princess.

"Thank you," she said. "I made a lot of it myself. Not the pond – Mother did that."

Alex detected something like venom in Holly's voice at the word Mother, but she said nothing, and after a moments silence Holly said, "Shall we play, then?"

"Sure, yeah. Whatever you want… Hey, there's your sister!" but the girl had darted around the corner in the whirl of a white dress as soon as Alex had caught sight of her. Holly waved a dismissive hand. "Never mind her. Just let her watch if she wants to. She likes it better that way."

"Oh, okay." Alex shrugged off her school jacket, marvelling at the heat. It had been chilly less than an hour ago, but now the wind on her arms was a blessing. She breathed deeply, closing her eyes for a moment. Just a dream. "Okay. So, how do you play?"

Holly clapped her hands with glee and took Alex by the wrist again, this time leading her across the clearing to the shed – an ancient thing made of dense wood and stone instead of metal. There was a window in the side, dusty and cobwebbed, but the shed was so shaded by the trees around that she couldn't see in.

The double doors groaned in a pleasant way as Holly pulled them aside. She motioned for Alex to enter.

The smell of flowers and freshly mown grass vanished as soon as Alex stepped inside, replaced by the evil stench of butchery and rust. A work bench took up most of the middle of the room, stained by varnish and cut in a thousand places. Every inch of wall space was taken up by tools of every kind except electrical, and many more leaned in the corners and lay under the narrow desk that lined the left wall. A tall wardrobe stood against the back. It was padlocked.

"Wow. Is this your dad's workshop or something?" Alex said. One of the tools, a hand shovel with a hook at the end, was swinging on its nail and she reached up to steady it. Her finger came away stained with grime.

"Yes. Mostly Greeny uses it, though. He's our gardener. You can meet him later."

"Okay, cool," she said, thinking I wonder how late it is. And on the tail of that: Maybe it's only been a single second. Or maybe I am in a coma and it's been three years. "Uh, so where's the game? Is it in the wardrobe?"

Holly laughed in the same way she might have read it out of a book, pronouncing each ha by itself: ha ha ha! A high, polite laugh. "It's not a board game, silly. It's a pretend game."

"Oh. What now?"

"First, we pick weapons." By way of demonstration, she turned and took stock of the wall behind her, one thoughtful finger on her lips, and then decided on a rust-speckled hand axe, which she removed from its spot.

"Okaaaaay. Are you sure your Dad won't mind?"

"He doesn't have to know. It can be our secret. Just like friends?"

Alex smiled. "Right."

She thought for only a minute before deciding on her own tool (weapon?): a pair of garden shears with blunt edges but sharp points. As soon as she'd selected it, the room darkened, and a clunk sounded as Holly closed the double doors behind them. When Alex turned around, Holly raised a finger to her lips.

"Why'd you do that?" Alex whispered.

"So, the Monster doesn't get out."

"What Monster? I don't even know how to play, yet."

"It's easy. The Monster is guarding a chest of silver. We are warrior princesses, and we want the treasure, so we have to kill the Monster."

"Oh. Are you sure it's safe?" It was coming together, now. Holly's sister must have circled around somehow and hidden in the wardrobe. When Alex opened it, she'd jump out and scare her. Funny, sure, but not if Alex had been more gullible.

"Its safe," Holly said.

"Huh. Let me guess, I have to be the one to open the wardrobe, don't I?"

Holly nodded, unable to hide the smile from her face. "Don't worry. I'm on your side. We'll get the Monster together."

Alex's neck itched as she moved to the wardrobe door and Holly stepped up behind her, holding a small hand-axe. What am I doing here? But Holly had given her the key to the wardrobe and now Alex was pushing it into the lock with her left hand, her right gripping the shears tightly. Jesus, this is so irresponsible. I should tell her parents.

The lock clicked open.

She stepped aside, pulling the doors open, ready to let off a fake scream when the strange little girl in a white dress popped out and yelled ta-da! With a mischievous grin on her face.

The door swung open.

The thing that lurched from the back of the wardrobe was barely human. Half pig, half girl, and mostly dead, covered in liquid sores and cuts, it fell forward. Alex took a step back, wanting to scream but somehow unable. It (she?) gurgled something that might have been words but for the black sludge that oozed from the corners of its mouth. It soon became apparent, however, that the pig-thing was far too dead to have anything to say. Alex bent under its weight and half stepped, half fell against the shed's wall. Points and blades and handles dug into her back as she struggled to hold the dead weight. Two brown eyes glistened lifelessly in her face and the black drool dripped onto her face. The smell was unbearable –

something sweet like fermenting fruit but earthy as a grave. Holly squealed in mock disgust from the back of the shed. "EEEWW!"

Alex was sure that she had to be having a psychotic episode. She imagined herself lying at the front gate that very moment, seizing and drooling while Holly blubbered through the phone to the ambulance.

Then, spurred on more by the thought of suffocating beneath this behemoth, Alex pushed the shears up into the soft pig's belly and heaved with strength she didn't know she had. A foul gas escaped from the wound, unloading more of the offensive sludge, but the shears gave Alex new leverage, and she was able to push the mountainous corpse to one side. Holly yelped and jumped back as it crumpled onto the floor in front of her. She scrunched up her face. "That's gross."

"What..." Alex let go of the shears and got up on shaking legs. "What is that?" Though now that she was able to see the dead pig in daylight, she realised that she was really asking the wrong question. She should have asked, among other things, what had happened to it . The greying flesh of the dead body had been heinously brutalised, and something about what had been done to it suggested the wounds were made pre-death. Torn beds where fingernails should have been, for example, and nails that had been hammered down the length of the backbone like spines on a stegosaurus. And, most tellingly of all, the words DIRTY PIG cut deeply into the back of its neck.

Holly raised her eyes to meet Alex's, disgust transforming into something hollow. "That's what happens if you aren't nice to me," she said in a plain voice. "I wanted you to see."

There was a beat of silence in which Alex processed this. Then, in a burst of speed that shocked her as much as it did Holly, she burst out of the shed door and down the path. A white face peered at her from the foliage as she raced through the clearing, appearing as no more than a blur through her tears. Holly called after her, a petulant wail: "Aleeeeeeex don't go!"

Please, oh please, let me wake up! I can't stay in this place. As she ran across the clearing, the garden changed around her. The grass and surrounding trees grew at an alarming rate, encroaching on all sides, so that by the time she reached what had once been a neat pathway in a field of flowers was now a narrow trail through a grasping jungle. She could no longer see the house. Tall blades of grass and vines curled around her wrists, legs, and neck. She tore through them, leaving stinging red marks on her skin, and then she was pounding gravel on the driveway.

The gate was closed, but with the amount of adrenaline coursing through her veins Alex had no doubt she could scale it if needed. She launched herself forward, intent on reaching that shaded, peaceful lane that lay just on the other side of the metal bars; and fell flat on her face, skinning both elbows and smashing her chin. She got up and fell again.

What? Come on! But this time she couldn't get up at all; something rough had curled around her left ankle, tugging at it.

It was a tree root.

It had followed her along the path like a brown python, and now it tightened its grip, turning her foot numb as it cut off her circulation. She sat up and tried to get her fingers around it to pull it loose, but it was impossible, and with each passing second it twisted tighter. The bark dug into her skin.

She reached for the main root, intending to lift it to bite it, but it drew taut with a sharp twang and the force of it yanked her leg straight and flung her onto her back. It pulled her, inch by inch, back down the path.

Whenever Alex had watched her beloved horror movies, she'd always been sure she would be the hard-core heroine. The girl who, instead of running and screaming while the killer pursued, would fight to the very end. But now, weak with fear and pain, confused, exhausted, all she could do was cry as she was dragged inexorably backward into the dragon's den.

And this, unfortunately, was how she knew for sure: perhaps she was lost in a nightmare – but it was not the sleeping kind of nightmare- nor the kind that visited mental patients in madhouses. No, this kind of nightmare was completely and undeniably real.

5
Sick

Two days, and Alex hadn't returned a single text. Her phone was offline. James couldn't do anything but wait, holed up in his room checking social media obsessively, wondering what had happened to her. Did someone she know die? Had she been forced to change schools again? He drew endlessly in his exercise book at the back of his classes, and spent the lunchtimes pacing the school grounds with his hood up and his hands deep in his pockets, worrying.

No one noticed. James had existed in this way for years before Alex moved to the school – like a ghost. Even the teachers ignored him, his grades neither good nor bad enough to earn him attention; as absent in class as out of it.

Finally, he couldn't bear it any longer. At lunch on the third day, he decided to ask Annie Walker. Annie was the closest thing to a friend Alex had besides James. The two girls were in almost every class together, but beyond that James had no idea how they could possibly get along. Annie was everything Alex was not: rich, popular, and intimidatingly cold.

He hovered at the edge of the quadrangle, trying not to appear creepy while he waited for her to be alone for a minute. After twenty minutes or so, he realised that Annie wasn't the type to be alone ever, so he just went for it.

She was sitting with four girls and three guys from their year level on a big square bench, laughing at something one of them had said, when James grew close enough to draw their attention. Two of the girls – the insanely beautiful blonde twins known to all as 'The Bitches', saw him first, smiles dying away and eyebrows raising in comical unison. A second or two later everyone else followed suit, including Annie. Silence descended.

"Uh, hey, Annie," he said, refusing to look at anyone but her, although they were all listening in on the conversation.

"Yes?" Her tone let him know she was responding only because they were both friends with Alex, and under any other circumstances she would have graced him with a blank look and nothing more.

"I was wondering if you knew what happened to Alex?"

"Don't you know? I sent her a text yesterday and she didn't reply."

"Yeah, me too."

She paused, biting her lip, then pulled her schoolbag out from under the bench and started rummaging through it. "Well, you know where she lives, right?" One of the guys laughed and nudged the other – a skinny stoner James knew from Maths named Harry. "Yeah, you do, buddy." When James nodded his ascent, there were chuckles all round.

Annie paid them no mind. "Well, can you go past there, like, today? Because she told me she'd do her part of the Chem assignment and it was overdue like two days ago. Here." She pulled out a sheaf of pages full of neat diagrams and highlighted headings and handed it to him. "That's my half of it, it's got all the data and equations and stuff, so she can use it."

"Okay, yeah. I'll just go now. Last two periods are Art History, anyway."

"I thought you like, liked art?"

Harry jumped in before James could open his mouth. "Yeah, but when you got art on one hand and sweet, sweet —"

"Can you not?" Annie said sharply, casting James a weary look that made him like her a little more. "Let me know if she's okay."

"Course."

He didn't go past Twisty Lane this day, although it would have been a quicker route. The thought of it made the hair on his neck prickle. Alex had mentioned she might go by the house after school. A vision of the strange girl — Holly — popped into his head, in which she bared canines the length of fingers and sunk them into Alex's neck. Man, you really should cut down on the horror movies.

Alex's house was the picture of suburban contentment: complete with the white picket fence, pristinely manicured front lawn, four windows and a pinewood front door with knocker. Part of him was envious, comparing the neat security with his own decrepit unit and chain-smoking father. When Alex's mother opened the front door, however, he wasn't so sure.

She stared at him for a long moment, her overly plucked highbrows peaked in a questioning arch. She had the build of an anorexic runway model, though the image was ruined by the stress lines at the corners of her mouth and the bags under her eyes. Her hair was pulled back in a bun so tight it would take no more than the slightest tug to scalp her. He realised she was waiting for him to speak.

"Uh, hi, Mrs. Miller. I just came to deliver Alex's homework. She's got a Chem assignment due." He held up the sheaf of papers in one hand.

Her face broke out in a wide but undoubtedly fake smile. "Oh, thank you…"

"James."

"James. Yes, I will deliver that to her directly." She reached for the homework, but he let his hand drop to his side and gave her a fake smile of his own. "Is it alright if I take it in to her? She hasn't been replying to my texts or anything and I just wanted to make sure she was okay."

Mrs. Miller's smile drooped into a frown and her hand retreated as though burned. For a second, he thought she'd refuse, but she gave a curt nod and stepped aside, gesturing for him to enter. "Ah – shoes, shoes, please!"

"Oh, sorry." He sheepishly removed his dirty school shoes at the front door – a custom as foreign to him as bowing and entered.

The interior of the house was as painfully clean as it appeared on the outside. Gleaming counters, spotless white tiles in the kitchen, and as James followed Mrs. Miller past the dining room he looked in and saw Mr. Miller, still in his suit, reading the paper. A gold-rimmed Crucifix sat on the wall just behind him, and he smiled at James with gleaming white teeth. "Who's this?"

"Friend of Alex's, dear, delivering homework." Mrs. Miller said. She hung impatiently at the doorway as her husband stood up to shake James's hand. His grip was smooth, dry, and hard as rock. "Wouldn't get too close, son, she's very sick."

"That's alright. Just wanted to say hi."

He nodded, continuing to shake James's hand for slightly longer than necessary. Then he gripped James's right shoulder with the same intense grip. "Have you been saved, son?"

What the hell? "Y – yes. Yes, I have."

"That's good. Good." His cool blue eyes were piercing, his gaze unwavering. "Alex has mentioned you once or twice. Said you wanted to be an artist?"

"Animator. For movies. Or book illustrator. Something like that."

He gave a tight nod. "That's good. Like Disney." It was a statement rather than a question, so James kept his mouth shut. Finally, Mr. Miller let go of him and returned to his spot at the table. "Well, I wish you all the best. Not too long in there, now, and keep the door open. She's very sick."

"Yeah. No problem…" He almost added a sir on the end, out of sheer pressure. He'd hardly been in the house for five minutes and he felt like he was drowning. How does she live like this? he thought as he followed Alex's mother briskly down the hall. It's like living in a compound, or… but before he could finish the thought, they were standing outside Alex's bedroom door.

Alex's mother stood rigidly for a minute, wavering. "I won't be long," James said with a smile he hoped was saintly enough.

She nodded at no one in particular, smoothed out her immaculate dress, and grimaced. "Yes. Alright then." She gave him a stiff pat on the shoulder and then hurried off to attend to whatever urgent business she had. James breathed a sigh of relief, though even being alone in the house was unnerving. He knocked on the door.

Ruffling bedsheets. A loud bump was followed by the sound of books tumbling to the carpet. That was normal at least, but what followed was not: a metal lock sliding into place. And then the voice – it was hers, and yet it wasn't. It was too small and high, as though she was pretending to be a little girl. No, not that either – maybe more like a little girl pretending to be older. "Is that you, James? I'm really sick."

"How did you know it was me?"

Silence. Then: "I really can't see you right now. Maybe in a few days?"

"Uh. Yeah, that's cool. I just came to bring you Annie's half of your chemistry assignment. Apparently, you have to hand yours in soon. Are you – what's wrong with you?"

"I'm really sick, I said. Can you slide it under the door?"

"Yeah, I know you're sick, but with what? Like, are you vomiting?"

"Quite a lot, thanks."

He paused, cocking his head to one side. It was a small thing, but the Alex he knew just wouldn't have spoken like that. She would have said tons, or yeah, it's so gross, or enough to fill the Hoover dam. But quite a lot, thanks? "Can I come in?"

"No. You'll catch it."

"That's okay," he said quickly. "I wouldn't mind missing school."

In the silence that followed, he could almost hear the cogs turning in her mind. Finally, she said, "just leave it there, I'll get it later. I have to throw up."

"Oh, okay. Hope you get better." He dropped the pages at the foot of her door and stared at them for a full minute before he turned and left. Mr. Miller gave him a brief salute on his way out, which he returned. When he was out on the street a light drizzle had started, and he pulled up his hood, jamming his hands in his pockets.

Small things, but they nagged at him. Quite a lot, thanks. It was more like something the girl from the house – Holly – would have said. Now that he thought of it, the voice from behind the door wasn't too dissimilar from hers, either, if she'd tried to disguise it. So what? A fourteen-year-old girl kidnapped Alex and is hiding in her bedroom? He was being stupid. He'd probably see her in a few days, and they'd laugh about it. Probably.

Probably.

Eyes were on him. He wasn't alone on the street – cars were driving by, people were on the sidewalk, dragging their bins out to the road and walking their dogs. But there was a sense, a primal instinct that had been honed to a knife point after millions of years of evolution, one that said clearly a predator is watching you.

A young boy in a hooded raincoat was walking on his side of the road about two blocks back, head down, no schoolbag. He had a pale face and slender build. It was his walk that gave him away: awkward, self-conscious, halting. You're being crazy. Why would a little boy be following you?

But the kid stayed with him, street after street. James passed his house once, then twice, and circled around, no logical route for anyone to take, and yet the boy was still two blocks back. And then he wasn't. At some point between Templeton Shopping Town and James's house, he vanished.

James went home. He ate dinner. He turned on his lamp and took out a fresh piece of paper and his pastels and he drew.

The pictures that emerged scared him. They were of Alex, small and wasted with tears in her eyes and a parasite eating her brain, and of the boy that had followed him, with red eyes and long claws peeking from the sleeves of his raincoat.

One week, he told himself. If he didn't see her in one week, he would go back to Twisty Lane.

He fell asleep facing his closet, and did not see the hooded face watching him from the window.

6
Doppelganger

Every move Alex made within the confines of her 'guest' room, the black eyes followed. She was the strangest person Alex had ever seen – if she was human at all: skin as white as porcelain, hair straight and neat as if it had been sewed on, lips thin and red – like worms. The first day, when she followed Alex into the adjoining bathroom, Alex tried to lock her in the cupboard, and she would have succeeded if Holly hadn't come storming in a moment later.

"Leave her alone!"

"She's creeping me out." Holly's presence was enough to put Alex on edge. The small girl was hardly intimidating by herself, but she had power over this house that Alex did not yet understand. She understood enough, though, after what had happened the day before, to be afraid.

"Let her watch you. She's just curious, that's all. Maybe if you talk to her, she won't be so scared." There was no mention of a threat, but it was there all the same, and so for two days Alex did as she was told.

Which, at first, was nothing at all. The room in which Holly had locked her wasn't exactly a prison cell: It had a four-poster bed, a closet, a desk with drawers full of pens and notebooks, and an ensuite bathroom with cream tiles and mirror cabinets. But the window was three stories above a rose garden, and the bedroom door locked from the outside. It had a reverse peep hole above the doorknob, and every now and again Alex looked over and saw a curious eye there.

Sister disappeared from the room at random times throughout the day, but she always reappeared at night, sitting in one corner or another to watch Alex, her dark eyes seeming to take in every movement, every breath.

The first night, pacing the room with adrenaline from the day, half mad with worry and fear, Alex had bombarded the girl with questions. "What are you? Who is Holly? Where are your parents? What is this place?" But the girl had only parroted her like an annoying child, mimicking her voice and facial expressions.

It wasn't until she returned to the room the following day, looking radically different, that Alex suspected there was something more than childish games at work. For one thing, the girl's hair was wavy and brown instead of straight and black, and tied in the same messy plait as Alex's. She was taller and more filled out – no longer pale and scrawny. She looked, in other words, a lot more like Alex. Only her eyes were unchanged.

This time, she was the one asking questions, and even seemed to be genuinely curious, like a nervous girl trying to make a friend. "What's your last name? What's your favourite colour? What are your friends like? Do you like your dad? Do you like James?"

Alex wasn't fooled. She lied through her teeth, but every time she did the girl raised both eyebrows – just as Alex herself did when she was suspicious – and asked again. And when Alex did answer truthfully, she found that the girl was willing to answer some questions of her own. It was a trade arrangement: Alex could either help this imperfect copy of herself become a more realistic imposter, or she could remain in her prison cell, helpless and in the dark.

They talked for hours after midnight on the second day, cross legged on opposite ends of the large bed. They were playing a game of truth and lies, and Alex didn't know who was winning. It was so hard to read those opaque eyes, especially after what she'd seen in the garden. Who was to say what was real and what wasn't in this place?

"What does Holly want with me?" She asked the girl.

"She wants to be your friend. What's your favourite hobby?"

"Knitting."

Silence.

"Horror movies. Are you… real?"

"Yes. Are you a nice person?

"Not usually. I don't like Holly." She kept her face straight, heart beating fast, but she hadn't told a lie. She didn't feel like a nice person at that moment after all. She wanted nothing more than to grab the unnatural thing in front of her and shove it out of the door. And she definitely didn't like Holly.

The girl paused, but when Alex asked the next question, she answered it without hesitation. "Is Holly going to hurt me?"

"Only if you hurt her. Do you like your parents?"

"I love them." Another half-truth. She loved them, but she didn't like them at all. Again, Sister swallowed it. Alex had no idea if this was a good thing or not. She just wanted to be alone back in her own bed, with the TV chattering downstairs and the comforting sound of cars on the street outside. It was so quiet here.

Sister returned to the house twice a day, and each time she brought a glass of sour, yellowed milk. At least, Alex didn't know what else it could be. In fact, it was thicker than normal milk, and it left her feeling full to the brim as if she'd had a three-course meal, bloated and a little sick, but warm and comfortable at the same time.

Sister's eyes were the last things to change. Late afternoon of the third day, the bedroom door swung open, and she entered with Holly in tow, carrying another glass of foul milk. Alex was struck by the resemblance immediately, as if the image hadn't made sense until the last puzzle piece fell into place. They looked exactly the same; they moved the same and she was sure if Other Alex were to open her mouth, they would sound the same, too.

Alex's eyes darted to the half open door. Holly had her back to the room as she set the glass down on the oak writing desk, but she called out in a funny sing song voice, "You can try if you like, but there's nowhere to go." Alex didn't try, and Sister closed the door.

Holly went to stand at the foot of the bed, hands politely behind her back and a pleasant smile on her lips. Alex regarded her with a neutral expression. For all the questions she'd asked her Other, she still couldn't tell what was going on behind the girl's innocent features.

Holly took a quick breath, as if she was about to give a speech. "Sorry I haven't seen you in a while," she said. She paused, but Alex said nothing. Oh, you've seen me alright. Plenty.

She went on. "I've had a lot of things to get ready. For you. And I thought I should get it all done before I explained it all. I don't think we got off on the right foot."

Alex shrugged. She wasn't sure that got off on the right foot was an adequate description of what happened.

Better wording might have been I don't think I should have forced you to help me kill a horrible pig monster in the garden shed with a pair of shears.

"And I'm sorry I tricked you earlier, to get you into the house. But I'm so sure you'll forgive me, once you see what it can be like. We can do anything here, anything at all! It could be just like the storybooks. We can go on adventures and climb trees and eat any food you like. You won't have to study or work or anything, and I have a library and toys and people – lots of people. I can make anyone you want, anyone at all, and I can show you things, and do things… isn't it grand?" She took a breath, eyes shining with genuine enthusiasm. "We can be just like Peter Pan – only girls…" She trailed off, noticing Alex's decided lack of joy. "What's wrong?"

Alex chose her words carefully. She was in the presence of something powerful and strange, and she didn't exactly know what, but she did know that if she put a foot wrong it could go very badly for her. As badly as the pig in the shed, even. "It's not you – you seem really nice – and I definitely want to hang out with you and play and all those things you said. It's just, my parents are probably worried sick about me, and I need to tell them I'm okay and, you know, say goodbye."

"That's okay," Holly said. "Sister can do it for you. They'll never know the difference."

"Okay… But I'd really like to go back for a little while. I have friends at school, and I have an assignment that's like, super overdue. And I always wanted to travel to other countries and have a career and…" She saw Holly's face falling and hurried on, "But I'd always come back to see you. I mean every day, even – I could go out for the day and spend afternoons and nights here, that kind of thing. You'd be my best friend. I promise."

"You can travel. The house can make things for you – beaches or forests or mountains – I'm sure it could. And I could make people to live there. If you stay here, you won't need a job. You won't have to do anything if you don't want – or you could do everything. Even if…" She swallowed. "Even if you didn't want to play with me all the time. I'd leave you alone if you wanted, I would." Her voice had taken a pleading quality, and Alex couldn't help but feel a pang of sympathy for the girl.

"I know. It's just… I just want to go home for a bit."

"This can be your home." Her eyes glistened.

"Can't I leave for a little while? To see my parents and my friends? Just for today?"

But Holly shook her head, frowning, and her next words sent Alex cold. "You can't go. Sister will see them for you."

"Wait, let's just talk –" But it was too late. Holly was already marching out the door, fists bunched, and jaw clenched. Sister gave a cheerful nod and left the room after her.

Alex launched herself from the bed, sure she could knock both of them over and maybe make it all the way to the front gate if she was fast enough, but her foot caught the blanket as she stepped off the bedside and then it was too late. Holly slammed the door shut, and a moment later the sound of a heavy bolt sliding into place echoed through the room.

7
All Better

James was sitting at the bottom of the oval in the rain when he saw her at last.

His unease had grown steadily as the days passed in her absence. He suspected he was being paranoid, but there was another, more persistent voice deep inside him that said otherwise. Something is wrong with the world, this voice said. And whatever happened to Alex sure as hell wasn't the flu.

But no sooner had this thought entered his mind than he looked up and saw her, striding unhurriedly across the oval in the downpour. Her hood was pulled down, so at first, he couldn't make out her face, but he was sure it was her. No other girl would leave a warm classroom and walk out in this kind of whether just to talk to him.

But there was something. He saw it as soon as she stopped in front of him, where he could see beneath her green school hoodie.

It could have been the shadow over her face, but he knew her eyes were grey, not dark brown. She was smiling, but it wasn't a smile he recognised – it was all lips. When Alex smiled, she showed every one of her teeth. Yeah, well I had three years of braces, I'm not gonna let that go to waste, she'd said when he'd called her on it once. "Hi," she said.

"Uh, hey. I didn't know you were back," he said as he stood up, wiping a mop of hair out of his eyes.

"I'm not," she said. Then she winked. "At least, the school doesn't think I am."

"Oh yeah? So, what, you were just pretending this whole time?"

"Nooooo. I was sick for a bit. I mean, really sick. James..." She put her hands on his shoulders, taking a deep breath as though she was about to say something serious. He felt the warmth on his skin through his jacket. He realised she'd never touched him – even like this – in all the time they'd known each other. "I almost died."

"What?"

"I got really dehydrated from all the... you know. And I fell unconscious and my Dad took me to emergency, but they said if I'd gone much longer without any fluid I could have just died."

"Jesus. Are you okay? It's only been a few days." He kicked himself for the messages he'd sent, nagging for attention.

"Once they got me on a drip, I was fine. But I thought I might as well play it out as long as I can. So, I'll be... kind of discreet for a week or so. I got my Mum to write a note, so I didn't have to do the stupid Chem assignment. I needed a break from, you know," she gestured back at the school, a dim collection of portables and asphalt in the grey mist, "all that. It's just. Almost dying that way made me think about time and relationships and just being alive, you know? It made me realise I don't have enough fun. I take everything too seriously. Right?"

He looked out over the oval, unsure of what to say. "I dunno. I guess."

"Look, we're all going to be dead soon, you know? I just escaped this time, but I won't escape forever, and I need to live." She dropped her hands. She was staring at him with an intensity he'd never seen before.

"You got a week off?" he said, trying to figure out if she was saying what he desperately hoped she was saying. "I could probably take some time off, too. I could forge a note or something, easy. I haven't been sick in over a year, so it'd be –"

"Cool." She looked over her shoulder. The muddy oval was empty. Then she turned back suddenly, and before he could figure out what the funny expression on her face meant she took his head in her hands and kissed him – the first kiss of his life, with the only girl he'd ever loved.

The feeling was alien at first, but not unpleasant, touching the soft sand of a foreign shore. Her tongue slid along his, and then pushed deeper into his mouth – too deep – so deep that it didn't seem possible that her tongue should be so long, but before he could react, she pulled back. Her face was flushed and full of new life, and she ran a hand along the side of his cheek.

"That was nice," she said. "But I think we need to practice."

8
Mr. Stretch

Alex heard and saw no one for the next twenty-four hours, and at the end of it she finally decided she was going to go out the window. She'd probably break an ankle, but at this point she was convinced it would be worth it for a chance at escape.

She paced the room, hers the only steps echoing through the house, stomach growling and scowl deepening. *If you stay here, you're either going to end up like that pig, or you'll lose your mind.* Finally, she unplugged the lamp from the desktop and took it over to the window. It was late afternoon, and the sun shone through a sky of grey clouds. She hoped she had the guts to jump. *Feet first. Just land feet first and you'll be fine.*

She drew back the lamp.

"Don't do that, Miss!"

She spun around so fast she almost fell backward through the glass pane anyway, dropping the lamp in the process. She scanned the dim room with a slamming heart. It took a minute to locate the source of the voice: the peephole was covered over. Someone had been watching her through the door. A man, by the sound of it, though his voice was dopey and oddly childish. "'Hello?" she said.

"Don't be afraid, Miss. I'm just a harmless ole buddy. Mind if I come in?"

She waited a beat, then edged around the bed so it was between her and the door. "Okay."

Alex was primed to charge the open door as the man entered, but when the lock slid aside the door itself barely opened a crack before he slid into the room. The sight of him alone was enough to freeze her where she stood.

He clicked the door shut behind him and faced her. "Didn't mean to startle you. I just didn't want you to make any mistakes seeing as how you're such a nice lady."

He wasn't quite human, but the resemblance was close enough that while he might have turned heads on the street, he wouldn't have elicited screams. He had a tall and narrow frame, and his limbs were impossibly slender, his skin so pale the veins beneath gave it a bluish tinge. He wore a baggy suit and a square hat, and when he smiled – as he did then – his whole face changed, the skin around his eyes moving like a loose mask.

"It's just that going out that way wouldn't do you any good besides broken bones, y'see? The second you break that window Holly will know just where you are and what you're about."

"Oh. How would she know that?"

"Well, it's complicated, but she and the house are all connected in ways. It's not the case, but you'd do well to think of her as the spider and the house as the web. Touch a thread here, and it vibrates all through, and she can move easily in and out. Best be on good behaviour, especially if you ain't in her good books. And I hate to tell you miss, but you ain't in her good books."

"Yeah, well. She's a brat."

"Sssssshhhhh…" He put a finger up to his mouth and cringed in an exaggerated gesture, looking over his shoulder into the hall. "Not so loud."

"She's not in the house right now, is she? I haven't seen or heard anything all day."

The tall man shook his head. "She's always in the house, somewhere. She can't leave, but she can… go away, sometimes."

"Where does she go?"

He shrugged and scratched the back of his neck. "Places. Sometimes the basement, or the attic. But you must never go looking for her there, miss, you'll not come out. If she goes, leave her be. Once you're free to roam, that is. They're forbidden even to the likes of me."

Alex folded her arms and cocked her head to one side. She didn't know what to think of this strange man, but the more he spoke the more harmless he seemed to her. She got the feeling he was as scared as she was, in some ways, and that he was telling her more than he should to keep her safe. She wondered if it was a trick Holly had set: a false friend to gain her confidence. "Who are you, anyway?" she said eventually.

He gave her a slanted smile and extended an arm so long he had only to lean forward for it to reach all the way across the bed. "My name is Mr. Stretch," he said.

"Alex," she said, shaking his hand. It was rubbery and smooth. No callouses, no sweat, no knuckles. She held on as long as she could bear it. "What's your first name?"

"Mister, of course."

"Huh. So, what are you doing here, anyway? Are you on sentry duty or something, to make sure I don't escape?"

He looked down at his shoes, and then up at the ceiling, like a child caught in a lie. "Yes… I mean no, not so much, now ya mention it. I'm to give you the grand welcome, you see. Holly thinks you need some space and to get accustomed. She said you should have someone else besides her to talk to and show you all around to see how nice this place can be."

"So, you were just spying on me?" To her amazement, she saw red shame creep onto his face, and she found herself restraining the urge to laugh. What was this place? Who were these… things? I can make anyone, Holly had said. But the truth danced just out of reach. She couldn't have meant what she said literally, could she? Why not? Who's to say what's real and what isn't, anymore?

"I wasn't so much spying, y'see,' Stretch said. 'I just had never seen a real girl besides Holly before and I, well I wasn't sure what to make of you."

"A real girl?"

"Now, listen, there's no…" He was getting flustered, and he kept twisting his neck around to look over his shoulder, though both of them would have heard someone coming from way down the hall. "What I mean is, there'll be plenty of time for questions at the end of the tour."

Alex didn't move for a long time and kept her gaze steady. Stretch shifted on his feet, his knees bending sideways in a manner they shouldn't have been able to. The oddness of his being was endearing in a way. Beneath his strangeness was something genuine that made her want to trust him.

"Okay," she said at last, and smiled when she saw him visibly relax with relief. It didn't occur to her until later that his relief had nothing to do with her and everything to do with Holly.

"Give me the grand tour then, Mister Stretch."

9
Love in the Dark

They were like prisoners on the run, or thieves, sneaking through the shadows behind James's house. She'd tried to get him to go back to hers, but after what he'd seen the other day, he would rather have slit his wrists. Besides, her bedroom window was too small to fit through, which meant they'd have had to go through the front door – not to mention her parents would probably ground her for the rest of her life if they found out she was seeing a boy, out of wedlock and unchaperoned, God forbid.

Her eyes were bright in the dark, her hands and lips warm in the cold air. They made it all the way to his bedroom window – not far from the living room which spilled light onto the brick patio – and then he pressed her gently against the wall and kissed her again. After a minute she pulled away from him. "Wait, what are we doing?"

"What? I mean… we don't have to do anything, you know? We can just chill if you want."

"Is it going to be more like this? Is it going to be like this?"

"Yeah. Even better, right?"

"Oh, okay then," and she kissed him again, and her long tongue pushed too far down his throat again, but he didn't mind, and his left hand was unhinging the metal catch on the window to push it open, and then they were spilling into his bedroom, laughing quietly and trying not to knock everything over. It probably didn't matter – the television was on in the next room and by now James's father would be apocalyptically drunk.

They found the bed and fell onto it, and she came down on top of him, her tongue once more probing him, unpleasantly. How is it so long? He wished it wasn't so dark, but he couldn't switch the light on in case his father noticed it. Mr. Harmon usually started to get paranoid at around a half litre of Jack Daniels. Besides, James couldn't have reached the light switch now: Alex was biting his lip, pushing him down into the bed. "What's next?" she whispered.

He laughed, pulling off his shirt. "I thought you were a horror movie fan," he said.

"So?"

"So, this is the part right before the killer slashes everyone."

"Killer?" Her tone jarred him. The Alex he knew would have laughed at that. There was no way she wouldn't have laughed, maybe even so loud he'd have had to clap a hand over her mouth. But he sensed only confusion now – even a touch of fear. Shit. This isn't any time for joking, he scolded himself. You gotta be romantic. He reached up and stroked the side of her face with his hand, felt her smile. "Sorry, just kidding. Now we take our shirts off, that's all."

They helped each other with that, and then everything else, and still, he didn't quite get it. It didn't click even then – even when his hands ran over smooth breasts, he only had a vague sense of something absent – he was too lost in the moment and the novelty of it all. This is real, he kept thinking. It's totally real.

But his hands kept moving...

There wasn't anything.

She was smooth, all over, everywhere. Her skin was too tight, drawn so thin he felt he could have split it with a fingernail. His hands discovered a midsection with no belly button and no belly – that part of her sucked inwards so deeply he could have curled his fingers around her ribcage. When she pressed up against him, groaning, he couldn't feel a heartbeat. She had no nipples. Her long tongue lapped his neck.

A surprised choking sound escaped him, and he pushed her aside, moving across the bed to see her better in the dark. He flailed for the light switch, but it was out of reach.

"I don't – I don't know…" she stuttered. She got off the bed and stood for a moment, silhouetted against the window. "What am I missing?"

"You're not her! Who are you?" The words were out of his mouth before he could stop them, but now that he could see her in the moonlight, he knew it was true. He wasn't looking at a real person: He was seeing a kind of imitation – a doll thing with all the main features and none of the details.

"I am! I am. I have to go!" She turned, scrambling out of the window before he could stop her. He could only lie half naked on the bed in shock and listen to the sound of her vanishing steps. She's running down the street without any clothes on. You should go after her. And then the horrible thought that followed: Not her. It.

A crawling sense of disgust consumed him. He felt like he'd eaten halfway through a steak and found a family of maggots nesting inside. What was that? But it was the question that followed this that took hold of him and kept him from sleeping a wink that night, even with the window locked and the lights on: where was the real Alex?

10
Birthday Girl

Winter, 1997

"Five Five Five Five Five!" Holly ran through the house at top speed, her rat-brown teddy swinging madly from one hand as she proclaimed her new age. Jane hurried after her, but without hope of ever catching the girl, only wanting to warn her of the coming storm if she refused to reign herself in. "Holly, please! Your father will be home any minute!"

"YES, DADDY! FIVE!"

She danced through her mother's clumsy grasp and hopped onto the staircase banister, scaling it on all fours like a monkey on a tree branch, Teddy clutched in her mouth. Jane thought, not for the first or last time, that Holly was going to be the death of her. And Gregory too, if his blood pressure maintained its current trajectory.

No sooner had the thought crossed her mind than she heard the front gates screaming open and then the revving of a car engine. Panicked, Jane gave up the chase and headed for the lounge room, Gregory's usual first port of call. She scrambled to get things into some kind of order – throwing toys, cushions and books into piles and hiding what she could beneath the couches. It was no good; his heavy footfalls were already clunking on the front steps. Jane surveyed the wreckage, hands grasping her straggly hair, breathing rapidly.

She turned just as he walked in the door, his expression already dark from whatever trials and num-wits (as he liked to call them) he'd encountered that day.

He shut the door and turned. His scowl deepened as he took in the state of the house.

Just then, at the worst possible moment, Holly presented herself at the top of the stairs in her underwear, both she and Teddy covered in multi-coloured finger paints, exhilarated from the day's activities. Jane's heart almost broke at the sight of her. The poor girl didn't know yet, had forgiven her father for the previous rages she'd seen in her short life, and would no doubt forgive him this one, too.

"DADDY! I'M FIVE NOW!" And she came thundering down the steps, screaming delightedly with each one. "FIVE! FIVE! FIVE!" Oblivious to the brewing hurricane that was already making Jane weak at the knees. She'd seen it before, the transformation of a good man into a monster, by the laying of one more straw on the donkey's back.

Moving to cut in front of Holly, a frantic smile barely concealing her underlying fear, Jane reached out for him. "Gregory, Dear, let me take your jacket and suitcase. How was your day today? Why don't you put your feet up on the couch and I'll pour you a scotch on the rocks, and by the time you finish all this will be –"

But when she reached for his jacket, he pushed her with enough force to send her sprawling on the hardwood. He didn't so much as glance her way, his fury concentrated for the moment on the manic sprite who was even then bounding off the lowest step with her arms outstretched, Teddy still clutched in her left hand. "FIVE FIVE FI –'

Halfway through the last five he struck her – a lazy backhand which sent her sliding across the floor on her rear, legs splayed out and her mouth locked in an O of surprise. The tears arrived without delay, though she was too breathless to cry out.

"What do you bloody well think you're doing, girl? You think I want to come home and see this? You think it's fine to run around covered in paint with your, your nakedness on show?" He advanced on her, his questions building in volume and begging answers that didn't exist, ramping up in advance of the next blow. Jane pulled herself to her feet and approached him tentatively, not wanting to get too close but knowing she had to drag his attention away from the petrified girl at his feet.

"Gregory, it's me! It was my fault, I told her it was alright…" She plucked ineffectually at his sleeve, wanting to make him face her. In an abrupt motion, he obliged: His left fist arced into the side of her head, dropping her instantly and turning her whole world into a merry-go-round. Later, she would find her pearl earring, broken at the clasp, in the corner of the room.

It had been a long time since he'd hit her with a closed fist, and she was stunned by the force of it. Not so much, however, that she didn't hear the dangerous tone in her daughter's pleading voice.

"Daddy, no…"

"Shut up! I'm not done with you, you little brat. Now I told you to help your mother clean the downstairs today for our guests tomorrow. How dare you disobey me…" He was hulking over her, too lost in his indignant fury to know what was happening.

But of course, he'd never seen Holly do IT before. And God help her, Jane would die before he ever did, because it would almost certainly mean a life in the madhouse for her, and a tiny grave in the backyard for Holly.

"Holly, don't do it! Don't make anything!" Jane cried. She had seen Holly's eyes change, her grey irises turning milky and the whites taking on a shine the way they did when she tried to make things. Any minute now the shine would become blinding headlights set into the little girl's face, and then something would pop into existence. A monster, perhaps, to dwarf the one that lived in her father.

When Jane launched herself at him, then, it was as much to save the man she loved as the daughter she feared, though she would never admit it to herself. She was just trying to keep them a family, that was all – she just wanted them all to be a happy family and for nothing bad to happen. So, she threw herself into Gregory with everything she had, dragging them both down in a heap of tangled limbs. Gregory shouted something, but it was lost in the horrendous crash that followed.

Jane sat up in a cloud of settling dust, blinking, and saw that one of the two great chandeliers had fallen right on the spot Gregory had been standing a moment before. Holly observed the wreckage, not with shock but with pouting disappointment.

Gregory extricated himself from his wife and sat up, dusty glass in his hair, staring around like a mad owl. His fury had vanished for the moment, and when he glanced at Jane, it was with a mixture of embarrassment and surprise. Mr. Hyde had once again become Dr. Jekyll, and Jane had never been so relieved to see him.

"My God," he said faintly. "That would have been the end of us."

Jane let out a shaky laugh. "We were going to replace those lights, anyway, weren't we?" Not mentioning that the only reason they hadn't got around to it yet was that those chandeliers had been bolted so tightly into the colossal beams above that they'd judged it too difficult a task to tackle at the moment. Nothing short of a wrecking ball will shake them loose, Gregory had said after huffing and pulling at the bolts for a couple of hours.

"I'm sorry, Daddy," Holly said in a small voice, and Gregory allowed her to hug him as he got to his feet. "There, there, that's alright girl. Now get yourself cleaned up, will you? You're getting older, see – from now on you must always dress and act like a lady. D'you understand?"

Holly nodded, sniffing, and he gave her an awkward pat on the head. "There's a girl. I think I'll have that scotch now, if you don't mind, Dear."

Jane nodded, rubbing her eyes, but when he'd settled in the lounge room a minute later she took Holly by the shoulders and shook her. "You don't ever do it in front of your father, d'you understand, Holly? Not ever."

And Holly nodded, tears springing to the corners of her eyes as Jane enclosed her in a tight embrace.

She kept it all hidden, after that, even from Jane, and for a long while it seemed she was an ordinary girl – or at least as ordinary as someone like Holly could ever be. Never again did she show her power in front of her father.

Well.

Never but once.

11
The Grand Tour

Alex had known the house was big, but it wasn't until Stretch led her through the second and first floors (the attic and basement being forbidden), that she really got a sense of its true size. Sitting rooms, lounges, dining rooms, there was even a wide-open hall that Stretch told her was a ballroom (a ballroom!) Everything made of rich wood and Turkish carpets, each room so quiet and dense, somehow a world unto itself.

Stretch navigated the maze of hallways and adjoining rooms with ease, but Alex was soon utterly lost, and was surprised when they arrived suddenly in the entrance hall and Stretch pulled open the front door. The light that spilled in reminded her of early dawn; bright but cold, and Alex breathed it deeply. So close.

But she was too wary to run, just yet. Not until she was sure she could get away. The raw red lines around her wrists and ankles had yet to fade.

"I know it seems all big and spacey now, but if you spend a while, you'll find the place can be nice and cosy, too, full of nooks and crannies to curl up in. If you're a good girl, Holly will give you all the freedom you want… in the house, that is.”

"And what about the garden?” Alex asked as she followed him down the stone steps and onto one of the brick pathways leading through the flowers. It was not, she was relieved to note, the way to the old shed.

"Garden's just the same. Go down one path and find a jungle full of rivers and vines, or another and you'll be in a place of trimmed hedges and cut grass. There's something for everyone!”

"How does she do it?” Alex said.

"Oh, she's a magical girl, Holly is,” Stretch said with an exaggerated wink. "House for parents and Nobodies for friends! Funny way to live, isn't it?”

'Nobodies?'

"Sure, that's like me and Miss… Like me and some of the others. She calls us the Nobodies because we had no bodies and now, we do!” He chuckled as though he'd said something funny instead of utterly terrifying.

Before Alex could think of anything to say to that, they rounded the Eastern corner of the house and she stopped mid-stride, halted by an impossible sight. Between the tall bordering wall and the side of the house stood a forest that would have looked less out of place on a European mountainside than a suburban mansion.

Stretch let out a strange donkey bray of delight at the expression on her face and slapped her on the back. "Mazing, isn't it? This is the Autumn Forest, what do you think?”

Rather than replying, Alex moved forward into the trees, crossing the threshold from a summery English Garden into this haunting landscape full of scraggly trees, red and brown leaves, and the ruin of an old well. Past that, a rusted iron gate opened into a miniature cemetery – around ten or fifteen graves with faded carvings on the tombstones. She hugged herself against the suddenly chill air, and when she squinted up at the sky, she found the sun had vanished and it was no longer dawn but dusk. "This isn't real," she muttered.

"Our Holly always loved nature, so she made the garden all the seasons at once. Front is Spring, here's the Autumn Forest, the back is Winter Snow, and the Western side with the garden shed is Summer. 'Course, the weather can always change at the drop of a hat, but Holly keeps it nice and calm mostly."

"Who's in the graves?" Alex asked, bending to read one of the inscriptions: Here lies Stupid Sarah Stiltskin, a too-tall girl that looked down on everyone. Now we're looking down on you. Ha – ha.

"Holly Bee gives everyone a fair chance," Stretch said. "But sometimes the Nobodies aren't very grateful." He shook his head. "Best move on from here, Miss Alex, the Graveyard always makes me sad."

"It's not exactly making me feel cosy and safe, either."

"Oh no! Holly doesn't want harm you – not if she can help it. You're alive, a real friend for her to have. She'd never waste such a valuable thing as that. And besides," he leaned closer, giving her the impression, he was about to impart some secret wisdom: "Holly plays the Nobodies like puppets, with her hands on their strings… but you have no strings for her to grasp."

And with that cryptic remark he led Alex through the Graveyard and on past the South-eastern corner of the building. Before they reached it, Alex saw a bed of roses lining the wall to her right and looked up, recognizing the tiny window two floors up as her own.

Just as before, the corner of the house marked a threshold, past which the trees were replaced by a snowy downhill, the falling leaves replaced by snowflakes gently drifting. At the bottom of the hill, the South wall was obscured by a dense collection of pine trees, some of which were as tall as the house itself. It was night, here. Three steps into the ankle-deep snow, Alex's shoes were soaked through and she was shivering. At her request, Sister had brought over a suitcase of Alex's clothes, but even her favourite windbreaker was not enough to keep the cold out.

"Ooookay, well this is pretty and everything, but can we get over to the summer side, like, now?"

Stretch gave her a pained smile, pointing down into the dark shadows of the pines. "Don't be so quick, Miss, there's a cosy cabin in those woods with a fire going and hot chocolates that never run out!" And, not waiting for her to reply, he took hold of her arm and pulled her after him down the slippery slope – only the second time he'd touched her at all, and this time with decidedly less care; he was like an overgrown child or a puppy.

"Alright – Hey!" She nearly fell several times on the way down, but the hill was short, and the snow was replaced by pine needles at the bottom, the ground shielded from the snowfall by the splayed branches and bristles of the pines. It was dark here, too, but only a few steps into the tree cover Alex caught sight of their destination. A pleasant little cabin with a single window that flickered with orange light. It was like something out of a fairy tale.

Stretch relaxed his grip on her arm, though she still had to hurry to keep up with his loping steps. He unlatched the cabin's front door and opened it for her, bowing and gesturing for her to enter. She thanked him and stepped inside, though a particular fairy tale had come to her mind just then, and it wasn't one she particularly liked: Hansel and Gretel.

Thankfully, the witch in question wasn't anywhere to be found. Instead, Alex sighed in the sudden warmth of the cabin, breathing deeply the smells of wood smoke, pine and, yes, delicious hot chocolate bubbling on the stove.

At least she keeps her prisoners in comfort, she thought, as Stretch closed and locked the door behind them. 'If she thinks I'm supposed to give up everything I've got for a stupid cabin and some hot chocolate, she –'

Stretch's enormous hand dropped on her shoulder and spun her around so quickly she almost fell over again. His expression was manic; wet eyes drooping horribly and mouth flopping down at the sides in a terrible parody of fear. All good cheer and jolliness were absent, and when he next spoke his words were short and urgent.

"No time for that, Miss Alex. We need to get you out the back, 'fore our Holly comes. Through the kitchen, now!"

"What? Why now?" Holly felt as though she'd just fallen through a frozen lake and plunged into the dark waters below. She let Stretch push her through the kitchen, brightly lit with the pot of dark chocolate simmering on the stove, then into a sitting room with a fireplace, where a second tiny window was set in the far wall, on the opposite side of the cabin to the one she'd seen from the forest. Only then did she realise what was happening: this window couldn't be more than several meters from the South wall of the property. And the pines that surrounded them were all at least as high as the top of the wall.

Stretch smashed the window with a bony elbow and used his sleeve to clear the glass from the edges. "Hurry!" he said. "She's set to meet us when you finish your hot chocolate. She can't see the place behind the cabin: The attic window – that's how she watches the garden, Miss."

Alex didn't need to be told twice. She all but threw herself headfirst through the window, though her hips (childbearing hips, her mother called them in her joking-not-joking way), jammed on the threshold. For a moment she hung halfway through the window, the sill digging into her lower abdomen, arms clawing at the logs on the outside, and then at last she tumbled out onto the muddy pine needles.

By the time she'd regained her feet, Stretch was already coming after her, his peculiar limbs contorting through the small opening, joints moving with the awkward grace of a spider. He dropped lightly into the dirt beside her and then the two of them were moving through the trees again, the chill air raising goose bumps on Alex's skin immediately.

"You can't stay here, Miss, or it'll be the end of you. She'll break you with pain and fear, or blackmail even – but if she can't make a friend of you, it'll be the Nobodies Graveyard. Here – this is the one!"

They'd reached the South wall at last, and right alongside its brick face was a tall pine, the tip of which towered well over the top. The wide branches spiralled up the trunk like a convenient staircase. "Once you're over the top, she can't come for you herself, but she can send others, so keep a wary eye. Please Miss, do what you can to burn this place from the outside, but if you can't, run far away and never come back, promise me won't you!"

"I promise!" And on impulse – a spur of the moment madness – she grabbed his big floppy face and kissed him on the mouth. If she hadn't been so terrified, she might even have laughed at the way his eyes bugged out of his head and his arms flailed helplessly.

But the moment was broken by the sound of a shrill voice, not too far off, that turned Alex's blood as cold as the snow. "Hello? Mr Stretch, where'd you two go?"

Alex pulled herself up to the lowest branch of the pine. The way up was easy after that, though the bark was covered in sap and she was soon sticky and covered in scratches from hundreds of tiny twigs. Mr. Stretch's voice reached her from the bottom of the tree: "Miss Holly, hurry! She's getting away!" The tree shook as he scrambled onto the bottom branches of the pine as if to chase her – though with none of the grace Alex had noted a minute ago.

It got lighter the higher up she climbed, and soon Alex saw the top of the wall, covered in a coil of barbed wire and yet no less promising. She would throw herself over it headfirst and break an arm if she had to.

When she heard Holly's heart stopping scream from below, she thought she would have to.

"GET HER! GET HER NOW, STRETCH, DON'T LET HER GET AWAY!" Alex stepped onto one of the smaller branches, just high enough for her to make the leap. She crouched, ready… and felt two hands grip her ankles.

Impossible. And when she looked down, she saw that it was indeed impossible – but it was nevertheless true all the same. Stretch was only halfway up the tree, but his arms extended, twisting through the branches the rest of the way up the trunk. The thought of jumping anyway crossed her mind, but when she saw his eyes, she knew he wouldn't let go, what she saw there was nothing but helplessness.

Stretch pulled her feet from under her and she came tumbling down the staircase of thick boughs she'd just ascended, scratching herself everywhere, grabbing at everything and gripping nothing, and eventually hitting the ground hard enough to knock the wind out of her.

"How dare you! How dare you run away! Come on, Stretch, let's show her, let's show her what happens!" Alex, only dimly aware of Holly's frantic admonitions, tried to curl into the foetal position, mouth opening and closing in the hopes of pulling some – any – air at all. Stretch dragged her through the snow back toward the cottage, and she clawed at the ground ineffectually, until she was hauled, soaking wet and burning with cold, back into the cottage. Stretch picked her up and pushed her to her knees in the small sitting room, by the fireplace, Holly following along with fists bunched and an expression of fierce indignation on her face.

Alex tried to stand but Stretch was standing behind her and leaning on her shoulders, keeping her in place. Holly came to stand in front of her, no longer screaming, but red in the face with rage. Alex gasped as her diaphragm finally released and allowed her first breath of air. No sooner had she taken it than Holly slapped her in the face.

"Ow, you BITCH!" Alex tried to get up but Stretch redoubled his efforts and pushed her back down, her knees striking the floorboards with a bang. Little dots of light flashed in front of her eyes from the blow. Holly stood back, arms folded, and lips drawn in a tight line.

"I told you that you couldn't leave. I told you."

"It was my fault, Miss Holly," Stretch said before Alex could reply. "I scared her. I didn't mean to, but sometimes I get excited, and I scared her, is all – I showed her the graves."

"It doesn't matter!" She said, her voice trembling. She levelled an accusing finger at Alex. "She shouldn't have run. I told her. And now," she went on, lowering her voice and speaking directly to Alex. "Now you have to see what happens when you don't do what I tell you."

Alex took a deep breath, fixing Holly with the sincerest look she could muster. "Holly, I'm sorry. I won't do it again, I promise."

"Miss Holly, please!" Stretch said. And it was that – the fear in his voice – that scared Alex more than anything else. "Don't you think we should be nice? Isn't it better to be nice?"

"Nice is for later," Holly said. "Put her hands in the fire."

Alex thought she hadn't heard right. For a long second, she sat frozen, trying to work out what Holly had meant to say – and in that second Stretch's big hands moved from her shoulders to take hold of her wrists. There was a metal grating in front of the fire, and Holly removed it, leaning it up against the wall.

"Wow, hey! Hold on a second. Holly, hold on one second, please!" Alex's mouth was suddenly very dry. Her throat seemed to be closing.

Someone – Stretch, probably – had thrown some large logs onto the fire before they'd arrived at the cottage, and now the flames had taken a hold of them and were tall enough to lick the entrance to the chimney. The charred wood flaked white ash and red-hot embers, the distinctive pine smell filling Alex's nostrils. It all seemed suddenly, terribly, real.

As Alex's hands moved toward it, enclosed in Stretch's iron grip, her mind scrambled to find something, anything, to say. But in the end, she could only repeat a single word over and over, as though it might somehow penetrate Holly's determination. "Wait! Wait! Wait! Please, God, just wait a fucking second –"

But then her hands were in the fire and all she could do was scream.

12
Stalker

James felt like he was going mad. He watched her from a distance and tried to figure out exactly what he thought – that the girl who looked and spoke exactly like Alex and who was at that moment in the C7 portable doing science wasn't Alex Miller? That the real Alex had in fact been kidnapped by a creepy twelve-year-old girl and held captive in a mansion? And that someone who looked exactly like James was stalking him? Surely there was no better word to describe these thoughts as madness.

James spent much of the school day talking to no one and pacing the school grounds, skipping more classes than usual, hiding out behind the cricket nets and taking out the knife he'd snuck into his schoolbag that morning at breakfast. Now you're acting crazy as well. This is what crazy people do.

Determined not to take the route past the house on Twisty Lane, he turned instead onto 'Tolley Avenue', a quiet winding road that passed Greenway Park. James usually avoided this way because drug addicts were rumoured to hang around the playgrounds there, and because it was a run down, dirty, overgrown jungle of weeds that no one in their right minds would want to pass through. But it was also the quickest way home, and the most discreet; no one could follow him without his knowing.

The entrance to Greenway Park was a steeply declining asphalt path that wound its way down a grassy hill and disappeared into the deep shadows of tall oaks and pines. There was a child's playground near the bottom, covered in rust; the tan bark concealing discarded syringes, condoms and cigarette butts. No children had played there in a long time, and if any had, they'd probably gone missing.

The place was deserted. This part of the park smelled like rotting vegetables and fertiliser. James stopped walking when he reached a peeling old bench beside a green pond. Back before the park had become such a dump. He used to come here down here with Alex. They'd play Bejewelled on their phones, legs stretched out on either side of the bench and backs pressed up against each other. Sometimes he thought he could feel her heart beating through her shirt.

She's not sick. He thought with terrible certainty. She's in the house on the hill. His reflection frowned back at him from the murky pond water. He felt rotten, stagnant, useless. His father's words came to mind, the last time he'd caught James with pastels all over his hands Quit this shit, kid. What, you're gonna make a living with this? He'd held up one of James's pictures – an image of a dead dog gnawing on its own leg. You're gonna have this trash up in galleries, huh? People swirling wine and talking about it? Listen to me... He'd started to tear it up, his expression one of mingled disgust and disappointment. Quicker you figure out how the world works, the better for you. You do work, it sucks, they give you money. You go to school, and you get a damn job, and you bring home the damn bacon. That's what being a man is. The torn strips fell to the floor and Frank Harmon wiped his hands on his work pants. If I catch you doin' this again, you'll regret it. And that had been that.

James was shaken from the memory by a sudden sense of dread. The hairs on the back of his neck rose with the delicate tingling of a spider running along his skin. He turned to look back up the hill from which he'd come, knowing that he was invisible from the park's entrance. It was late in the day, and he saw the shadow stretched out on the path, a slender silhouette.

The boy. Even before James saw the distinctive blue hoodie and faded jeans, he knew it was him because of the way he walked. He had an uncertain gait, the stride of a small child who'd just learned to walk, swaying side to side, occasionally taking a step too long or too short.

The boy stopped abruptly at the entrance to Greenway park. Didn't look back, didn't take his hands out of his pockets or pull back his hood. James could not see his face, but he sensed the boy was searching. Looking for him.

James ducked his head down and hoping the trees and the playground would cover him, continued along the path as quickly as he could. If he had to, he figured he could outrun the kid. They looked about the same size but judging by the way he moved the other boy wasn't so co-ordinated.

As he walked, James unshouldered his bag, took out the kitchen knife he'd packed into the front pocket, and tucked it into the back of his belt.

The path narrowed and led to a short bridge that crossed a gurgling creek. James considered jumping down and hiding beneath it but was immediately confronted with the image of a grinning warped face dropping down over the side: I found you! Better to stay moving than to hide. Hiding made him feel too much like a victim.

All too aware of the hollow thumping of his feet, he hurried over the bridge and started up the hill on the other side. It was a steep rise through rows of newly planted saplings, but at the top a twisted fence opened onto a cul-de-sac just one street over from his house. He could almost make it out, the last of the sun's rays just reaching the tangled metal barrier and…

The boy was there. No fucking way.

James ducked down behind a blackberry bush on one side of the path, peering through the leaves. The boy was standing beside the opening in the fence, leaning against a tree with his back hunched and the hood hiding his face. He seemed to be staring at his feet.

James doubled back. There was only one other way out of this place. He would have to follow the creek upstream until he reached the wide sewer opening from which it came, and then hope the concrete wall above it was not too difficult to climb. If he could get over the fence above it, he would land on the sidewalk along busy Randall Road.

As he made his way along the overgrown creek bed, random details of the landscape jumped out at him: stones lying beneath the clear water, the lush green ferns he brushed aside, the sting of a thorn scraping his palm – everything coloured and intensified by his fear. It was like being in a vivid dream from which there was no escape, no waking up.

A splash sounded far behind him, but the bridge was hidden by the dense plant covering. He quickened his pace, moving higher up the bank so that he wouldn't leave tracks in the mud. The sides of the creek were getting steeper by the minute, and he knew that by the time he reached the sewer opening they would be too tall to scale. But if he left the creek here, he would end up right back at the playground, and he had a feeling the boy would be waiting for him at the park's entrance. He pushed on, the banks on either side of him rising into clay walls. Every few meters he glanced behind him but saw nothing and no-one.

At last, the hill peaked, and he caught sight of the sewer opening. Shit. The fence was a good five meters from the top of the dark tunnel. Just above it, the sound – so close and yet so far – of busy traffic reached him, along with the last fading rays of sunlight. There was no way he would make it up there.

James stood for a long minute in the running water, his shoes soaked through, the knife now gripped in one hand. It did nothing to make him feel more secure. He stared at the entrance to the sewer. It was just large enough for him to curl up in, and he'd only have to go a couple of meters in to be concealed by the dark.

Guess he was going to hide, after all.

Minutes inched by. James's pants and feet soaked in the cold greywater until he couldn't keep from shivering. He didn't move from his position, watching the entrance to the sewer and the creek beyond until dusk turned to night. Not a soul in sight. Can't stay here forever. No, he couldn't. But it would be an awfully long time before his father dragged himself up from his hangover tomorrow and wondered where James was. The kid's gone. Has to be. He must have lost your tracks, probably went home to tell his creepy sister about it at the house on Twisty Lane.

James pushed himself out of the sewer, wincing as pins and needles exploded in his cramped legs. The back of his shirt and pants clung to his chilled skin. He shook his head at the state of himself, letting out a shaky laugh.

The flint rocks jutted from the water in a series of heavy stepping-stones, and James had hopped just a few of them when something echoed from the tunnel. His entire body flooded with adrenaline as he turned, mind racing. It made no sense. It was impossible for the boy have crept into the tunnel, unless… James recalled passing another sewer entrance, a manhole sized grating in the mud beside the playground put in place to keep the park from becoming a swamp.

He (It?) must have been sneaking up on him for hours – moving with painstaking slowness so as not to make a sound. Five more minutes, perhaps, and James would have felt cold hands close around his throat in the dark. Now the boy was crouching at the tunnel entrance, leaning forward over the lip and staring at James, his face a pale moon. Only too late did James recognize his awkward crouch for what it was: A predator getting ready to pounce.

The boy launched before James could move, slamming into him with enough force to knock the air out of his lungs. Somehow, he avoided the stepping-stones, any one of which would have neatly cracked his skull and landed on his back beneath the icy water. A weight like a sack of rocks landed on his chest.

James flailed weakly but the boy knocked his arms aside and then placed both hands on his face, pressing his head back into the sand bed. James felt as though all of the strength had been drained out of him in seconds. Panic seized him. He tried to buck the boy off him and failed. He tried to get his arms up to pull the hands away from his head and failed. His lungs heaved; a deep blackness closed around the outside of his vision, framing the blurry visage that was visible through the surface water that ran just over his face.

He was dying. He had a vision of his body, bloated and floating downstream to bump against the wood that collected down by the bridge. Bluish skin waterlogged and heavy, his black hair waving in the current, the tips of his fingers already nibbled away by small fish.

It was this image – which his mind presented to him in typical fashion as a painting rather than a photograph – that dispelled the panic. It was so clear that he could even see where he might scrape the black pastel and rub it into the paper, to give his empty eye sockets that hollow, shaded look.

He closed his eyes. The knife. You dropped it after you landed – it can't be far. Rough sand slid through his numb fingers as he searched the creek bed with his right hand, opening and closing his fist, systematically searching each palm sized patch. Not down by his waist, try higher. Not there, try closer in… There.

He held it; took his time, with detached care, to make sure that he had it securely in his grasp, all the while staring up through the shining film of water at the boy's blurred face.

And then he brought it up with every inch of his remaining strength, again and again, not knowing whether or not he'd connected until the water in front of his face became red and warm and the weight on his chest rolled off to the side.

James came up on top, gasping, and took hold of his collar. He pulled his head out of the water and pressed the knife against the boy's neck. For a shocking second, he locked eyes with his mirror image.

The Other James smiled in a confused daze and then coughed blood onto the knife. "You stabbed me."

"I… I'm sorry." James's mind had gone terribly blank. It was as though he were watching everything happen from the banks of the creek, helpless to intervene.

"It's okay," the boy said. "I can be free now. Holly can't punish me anymore."

"Holly? The girl on Twisty Lane?"

The Other James nodded, blinking slowly. James felt his body soften and deflate beneath him. It was like sitting on a leaking waterbed.

"Does she have Alex, too?"

"She's evil – Holly is."

"I'll get the police. I'll tell them she kidnapped Alex."

But the boy shook his head urgently, more blood leaking out of the side of his mouth. "They won't find anything. The house… She can show them whatever she wants… Like a, like a…"

"Like a movie?"

The boy smiled again, his teeth stained red. "Like a movie…" He swallowed, clearly struggling now. His head was a dead weight in James's grip, and James dropped the knife so he could hold him up properly. It occurred to him that he was watching himself die. That it wasn't really him made no difference whatsoever: his mortality was suddenly the most real thing he could imagine. This was not death to some old man in a bed on some distant future date; this was death, as it was now, right in front of him.

But Other James had something more to say, and he summoned the last of his strength to raise his head an inch closer to James's face. "The truth is in the basement," he said. "You must kill her. You must…" His mouth kept working to finish the sentence, but instead of words only blood poured from his lips, and his eyes rolled back into his head. A minute later, James let his head fall back into the water.

He wanted to do something – to bury him, maybe, but in the end, he dragged the body into the bushes and covered it with sand. That's all death was in the end, he thought: a non-event, as mundane as going to sleep.

James jammed his hands in his pockets and started for home. Shocked and numb as he was, he did not notice the girl in the raincoat sitting on the swing of the broken jungle gym as he passed by. Even if he had, perhaps he wouldn't have recognized her, because she had the hood up and her head down, and the real Alex Miller hated that raincoat and had never worn it in James's presence.

13
Security Measures

Holly locked Alex in her room and forbade Stretch to talk to her for at least a day. "And you're lucky I don't give you over to Greeny," she added sharply. "Honestly, letting her get away like that."

Stretch hung his head in shame, but she forgave him soon enough. She knew he was still upset about Miss Pinky. It wasn't his fault he was so clumsy all the time, after all. Still, better to let him stew in it so he wouldn't be so careless next time. She left him to his own devices and spent the rest of the day brooding in her treehouse, away from everything and everyone.

It was a neat little place, buried deep in the jungly western corner of the garden, at the top of a jacaranda. Usually, the tropical climate of the summer quadrant cheered her up, but when she settled her head in her hands and peered out of the little window, she saw heavy rainclouds above. She sighed.

Why was Alex so desperate to leave the house? Wasn't it nice enough? Wasn't there enough to do? Perhaps she didn't know. Stretch's grand tour was only the scenery.

Holly hadn't had a chance yet to show Alex everything that could be done here; all the adventures to be had and games to play!

She smiled at the thought, letting her mind wander for a moment. That would all be fine. Once she really saw, then everything would be alright.

That would have to wait until after her time out, though. A few chores, working with her injured hands – that would teach her, just like Cinderella having to sweep the floors. Then she would be nicer and appreciate what Holly was offering her.

Pondering this, Holly opened the trapdoor and descended the rope ladder to the base of the tree. As she picked her way through the humid jungle, her mind was elsewhere. It wasn't Alex that was bothering her – Holly was sure she'd come around soon – but it had disturbed her how easily she'd almost escaped. Not only that, but the double Holly had sent out to get James still hadn't returned. She would have to ask Other Alex what was happening out there, later.

Heavy thunder rolled across the sky and a few scattered drops of rain hit Holly's bare arms, but she paid no mind. Rain was good for reading, and she intended to curl up with a good book up in the library before long. First, though, she'd have to do something about the walls.

She headed deeper into the western corner, the tall grass and elephant ear trees growing taller on all sides until she reached the brick wall at the edge of the property. She regarded it with her hands on her hips, scowling as she remembered how close Alex had come to leaping over the edge. That won't do, she thought. That won't do at all.

And as she pondered the problem and glared at the formidable wall, the house, as always, came to her aid.

She heard it before she saw it, mistaking the sound for the pattering of heavier rain until she saw that it was actually the movement of a hundred or so roots creeping out from the undergrowth all around her. Like tangled brown snakes, they curled and twisted and climbed from the base of the wall all the way to the top, sprouting thorns and green leaves as they went, and even a few white flowers, as though the house itself was offering up an apology. *Gee, Miss Holly, sorry I almost let her get away. Is this better?*

Holly cocked her head to one side, thinking that if anything the vines should make it even easier for anyone to escape. As if to test this for herself, she reached forward and took hold of a couple of thick tendrils, testing to see if she could use them to climb the wall.

As soon as she had both hands and one foot in the hanging vines, the tender plants swung into motion, loops closing around her hands and ankle and flipping her backward. She let out a scream, but before she touched the ground a hundred slender arms caught her, the thorns turned away from her body, and flipped her upright again. They planted her softly back on her feet and a curling vine extended her way with one of the white flowers at its tip, eliciting from her a delighted giggle.

"Oh, why thank you, Mister House," she said, plucking the flower and bringing it to her nose. It smelled like strawberries and cream. One of the leafier roots waved at her from the top of the wall, as if assuring her that no one was getting over that way, either, or she waved back.

There, you see? she thought as she started back up toward the house. *Everything's getting better already.*

14
The Artist

James pushed through the unlocked front door, soaking wet, muddy and scratched to hell. His father lay unconscious on the couch. One hand down the front of his pants, empty bottle of Jack on the side table, his head hung so far backward that though James had entered from behind, they were face to face – the whites of Mr. Harmon's eyes visible beneath his drooling mouth. His snoring was drowned out, barely, by the infomercial –AB SHREDDER FIVE THOUSAND GET RIPPED GET FIT TODAY- blaring on the television.

I could be dead, James thought numbly. I could be bleeding out in the creek. He headed up to his room, his sanctuary, where everything was as it should be total chaos. Every inch of his wall and ceiling was covered in pieces of paper, not an inch of white visible beneath the layers of pastel pictures he'd drawn over the years. Clothes and books buried the floor and bed. An old school stereo with giant speakers was surrounded by piles of CDs, nothing but Blues and Punk Rock. And his desk, covered in a hundred pastels and papers, the wood itself so stained by rubbings and powders it would have looked like a Jackson Pollock painting if you could see it at all beneath everything else.

His father's warnings had had, if anything, the opposite effect on his production. These pages had always been there for him, and he wouldn't stop for anyone. Each picture up on his walls reminded him of the day on which he'd drawn it. Whether he was sad, or scared, or wanting; every time the walls had closed in on him with no escape – the pages had given him a way out. They'd shown him a window into his own soul.

And so, James did what he'd always done, in times of stress and fear: he drew.

The first pictures that emerged disturbed him. They were of his doppelganger – but instead of eyes he rubbed black powder into dark circles in the Other James's white face. Then he drew him dead, deflated, and streaming blood into the creek, a crooked half grin stuck on his face. He drew Alex's doppelganger too, and then Alex, comparing them side by side and noting where he'd put the tiny differences: in her eyes, in the way she smiled, how she stood.

Last of all, he drew the house on Twisty Lane.

This was how it always went. First came the things he knew, the thoughts on the very surface of the mind. These always led deeper, to the things he knew in his gut. And finally, like a diver sinking to the bottom of the Mariana Trench, he arrived at the dark places in the pit of his soul, where he found the truth.

He drew the last pictures in a kind of fever, no longer shivering but sweating from the effort, his heart rattling in his chest, breaths coming fast but even, unconscious of the rest of the world. Now he drew his own body in the creek with his ghost standing over it with the knife, looking down. On the next page the ghost was at the gates of the house on Twisty Lane, looking up at the great mansion, which glowed with a sinister inner light. Then there was Alex, tied up to a bed and screaming while the creepy girl, Holly, bit into her with vampire teeth and white eyes. And finally, James drew himself and Alex embracing, the little girl's body laying between them, monstrous face twisted in rage.

He finished the last rough strokes with the red pastel and then dropped it, hand cramping up. The finished pictures lay all around him, each one tossed aside as he'd grabbed the next. He hadn't thought of what he was doing, as caught up in the images as if he were dreaming them, but now that he could see the story laid out in front of him, the truth of it was obvious.

No one could help him get Alex out of the house on Twisty Lane. And whatever was happening up there... Holly can't punish me anymore... The truth is in the basement... It sure as hell didn't sound like anywhere she'd want to be.

He was going to have to go alone.

15
Despair

The burns kept Alex from sleeping. Mr. Stretch, weeping and terrified out of his mind, had dressed her hands, and wrapped them in bandages, but despite the cool cream and soft material, it felt as though she was still on fire. She sat on the edge of her bed late into the night, rocking and sucking in short breaths.

Holly had calmed down substantially in the aftermath of the torture, announcing that Alex could make up for her disobedience by helping 'Greeny' – whoever that was – clean out the garden shed. "And you and I can play down in the summer gardens and I'll show you how nice it can be. We'll have a picnic – doesn't that sound grand?"

And Alex had nodded through her tears and said that yes, that did indeed sound very grand, and did she mention how sorry she was about it all.

"That's alright," Holly had said, stroking her face with the back of her hand. "You're a good girl at heart, Alex – I just know you are. See you in the morning."

Alex had never felt so helpless and so ashamed. Just like that, everything had been taken away from her. There was no way to escape – and even less so now that her hands were nothing but big balls of gauze. I could still choke her. If we could be alone for a few minutes…

But the thought had no bite to it. It was more of a helpless longing – a prisoner staring out through the bars of her cell and dreaming about how it would feel to walk free. Seeking distraction from her pain, she stepped over to the small window and pressed her bandages up against the glass, hoping some of the cold would seep through to her throbbing hands. She remembered staring at them in shock when Stretch had finally allowed her to pull back from the fire; a pair of swollen red lobsters.

The next morning when Holly came to collect her for the picnic, she carried an air of seriousness that was almost maternal. As though she'd chastised a small dog but was willing to toss it a treat if it behaved itself.

"Good morning," Alex said with an apologetic smile.

"Good morning to you, too." Holly paused, waiting.

"I apologise for last night." Each word delivered with absolute sincerity, no trace of bitterness whatsoever.

Holly immediately broke out in a brilliant smile. "I forgive you. See, we can be friends!" And just like that it was over; she wrapped Alex in a tight embrace for a second or two and then took her by the arm. As she led her through the house, she rattled off all the different ways they were going to be friends that day.

"First, I think we'll have a picnic and talk about all kinds of things and then maybe I'll show you how I make Nobodies and you can show me something you know how to do, maybe, and we can teach each other all about our different worlds. Mine has a lot more than yours, I think, but first we have to decide where we're going to have the picnic."

They stepped out of the front doors into crisp sunshine and blue skies. As they crossed the field, Mr. Stretch emerged from a side door carrying a basket and a chequered blanket. He handed it to Holly and bowed, shooting Alex a sympathetic glance before departing. Holly didn't seem to notice the exchange. "So," she said. "Where would you like to have our picnic?"

Alex hesitated. "Um… where can we?"

"Anywhere you like. Up in a tree? By a river?"

"By a river sounds nice… but where could –"

"Oh, you'll see." Holly chuckled, clearly pleased with herself, and led Alex past the garden shed and along a narrow path through pretty acacia trees. Sure enough, before they'd walked another minute Alex became aware of the sound of running water, and a minute after that they arrived at the most beautiful scene she'd ever encountered.

"The House provides," Holly said smugly, setting the picnic basket down in a patch of lush green grass.

There beside them, a crystalline river flowed through the trees, which were spaced just widely enough for the warm sun to shine through. Even more shocking, when Holly opened the picnic basket it was filled to the brim with fresh fruit: strawberries, apples, peaches and even a container of cream (though Alex suspected that it would taste very much like the milk she'd been living off so far.)

The rest of the afternoon was like a dream, the pleasant kind, for once. The fruit was juicy and sweet, and Holly kept up the conversation with a monologue that Alex found at least as fascinating as it was disturbing. She spoke about the first Nobodies she'd ever created, and how they'd come out fatally deformed in the beginning, until Holly had learned how to channel her power better and better. Alex barely had to say a word here and there to encourage her – the girl was content to talk exclusively about her own world.

The highlight of the day, however, came when the food was all finished and Holly produced from the picnic basket the last thing Alex would have expected, a small grey battery-radio. It was the kind that ran off cassettes, and Holly had already slotted one in. The music that crackled from its dusty speakers sounded like something from the 1920s, Jazz, with a warbling female voice in the background.

"Isn't it wonderful?" Holly said. And then, to Alex's surprise, she got up by the river and began to fling her arms and legs in all kinds of odd directions. At first it seemed like she was having some kind of psychotic episode or a break from reality. Her eyes rolled in her head and her hair whipped around as she twisted her neck and body like a marionette. But then Alex understood she was dancing.

But it wasn't like dancing should be – it wasn't in time to the music; it didn't even make sense. Of course not. She's never seen it before. The realisation struck Alex with perfect clarity. Holly had grown up in this house, had never experienced the outside world except through books. She had no movies to reference – her only knowledge of dancing had to have come from the written word, descriptions of swaying hips and twirling hair. She'd had to imagine it for herself, and this, this insane ballet, was the result.

Alex couldn't help it. The look of utter conviction on Holly's face was what did it – she started laughing. A snort, then a delighted peal of laughter, and then she was tearing up at the eyes and doubling over. Holly stopped dancing and took a moment to stare, head cocked to one side.

This was bad. So bad. Alex was sure she would be punished severely for daring to laugh, but she couldn't stop, she rolled over onto her side and curled into a ball, her sides aching with the force of her laughter.

And then, thank god, Holly began to laugh as well. Soon, the two of them were side by side in the grass, weeping tears of mirth and begging for it to end. But every time their eyes met one of them would break up again and it would start over. Eventually Alex recovered enough to sit up, wiping the tears from her eyes with her arm, and their laughter gave way to the cheerful bubbling of the river.

"I can't believe this is all real," Alex said.

"Much better than your world, isn't it?" Holly said. "And just imagine, I can make anyone you want, anything you want. We can have days like this all the time. Do you want to see me make a Nobody?"

Despite her genuine curiosity, Alex couldn't bring herself to say yes. Imagine bringing a thing – a real living thing like Mr. Stretch – into the world? And what would Holly do with it, (or him or her?) when her little demonstration was over? It didn't bear thinking about. "That's okay," she said. "Maybe another day, we've got lots of time, after all."

Holly smiled. "Yes, we do, don't we? Well, it's getting late, why don't we head back, and we can read in the library until dinner time?"

And that wasn't unpleasant either. The house had all manner of fascinating books, and Alex found herself so engrossed in A Tale of Two Cities that she was still reading it by the fire when bedtime came and Stretch escorted her to her freshly made bed. Only then, in the solitary quiet of her room, did the spell break.

It rained that night, and the graveyard was barely visible beneath her window. Alex pressed her head to the glass and took a deep breath, but the tears came anyway, and she soon gave up trying to restrain them. They hit the window and trickled down the glass, mimicking the raindrops on the other side.

Her thoughts wandered to James. Had he been taken, too? She knew Holly had sent another of her creepy minions to kidnap him, but he hadn't returned yet. Maybe James had tricked him, somehow gotten the truth out of him. The thought gave her hope, but it was short lived. After all, what could he do? As far as she could tell, Holly had total control of everything on the estate, from every blade of grass from the back wall to the front gates. They might as well have been on another planet.

You have to play nice, now, Stretch had said as he'd fixed her bandages, nodding vigorously as though trying to convince himself as much as her. You'll have to be her friend the way she wants… You will, won't you, Miss Alex? I don't want you to get h-hurt again. I don't want to…

"It's okay, Stretch," she'd sighed, though her heart had sunk to the pit of her belly at the thought of being controlled – no, enslaved – by that sadistic bitch. "I'll pretend."

So, in the end Holly was going to get what she wanted.

Where the hell are you, James? And then a terrible thought occurred to her. What if the doppelganger hadn't meant to kidnap James but to kill him, to make sure he didn't figure out what was going on? And then another: what if James was fooled by the Other Alex? Perhaps she'd seduced him, even. Maybe they were even now going out to movies together, making out, dating… God, that would be just like him. He was so lost in his own stupid head all the time – he'd probably end up marrying the cardboard cut-out that was pretending to be her.

The thought shocked the tears from her eyes, and she lifted her head from the window. For the first time the truth of her isolation hit her in full force. It wasn't just that she was, as she'd thought of it before, on another planet. It was that and the fact that no one even knew she was missing.

"Oh, God." She'd never been a religious person. Being an avid horror movie fan, Alex had always had an acute awareness of the existence of evil and had found it too difficult to reconcile with the notion of a divine plan or being. Still, she found herself praying now, with her eyes shut tight and her mouth forming desperate whispered words to anyone or anything that might be listening: Don't let me die in this place. Please give me one more chance. I swear there's nothing I won't do if you just give me one more chance. "And please don't let James be a fucking idiot…"

But her only reply was the steady pounding of rain on glass, and truth be told she didn't think there was anyone out there to hear her.

She was truly alone.

16
Sister

Sister did not think of herself as the Other Alex – or even Sister, anymore. After all, no one treated her that way except the girl she was supposed to replace – the one who looked at her as though she were some kind of monster. Well, that was fine. She was with Holly forever now, and her life – as Holly had said – belonged to Alex. The new Alex.

"Just make sure he doesn't find out," Holly told her. "At least until he's with me, too. After that you can do what you like, as long as you never betray me." There was no need to threaten, of course. All the threat in the world lay behind Holly's bright eyes, the very eyes that had lit Sister's way into existence in the first place were the same doorways through which she may leave at any time.

And Sister had already screwed everything up.

The look on James's face haunted her as she tossed and turned in bed that night, and in the days afterward. His rejection of her, the truth of her otherness clear and plain in his horrified expression, and the looks he cast her at school afterward, looks of suspicion and hatred, as though she wasn't just as real as he was... Like she was some kind of freak.

She hated him.

But she couldn't tell Holly any of this, in case those big eyes glowed screaming white and sucked her away into oblivion.

These were the thoughts on Sister's mind as she carefully conducted the theatre of life. As she laughed at jokes, brushed her hair back out of her eyes, spoke with the correct cadence, walked the right way, said the right things. Being Alex was a matter of acting a mask instead of wearing one – like the ones she and Holly used to play with when it was just the two of them – sisters together – and Alex had been her friend instead of the Other. While she daydreamed with a distant smile on her face in class, she stewed with bitterness inside.

She would get him, she decided. One way or another, she would get him.

17
Thief in the Night

Dad,

I know you're going to think I'm making up stories or being crazy, but I hope that if I don't come back from where I'm going, you'll look at this note more seriously. Listen, my friend Alex Miller has been kidnapped, and there's someone pretending to be her. Like a twin or something – they look exactly the same and act the same but it's not her. Just show this to the cops and they'll do a blood test or a medical exam on her or whatever and they'll find out the truth. Please trust me on this. And by the way, if I do go missing, I'm at 243 Twisty Lane. That's where I'm going tonight, to get my friend back. I know I sound paranoid, but just get the cops to search it and I bet they'll find something. Please believe me.

I know how it sounds. I know I haven't been the best son, and we don't really talk anymore, and I know I'm not who you want me to be. But just trust me this one time and I swear I'll never ask for anything again.

Or maybe I will come back, in which case you'll never see this. Fingers crossed. But if I don't? Well, thanks for giving me food and a place to sleep.
James

To say that James Harmon 'lived in his own head' was an apocalyptic understatement. The truth was that he saw all reality, all existence and experience, through the lens of art. He flipped through his own memories like the pages of a comic book, each one a still image, larger than life and more colourful. That he was here now, hurrying along dark streets alone, was testament to the depth of his illusions. The pastel images he'd left behind in his bedroom were not trivial to him – they were depictions of truth, drawn out from the wells of his own mind. So, it was odd but not unusual that when he arrived at the house on Twisty Lane, it appeared to him like something straight out of a horror movie.

Twin gargoyles snarled down at him from their perches on either side of the formidable iron gate. The enormous mansion stood aloft at the end of a long drive like Dracula's castle, the windows glowing with hellish light. James knew instinctively that this was a front presented for the benefit of passers-by. People live here, but no one you want to meet, so keep walking.

He put one hand on the gate's cold steel and then hesitated. Everything that had happened since the end of school bell rang felt surreal. It was as if he'd fallen into one of his own pictures and was condemned to act out what he'd drawn. Maybe that was all life was – a series of images through which you were compelled to race, one to the other, each one bringing you close to the last, which was nothing but a page coated in black.

Dude. You're losing it. Just get in, find Alex, and sneak out with her. Tomorrow morning it'll be over, one way or the other.

He nodded to himself, patted the knife in his belt for reassurance, and started up the gate, hand over hand. He cringed at the metallic rattle, though he didn't think it was loud enough to reach the house. The top of the gate was lined with razor sharp spikes, which he avoided by stepping onto the concrete pedestal on which one of the gargoyles crouched. Stepping on his tip toes, he managed to slide around it and lower himself down into the soft grass beside the driveway.

There was a moment, as he landed, when the whole world seemed to tip on its axis. The grass swayed ponderously beneath his feet, and he dropped to all fours to keep his balance as it swung too far in the other direction. The urge to vomit rose suddenly and urgently from his belly and he heaved forward to deposit his meagre dinner into the weeds. No sooner had he done so that everything righted itself and he was able to climb back up on shaky legs. "Ugh. What the hell was that?"

When he looked up, all the lights in the house were out.

He froze, half-crouching in the long grass, eyes scanning the surrounding landscape for movement. Minutes passed, but the house had no more surprises in stock; so, he thought, until he glanced over his shoulder and saw that the gate and wall just behind him were covered in ivy. Impossible. Had it just grown then, in total silence, in a minute? It hadn't been there when he'd been climbing the gate on the other side.

Feeling more and more off kilter, he moved toward the left side of the mansion, stopping beside the huge stone fountain. It was nearly as large as a small swimming pool, with a thick concrete base. Actually, it was quite beautiful.

Each of the nine levels were ornately carved stone and lit from beneath with different coloured lights. The wide trough at the bottom was red, and when James inspected the ornate figures in the carvings there, he realised that each of the levels was a representation of the Nine Circles of Hell from Dante's Inferno. He'd never read through the book, but the school library had an ancient, illustrated edition of it and he'd stared at the pictures for hours on end and even tried to recreate some of them in his own drawings. Creepy.

He crossed the open space to the Eastern corner of the house as fast as he could, though he didn't think anyone could see him. The whole place seemed to be in a deep sleep, the melancholy blanket of night thrown over the house itself, as though it were a living thing – a beast slumbering away in its cave.

Creeping along the Eastern wall, he came to the graveyard. Someone had left the rusty iron gate open, so he entered silently, but once he saw where he was, he wished he hadn't. Holy shit. She's some kind of serial killer. He tried to reconcile this new information with his memory of the girl he'd met so briefly at the gates; in his mind a picture of innocence in a white dress, neat hair and royal manners. It seemed impossible. Maybe her parents were the killers?

Then he found, walking among the tombstones, a freshly dug grave. A hand tightened around his heart and squeezed as he knelt to read the stone already in place, but when he saw it, he breathed a sigh of relief. It wasn't for Alex, but for someone named Miss Pinky, which was disturbing in its own right. What had happened to her? Miss Pinky forgot she owed her life to Miss Holly, and now she's just Miss-ing. Rot in Pieces. Underneath this, carved in letters so small James could hardly read them, was another message: Sad Goodbye to Good Friend of Mr. Stretch.

James stood up quickly, suddenly not interested in exploring. He needed to find Alex and get out of here as quickly as possible. But there were only two windows on this side of the house. One at least two stories up, the other a narrow rectangle of glass half concealed by a rose garden at the base of the wall. It could only lead to one place.

The truth is in the basement, Other James had told him.

James crouched down by the rose garden and peered through the thorns at the muddy window. It was pitch black inside, and all James had brought with him was a shitty little penlight. He said the truth, not Alex. Maybe. But perhaps the truth – whatever that sinister word implied – could lead him to her. At any rate, this was the only way he could be sure of getting inside the house without being caught.

It wasn't the kind of window you could open, the edge fused into the brickwork – but it was old and thin, and a cobweb of tiny cracks branched out from the upper left corner. It wouldn't take more than a few raps with the back of James's knife. He crawled forward, careful not to let his clothes snag on the thorns, and pressed his face up against the glass, hoping for something, anything that might give him an idea of what the hell he was getting into.

Total darkness.

Everything in him wanted to get out of here, to sneak quietly out of this evil place, climb the gate and run back home to the comfort of his bedroom. But just as he was on the point of backing away, a memory found its way into the forefront of his mind. As always, he envisioned it in pastel, the vibrant colours and thickness giving the memory an added layer of emotion – more true than true.

It was a portrait of Alex as she'd been on the last day, he'd seen her – the real her – looking through the thin veil of dark hairs the wind had blown across her face, smiling at something he'd said, her eyes full of warmth and her cheeks glowing pink in the cold. Smiling at him.

And then the other – the picture he'd drawn just a few hours ago back at his house, of her being tortured by Holly.

The truth is in the basement.

"Alright," he whispered to no one in particular. "Alright, then."

And he went.

Love and Suffering

18
A Place of Her Own

Summer, 2001

She begged her father to build her a treehouse, and after that her mother, and eventually she gave up and went down into the basement instead. He had no time and she had too much to do around the house as it was, sorry honey.

Sorry, honey, she mock mimed her mother's words to herself as she stood with hands on hips at the bottom of the basement stairs, observing her new playroom. "We have a rumpus room, for Christ's sake," her father had said. "And, more importantly, a library. Lord, Holly, if you get any more spoilt, I'll have to sell you to the circus." And he'd given her cheek a pinch and winked, one of those heartbreakingly warm moments that made her think why can't you be like this all the time?

But he didn't understand. The library was one thing. She spent hours there every day as it was, often studying and doing the homework her mother set for her, and then in the afternoon and early evening when she just wanted to get lost in the wondrous worlds of Peter Pan or Merlin or any of the thousands of fairy tales and fantasies she so adored. How she longed to make friends with Wendy and fly to Never Never Land, or with Dorothy and Toto, or Pinocchio and Geppetto.

These worlds, however, were not enough. Not when she could do the things she could do, make the things she could make. What she really needed was a place to play, to experiment, to create. Alone.

She sighed, scanning the cracked and leaking basement with a critical eye. "Well," she said to herself at last, "I suppose it'll have to do."

Over the coming months and years – her father might call her spoilt, but Holly Anderson could be as patient as a Buddhist monk when it came to getting things just right – she began to make the basement her special place. Somewhere just for her.

And of course, her… experiments.

She wasn't worried about being found out, because she knew the house would help her. The house had always helped her, was the only true friend she ever had, a secret friend and one that she couldn't talk to or play with, but a benevolent and loving force all the same. It was the house, she never forgot, that had almost got her father with the chandelier.

So, once she began to really get to work, laying a carpet and cleaning and dusting the cold stone, she found the leaks disappearing, the cracks sealing, and the air growing warm and welcoming. On the rare occasions her parents had tried to enter while she was inside, the door had a funny way of jamming on them until Holly could make sure there was no evidence, and eventually they got the picture. Little girls, Gregory said dismissively, could have their alone time if they wanted. Holly wasn't fooled. She had eyes to see her mother's bruises, and ears to hear what went on above her late at night, when they thought she was in bed but was in fact just beneath them. Father was glad to have Holly out of the way, and free reign of the house, and his wife. Perhaps he hadn't forgotten the Chandelier, either.

And when everything was ready, when she had herself her secret little dungeon room where she could go and disappear from the lives of her quiet oppressors, her own world – her own universe… she began to play.

It was a feeling unlike anything else she could imagine. A welling up behind the eyes, a blinding whiteness and a fullness of body, a rushing – volts of electricity powering through her body from the tips of her toes up into her spinal cord and out through her eyes. She'd hold the image of what she wanted in her mind, and for a minute it would consume her thoughts and she'd become lost in the act of creation. A fleeting moment of nothingness, like the black space between two slides on a projector, and then she would blink, and it would be there in front of her; a living, breathing, entity.

The first ones were all broken and small, like disfigured babies – and it took her some practice to make sure they emerged voiceless. It wouldn't do to have her parents hear such noises, though she was sure the house would muffle them for her.

The hard part was disposing of the bodies, until she discovered that if she just cut them deeply enough, they would bleed out, their insides nothing but hot red blood. A drain appeared in one corner of the basement where the floor was sunken in, and this became her disposal area. The loose skins that remained could be collected in bags and buried in the garden.

It was a disheartening process, to begin with, but the desire to make something real, a friend she could talk to – or maybe even, one day, a Wendy or a Peter Pan or an Alice – was too great to ignore. She couldn't stop. Her experiments grew more bold, more complex... more intelligent.

There was an element of chaos that she could never eradicate no matter how hard she tried. They always came out different; sometimes mean, sometimes happy, sometimes wild, sometimes scared. Their bodies were never quite as she envisioned them. Broken, slanted things, brain damaged monsters. Many of them sickened her.

One day she saw the corner of a wooden trapdoor peeking out from beneath her bookshelf – the one she used for her most treasured tales – which hadn't been there before. She discovered it on the morning of her tenth birthday, and a great smile broke upon her face. When she'd moved aside the shelf and dropped into the small room below – the secret within the secret, as she thought of it – she knew it was just what she needed. A containment area. She returned to the basement and smiled up at the lone orange bulb that lit the room.

"Thank you so much, House, I love it," she'd said, and the bulb flickered happily in response.

19
The Truth

The glass cracked softly, the pieces tinkling into the basement with a sound like Christmas bells. James pulled his jacket over his hand and swiped the remaining shards from the windowpane. He was met with a rush of warm air that smelled like mould and cardboard. Here goes.

He slid through the narrow opening, face down and feet first, saved from scratching himself by his thick jacket, which snagged on thorns and slivers of glass on the way through. As soon as his feet touched the floor, he let go of the windowsill and dropped into a crouch, though of course no one could have seen him in such total darkness.

Knife raised in his right hand, he reached into his inner pocket with his left and brought out the penlight. He switched it on.

The basement was a hoarder's paradise. Except for the small space in which he crouched and a central corridor through the middle of the long room, it was packed with stuff; cardboard boxes, piles of old books, garbage bags filled with who knew what... There was a desk buried in old exercise books and newspapers and, strangest of all, a bookshelf obscured by stacks of old bird cages. Some of the cages had been stuffed with random articles of clothing and sewing materials, others with anonymous lumps of fur and leather. To the right, a short flight of concrete stairs led up to the doorway. To the left, James's penlight illuminated a sunken drain in the floor and, at the opposite corner, a trapdoor.

The truth is in the basement. He wanted to go up the stairs. If that door was unlocked, he would be able to search the house for Alex undetected. He even started to go that way, stepping out of his nook and tiptoeing along the narrow corridor with the light pointed just in front of him… but a creeping on the nape of his neck made him turn back to the trapdoor.

Something was in there – the Truth, sure, but the truth about what? About Holly, the house – what all this was? Something powerful, for sure – James could feel it radiating from the far end of the room. There's no one down here, he thought. No one to stop you finding out. And then, the thought that finally pushed him over the edge of indecision. It could be Alex.

He headed back down through the towering aisles of ancient junk, heart thrumming, and it occurred to him that he was excited. He'd never felt so alert, so locked into the sights and smells and sounds around him, in the passing of each present moment. He felt like an explorer deep in some Egyptian pyramid, seeking to break into the long-lost tomb of a dead pharaoh.

It was, as he'd suspected, much warmer at the far end of the basement, but the warmth was not coming from the trapdoor but the drain in the opposite corner, beside the stacks of bird cages. James knelt beside it and felt a dampness on the concrete. The penlight revealed a film of slime around the metal drain, the colour and consistency of tar. He rubbed it between his fingers and sniffed it, but the smell was foreign to him. The closest thing he could think of was the smell of the fertilizer his mother used in the garden.

He held his hand over the drain. Sure enough, a warm breeze wafted steadily through his fingers. A low moan echoed through the pipes below and James froze. Just some kind of heating system. It's an old house, that's all. But his skin broke out in goose bumps all the same, the body betraying the mind's lie. He slid forward, lowering his ear over the drain in case the sound came again.

"Hoooooollllllyyyyyyy…" James pulled back from the drain, the beam from his penlight shaking visibly. There was no mistaking it, that time – that was a human voice, alright – but it wasn't Alex's. It was the whispery croak of an old man, someone close to death by the sound of it. For the first time it occurred to James that the drain was not necessarily connected to a sewer. It might lead, instead, to the room beneath the nearby trapdoor.

James crept over to it – nothing more than a few boards of old pine with a metal ring in one side. He expected it to be locked, but when he pulled at the ring the door swung upward with a rusty creak, hot air from within blasting James's face like an oven and pushing the fertilizer stench up his nostrils with enough force to make him gag. He shone the penlight through the opening.

"Hooooooollllllyyyyyyy… pleeeeeeeeassse…"

Perhaps the old man had once been human. Now, he was little more than a torso and a withered head. He lay face up on the floor of a rectangular room below the trapdoor, with his feet on James's side and his head below the drain. He was half submerged in the floor of the building, which was coated in an inch or so of the thick black substance that had surrounded the drain. His body was covered in wounds too numerous to count, but far more than he should have been able to survive; coin sized pieces of his flesh were missing here and there, and burns, blisters and cuts covered what remained. A pair of eyes peered out from a mincemeat face. When James's light touched it, the corpse-thing opened a mouth half full of broken black teeth and moaned again, much louder this time: "Heeeeeeeeelllllllppppp meeeeeeeee."

And as the last of that terrible plea was floating out into the darkness, James heard things stirring in the basement behind him. Bird cages rattling as the mysterious lumps of material he'd seen before roused themselves from slumber. There was a tearing of cardboard and a peeling away of drapes, a chittering and sliding of flesh on flesh and forgotten, dead things came back to life to see what had disturbed them.

James did not wait to find out what they were. He let the trapdoor fall with a heavy thud, not caring that it was even louder than the old man's cry, which continued to echo up through the drain. He headed back for the window in a mad rush, the penlight revealing in brief flashes deformed bodies and lopsided faces emerging from their hiding spots amongst the stacks on either side of him. Some of them reached out and one scuttled out in front of him like a startled cat. He tripped over it and landed hard, slamming into a tower of old suitcases which tumbled over everything. Something squealed and he felt a warm mouth close around his ankle. He kicked it away and struggled to his feet.

He'd dropped the penlight and was now in total darkness, but before panic could consume him completely, he looked up and caught sight of a blue rectangle of night sky shining in from the window. He ran for it, kicking something furry and large as a small dog to one side and eliciting a yelp. A barb stung the side of his neck and he lashed out with his knife. They were all around him, now –

he could hear them shuffling closer, wet mouths opening and closing and furry digits pawing at him. He could feel their bodies closing in. Inhuman voices cried out, "Intruder! Help us!" and, with a rush of breath against his right arm, "MEAT!"

He lashed out again and the voice cried in pain. James leapt up for the window and pulled his upper body out into the rose bushes. Not so careful this time, he let the thorns shred his arms, face and clothes; all he cared about was getting away, getting out, escaping this impossible nightmare.

And then, kicking the last of their grabbing hands and mouths away, he was free.

The colder air in the graveyard whipped into his face as he sprinted through the trees and then out across the open grass. When he reached the fountain, he looked across the garden and saw lights flicking on inside the house. Screw this, he thought frantically. Screw all this, screw everything, shit, shit, shit… But here at last was the front wall of the property, and with one long stride and a leap he was halfway up the wall already, pulling himself up the web of ivy that covered the bricks.

His hand got stuck. He pulled it away, only to find that he couldn't lift his feet. Tendrils of leafy foliage were curling around his ankles and tightening. While he struggled, others snaked into his ears and nose and around his neck.

Later, he would think of those moments and wonder what might have happened if he hadn't kept hold of his knife in the chaos beneath the house. Would the plants have simply restrained him, or penetrated him completely, slithering down his throat and into his brain?

Mind blank with panic, he hacked madly at the tentacles of investigating vine until he managed to detach from them completely. He fell backward, landing hard enough to knock the wind out of him for a minute. Somewhere far away, the front door swung open, and steps hurried down the driveway. A young girl's shrill voice called out. "Mr. Stretch! Check the Summer Garden and wake up Greeny!"

James poked his head around the fountain in time to see Holly turn back into the house, slamming the door behind her, while the silhouette of a grown man loped off in the other direction. The vines meant running was out of the question, and in that moment, James could only think of one place to hide.

He rushed back across the grass, all too aware of the fact that he was moving closer to the basement. When he reached the graveyard, though, the broken window was empty. No monsters crawled from the dark to get at him, no red eyes peered out. Glancing once over his shoulder, he lowered himself into Miss Pinky's grave. Working quickly, he pulled as much of the soft soil over him as he could and then lay back, only his dirt-stained face exposed to the air.

An hour or so later, he heard Holly ordering the oddly named Stretch and Greeny in all directions. When a slender face with overlarge mouth looked into James's grave, his heart stopped in his chest. He – or it – regarded James for a minute; a strangely deformed creature with uneven features and, of all things, a top hat.

He was sure the man could see him, and for what seemed like a long, long time the two of them just stared at each other. Holly's voice called to him from some other part of the graveyard, and as if waking from a dream the man snapped back up and away from the opening.

"No, nothing, Miss Holly," James heard him call out.

They padded away to another part of the house, and James was left to the dark and the worms and the hours of waning night.

He did not sleep or move, or even cry, but stared straight upward at the sky as though he was already dead.

20
Greeny

"Greeny, at your service, Miss Alex." He extended a hand and then, seeing the state of hers, bowed instead, his back creaking like an old tree in the wind and his head nearly touching the ground. He was more plant than man; twisted bark for skin, gnarled and leafy limbs, and grass instead of hair. His eyes were two black holes in his head about the size of buttons, and his mouth was lined with sharp twigs for teeth, a couple of worms serving as lips. Insects crawled in and out of his various orifices and hollows at will, but he didn't seem to notice.

"Nice to meet you," she managed and Stretch gave her shoulder a reassuring squeeze.

Greeny scratched his head, regarding her for a moment, and then looked at Mr. Stretch. "What was it you said I'm to do with her?

"She's to help you clean the… Clean everything, as punishment." He sounded oddly strung out to Alex, as though he were on the brink of crying, or perhaps screaming. "She says to be nice, and if she works hard to be let out in the afternoon so she can play with Miss Holly."

They were standing out in the summer garden by the shed, hot sun streaming down on them and making Alex's bandaged hands itch with uncomfortable heat. Greeny stood beneath the shade of an oak, the shadows making him seem like part of the tree itself. He smiled, bemused. "Cleaning? For punishment? Does that mean –"

"No," Stretch cut him off. "It means cleaning, that's all." Then he turned to Alex and gave her a reassuring smile. "Just do your chores and play nicely, Miss, and it'll be a good day, today. Holly says if you're a good friend I'm to make ice cream sundaes for dessert!" And with an overzealous pat on her back and a ridiculous smile on his face, he turned and headed back to the house.

Alex, heart sinking, looked over at Greeny, who was regarding her with his strangely expressive eye holes. "Well, well," he said, muttering as much to himself as anyone. "A real live girly we got here… What's yer name, then?"

"Alex," she said. She took a deep breath and then held it for a second as a spider scuttled down his cheek from one of his mushroomy ears. Then she said, "So, what do I have to do?"

Though by then the smell from the open shed door had reached her, as had the low buzzing of a hundred flies, and she suspected she already knew.

There wasn't a lot left of Miss Pinky besides blood and skin. Whatever had been inside her had spilled out in a liquid, organless mass and sunk into the floor. Flies filled her eyes sockets and mouth and covered the site of the wound.

"Oh My God." Alex put both hands up to her mouth and restrained, barely, the urge to vomit. One of the flies flew too close to Greeny's mouth and with a snap and a crunch it was gone. He chewed slowly, savouring it. "Imagine my bloody surprise when I came back from me holiday. Was gonna clean it earlier but I had to dig a grave first, so I've had to be livin' with the poor thing. S'too bad. She was a good one." He pondered this for a moment and then, all business, clapped his leathery hands. "Right. You take the legs an' I'll get the head."

Alex couldn't hold anything with her burnt hands, but Greeny wasn't having excuses. He made her tuck Miss Pinky's slender hoofed ankles under her arms and carry that way. The body was so light without the blood, – more like a wet carpet than a corpse. They dropped her into the freshly dug grave Alex had seen the day before, and then Greeny started back for the shed. "I'll put the dirt in later. Shed first."

Alex didn't follow right away. She was looking for something, but she didn't know what until she saw it. Last night, she'd heard the quiet cracking of glass, and footsteps, but hadn't been able to make anything out in the dark. Now she looked from the empty windowpane two floors beneath her own window and then, her heartbeat doubling in a moment – at the clear shoe prints in the dirt. They led in two directions, one heading toward the front of the house, and the other seeming to head out of Miss Pinky's grave and toward the Winter garden behind the house. James, she thought. It has to be.

But then Greeny was calling, and she hurried after him, not knowing whether to be glad or horrified. She had not missed the vines that had crawled up overnight to cover the outer walls of the house, and she was smart enough to know what they meant. If James was really here… He wasn't going anywhere anytime soon, with or without her. Still, the knowledge that he had come for her was like a flame, igniting a warmth in her heart that couldn't be reached by the harshest winter chill. He came for me, she thought over and over, the sky seeming suddenly bluer than before. He came for me…

Greeny wet a large sponge for her and splashed his mop across the quagmire of congealing blood and some other, thick black gunk that was mixed in. Flies exploded in an angry flurry and then settled again on the remaining islands of leftover flesh. "You just press on that, back and forth, and it shouldn't hurt yer hands too much," he said, smiling cheerfully.

"See? Ol' Greeny ain't all bad. Just got a nasty job, is all. Right good old fella, I am." His accent reminded her of a stereotypical pirate – Captain Barbosa from Pirates of the Caribbean, maybe – or Davey Jones. Perhaps that was where Holly had gotten it from. Was that how it worked, she wondered? Could she simply make these – these creatures come out of her mind the way an author wrote characters into a book?

They scrubbed and mopped in silence for a while. Alex found that if she put most of her weight on her wrist instead of the balled-up wrappings of gauze, she could manage the pain. Still, it wasn't comfortable, and the mingling of detergent water and blood made her head spin with nausea. Talk to him. Maybe he'll let something slip. It was better than slaving away in misery, anyway.

"So, uh, Greeny? What do you think of… of all this?"

He smacked his wormy lips and gave her a quick smile over his shoulder before answering. "All this? Do you mean, young lady, the glorious and diverse world that Holly has given us, along with our lives?" If those black holes in his head could have twinkled with mischief, she suspected they would have. "Or do you mean…" And he turned his gaze to the abattoir before them.

"Both. All of it. Who is Holly, really? What is she? How do I…" How do I kill her, was one question? How do

I get out of here, might have been another – but Alex restrained herself. Even if he was good, and no more than another of Holly's unfortunate prisoners… well, Mr. Stretch had still put her hands in the fire, hadn't he?

Greeny pondered the question for a minute, mopping the blood and skin into the corner of the shed so Alex could wipe the stained floorboards. "That's a lot of questions, now. But I s'pose I'd have a few myself, in your position. Perhaps you'll tell me a thing or two about the world outside, if I tell you some of what I know. Just a friendly conversation, like?"

"I'll tell you whatever you want to know," Alex said. Her heart hopped to a steady beat in her chest, and she thought with bitter triumph, See, you bitch, no one likes you. They all can't wait to get out of here.

"Is it true that out there in the world there are Kings and Queens and Dragons that burn folk and guard treasure? And are there monsters?"

Alex paused, then shook her head. "No, none of that's real. Well, I mean some of it is, but it's not what you think. There is treasure, I guess, but you have to work for it – like at a job. It's pretty safe, but there are monsters. Not dragons or anything like that, they look just like people, but they're monsters inside. But it's free, out there – that's the best part. You can do whatever you want and…" But even as she said the words, she heard the lie in her own voice. What was she talking about? She wasn't free, was she? She was as much imprisoned in her life out there as she was in here with Holly.

Still, she persisted with determination: "Anyway, everything about it is way better than in here. There are billions of people to meet, more things to do and see than you could in your whole life and it's bigger than you can imagine… I mean, yeah, it's awesome," she finished lamely.

He regarded her for a long minute, chin resting on the handle of his mop. "I don't believe you," he said, not unkindly. "You're trying to turn me against Holly, like she warned me. Not that I believe Miss Holly, either course. Lies, lies, all day long." He muttered to himself and resumed his chore. "As to your questions, I will tell the truth since I have no cause to lie.

"Holly is a spoilt brat. But she is an all-powerful spoilt brat, and one with power beyond your imagining. That, and she has the house on her side. As for me? Well, I know just how to keep my Holly happy – and it's a good thing, too, because despite being a spoilt brat –" Every time he said the words 'spoilt brat' he glanced up at the shed's only window. "She can give a good life to a thing like me. I eat whatever I want, and I can have what comforts and pleasures I like, for the cost of just a little work here and there."

Alex stood up, pretending to stretch but actually just trying to get a view through the window herself. Sure enough, Holly was visible on the other side of the summer field. She was talking to Sister – the girl now looking, if possible, even more like Alex than ever. Alex wondered how the other was getting on with her old man. Fine, take my life, she thought, and a wave of sadness washed over her as it occurred that her life wasn't all that terrible a thing to lose. Enjoy it. She got back down on her knees and scrubbed more vigorously. She ripped another blister, and her right hand started to get terribly itchy, but she didn't stop.

"And how do you keep the brat happy?" she said.

"My jobs here in the great House of Holly," Greeny said, "are groundskeeper and disciplinarian. And the shed is where I do my jobs – both of 'em."

It took Alex a minute to put the two together – how being a disciplinarian and groundskeeper could be accomplished in this dusty shed with its bench and old tools and… Oh God. She remembered Miss Pinky launching at her from the cupboard at the back, not attacking but lunging like a drowning person for a lifeboat. And how covered in wounds she'd been, her pink skin butterflied by shears and scissors, her joints torn with pincers, her snout flattened and broken, perhaps by the slow pressure of a vice. "You're a torturer," Alex said.

Greeny set the mop aside and reached for a great big bag of what appeared to be beach sand. He upended it over the thick pool of gore in the corner until it was mostly buried, and then he set the bag aside and waited for the grains to soak up what they could. "The Nobodies, they come and go," he said. "But not I. Greeny stays, and lives and thrives, he does. Dirty work, see, but I'm willing to do it, and that's why Holly keeps me."

And then he gave her a smile she'd never forget as long as he lived; odd twiglike teeth sticking out at funny angles, a sluggish tongue sliding out to moisten his lips. "Enough about me, though. Tell me about yourself, Miss. First time I've had the honour of meeting a real live girly, besides Holly – and I think she's something different…"

And so, as Alex scrubbed the stains into the dark floorboards and Greeny scooped the bloody mud into a garbage bag, she told him all about her parents, and James, and school. He listened so intently, stopping her only occasionally to ask a question that she lost herself in her own story. It had never occurred to her until now, when she had to relate her life to someone else, how small and dark her life had been. No matter how she spun it, she knew he was seeing the parts of herself she tried to obscure. How she'd always shrunk away from her parents, done everything she could to keep them happy, and the same for everyone else. And how she disappeared into her horror movies and her music to escape when things got too hard, the same thing she suspected James did with his pictures.

She paused at last when, in an effort to get out the last of the stubborn blood stains, she pushed too hard again and a patch of burnt flesh moved inside the bandage on her right hand. She gasped, clenching her eyes shut against the pain. A second later she felt knobbly hands pulling her gently to her feet and then Greeny was unwrapping the now dampened bandage. His black tongue protruded comically from the side of his mouth in concentration, and his sticklike fingers worked with deft tenderness, until her hand was out in the open air.

It was bad. Her entire hand had swollen to twice its original size, and every inch of it was covered in blisters and red flesh. The slightest twitch of a finger would split skin, and even Greeny's light breaths were like sandpaper on the burns. He grunted. "No good, no good."

Leaving her to hold her hand out over the bench, he ducked down and rummaged through a cupboard, emerging with a tube of burn cream and fresh bandages.

"Why bother healing me?" Alex said, unable to conceal her bitterness. "Isn't the whole point to punish me?"

"Better to heal quicker. She might have been the one to burn you, but that won't stop her from getting annoyed if your wounds get in the way of her games. She likes her games, does Holly…"

The cool cream was heaven on her burns, and after Greeny had carefully re-done both of her dressings, she sighed with relief. "Thanks so much," she said, and then paused, her gaze drifting to the dark patch that was now all that remained of Miss Pinky. He's tortured living things all the way to death. Who knows how many times? How many bodies had to fill those graves?

"No problem, Miss. Just remember to play nice, now…"

And as if those buttonhole eyes of his could read her thoughts, he leaned forward and whispered, "Pleasant as you are, I hope for your sake I don't see you here again, for any reason."

21
Promises, Promises

Holly bounded from her bed with fresh exuberance. Her rage from the day before had died down – it always did after she visited Mother and got her beauty sleep – and now she was ready to attack the day. Attack was the word, too, after the mysterious break in last night. The house would have healed its broken window by now, but that didn't change the fact that someone had gotten all the way into the basement and, if the frustration and hunger of the Babies were anything to go by, escaped. But whoever it was couldn't have escaped the estate all together – no more than a fly could escape a spider's web, once caught. She had only to wait for the vibrations to lead her to the culprit.

And she thought she had a good idea who that would be, even before she opened the front door to a calm summer breeze and saw Sister making her way down the driveway. Holly went out to meet her, wanting to stand out in the sun and flowers. Judging by the frown on the other girl's face, the news wasn't good.

"Shouldn't you be in school or something?" Holly said, picking a dandelion as Other Alex drew within earshot.

"Yes, but they let me go because everyone knows I'm James's friend."

"What does that have to do with anything?" Holly said, half smiling because she already knew the answer, and it was just as good as good could be. Mine, mine, mine, her inner voice sang. A future filled with games and happy memories with her brand-new friends sprung up in her mind, her imagination already running away with her.

"I found his body," other Alex said plainly. That was unexpected. Holly blew the head of the dandelion away and stood up straight. 'Whose body?' she said.

"Other James. Not him - he must have killed it."

"Did you see? What if they find it?"

Sister shook her head. "All they'd see is skin and blood."

Holly nodded, reassured. That was all Nobodies were in the end - skin and blood and a little magic to hold it all together. A mask with not much behind it.

"And the real James is missing, isn't he?"

"How do you know?" Sister's tone had an edge to it that Holly didn't like. Sister was getting too used to the outside world already, perhaps, forgetting that she wasn't a real girl, after all. If she kept that up Holly would have her pay Greeny a visit about it.

"Someone snuck in last night," Holly said. "Most likely still here somewhere. So, they can search all they want," she added.

"Do you want me to find him?" Sister said, brightening.

"No. Your only job is to spy on the outside and make sure no one disturbs me. And if I feel like having more real people –" she emphasised the word 'real' so as to eliminate any doubt that may be in the Nobody's mind that that was exactly what she was: A Nobody. "Then you can help me bring them in."

She cocked her head to one side, appraising her creation in a different light, frowning. There were dark bags under Sister's eyes that hadn't been there before. She looked malnourished – anorexic, even. Her skin had none of the living glow it had had a couple of days ago. "Have you been eating enough?" She said eventually.

Sister nodded. "Lots," she said. "They make me food twice a day, and pack my lunch, too. I eat just like them!" she added proudly, but Holly was having none of it.

"See Mother before you leave," she said.

"But I'm fine! I don't need –"

Holly slapped her hard enough to make her reel backwards. There was some colour in her cheeks now, alright, and real tears in her eyes.

"Don't talk back." But she'd seen that look on another's face once before, and it brought no small number of unwelcome recollections. Like pets, remember, just like Greeny told you. You have to toss them bones as well as kick them.

So, she forced herself to smile, and reached over, ignoring Sister's involuntary flinch as she did so. She stroked the cheek she'd slapped, the heat she felt there sending a thrill up her spine. She was looking forward to playing with Alex, soon. "I'm sorry, little sister," she said. "Tell you what… If you visit Mother twice a week or more and do your job on the outside – and if you help me with Alex, later… I'll let you have James all to yourself two days a week."

Sister's eyes widened, full of hope. "Really?" she said. "And I can do whatever I want with him?"

"As long as you give him back in one piece," Holly said. "You can do whatever you like."

22
A Back Way

As James pulled himself out of the grave in the crisp early hours of the morning he felt, appropriately, like a zombie. Every joint was stiff, his extremities numb, and his mind dull with shock. The basement window had, impossibly, restored itself overnight. Now, a crisp grey morning set a thin layer of frost over everything, including the glass, and the interior was just as impenetrable as it had been the night before.

He'd meant to hide, just until he was sure those searching for him had well and truly gone. But in the comforting dark of that deep hole in the ground, where the soil was strangely warm against his skin, he'd found himself drifting off beneath the winking stars. His mind ran a hundred miles a minute even while he dreamt, as though his subconscious was trying to make sense of everything that had happened to him and all he'd seen. The result had been a cascade of bright and vivid nightmares: grinning strangers in top hats with necks that were too long, scowling girls with neat hair and big knives, and a world in which everyone he knew had been replaced by clothing store mannequins.

Now, as he crawled from the damp earth, his fear was exhausted. He simply didn't have the energy to be terrified any longer, and his desire to find a way into the house had as much to do with getting warm as it did with finding Alex. Just in the nick of time, too; no sooner had he slipped through the graveyard's iron gate did he hear the house's heavy front doors swing open.

He hurried along the side of the house, giving the basement window a wide berth, repaired (though that cobweb crack in the top left corner had returned along with the glass) or not.

When he rounded the back of the building, he came to an abrupt stop. It had been cold a moment ago – now it was freezing. He gasped for a moment in the frigid air, his breath steaming in front of him. There was snow here! He looked back around at the graveyard, and saw dying leaves covering the ground, but no ice. The transition was more obvious in the form of a muddy line where soil met snow that ran from the corner of the house downhill into the trees.

He was on the point of rushing past this place in the hopes that the Western side of the house would be warmer – and what a crazy thought that was – when he saw a window set into the cracked stonework that made up the back wall of the house.

It was open. Not a lot – just a crack – but enough that he could get his fingernails under and slide it all the way up.

He crunched through the frost and wiped a circle in the glass so that he could see inside. Though the room on the other side was dim, there was enough light for James to make out several towering shelves of books. A kind of home library, and the perfect place for him to hide out.

Even if someone else entered, it couldn't be that difficult to keep just out of sight behind the stacks. He blew on his fingers to thaw them out and then wedged them into the crack beneath the window. It slid up as if it had been oiled the day before – silent.

James allowed himself a small smile. Finally, he thought. Something's going my way.   Lowering himself stealthily into the quiet room, he made sure to slide the window shut after him. When the bolt slid neatly into place with a sound click, he was already too far away to hear it.

23
Experiments

Spring, 2002

Down in her special place below the house, where the thick walls and windowless chambers kept everything nice and secret, she'd torture them. Some of them died all on their own, and she dug her first graves just outside, planting the rose garden and tending to it enthusiastically so her mother wouldn't be suspicious. She kept some of the more interesting specimens in boxes and crates – a museum of the things that didn't work. But occasionally she'd take one and try things with it. She'd show it around and see how it reacted. Poke and prod it. Tie it up, release it. Try to talk to it. She was a curious girl – she always needed to understand what and how and why, and her own creations were a source of constant mystery.

Mystery, and newly discovered joys. They could feel things, she discovered. Through her extensive experiments, she found they could feel misery and joy and pain, and some of them – her best works – could even think, to a degree.

Down there, where she dug her first graves and met her first real Nobodies, down there she learned about control. The whiskey controlled her father. Her father controlled Holly and her mother. And Holly controlled the Nobodies. Control and power, that was what it was all about.

And you couldn't have control without fear and pain.

Miss Pinky was an accident – albeit the kind of accident that is bound to happen in time. Throw enough darts at the board and you'll hit the bullseye eventually, even if you're blindfolded. And Holly, with her obsession and her experiments and her determination to get there, to create the thing she really wanted, something real – was not blindfolded.

She wasn't trying to make anything in particular – merely struggling to distract herself while her mother's muffled cries creeped through the floorboards. If she could just drain herself, create something so large and complex that it exhausted her, then maybe the rest of it wouldn't matter. But then on the fifth try, just when the first tears were pushing behind her eyes – half from fear and half from determination – the fire exploded in her mind and the world went white and…

Miss Pinky was there.

She rolled over, still steaming, pink and naked, her snout like face and cloven feet forming last, gap toothed mouth opening and closing like a fish as she took her first breaths. Giggling, amazed at herself – Holly pointed an accusing finger at the Nobody's exposed nipples.

"You're naked!" she said. The four breasts – like hog's teats – fascinated her. What a thing to have made! Miss Pinky reddened appropriately and reached for the nearest means of cover – a large brown beanbag that Holly liked to sit on while she read – and pulled it over herself. Her beady eyes darted around her surroundings, settling at last on Holly.

"What's your name?" Holly said.

A kind of muffled grunt escaped the creature's mouth, and she looked as surprised to hear it as Holly was.

"Hm. Well, I'm going to call you Miss Piggy, because you've a snout and trotters." She giggled again, and then, feeling oddly guilty: "Well, maybe Pinky instead – that's nicer."

Miss Pinky smiled back nervously, and just like that; they were friends.

Holly learned, as she grew older, the art and value of escape. The more she could make herself invisible, the better for her. If her father paid attention to her, she made herself invisible by portraying the doll-like perfect daughter that he expected her to be. Yes sir, no sir, I have done my studying, I did have a wonderful day, and isn't this food delicious? It was the same act her mother played – that of the perfect wife, only her mother could not escape the way Holly could, late at night, when Gregory began to drink.

But soon Holly had created a world for herself away from whatever horrors occurred above ground come nightfall. She would lock the door behind her and push a mattress up against it to keep out the sound, and then she would turn on her Jazz records and play with Miss Pinky, or read a book, or dance or write in her diary or, more often than not, create.

Miss Pinky was the first Nobody that had lived long enough to require some kind of food, though luckily, she could eat just about anything – from meal leftovers to garden waste and worms. Better yet, Holly discovered that Pinky could feed some of the other nobodies with her teats – just like Holly learned from reading the farm books her mother gave her for Biology Class. Holly didn't try to create any more Miss Pinky's – they'd be too difficult to contain, and who knew what would happen if they got out and her father found them. Instead, she experimented on a smaller scale, making squirming little creatures she called her Babies. Some of these – the ones with mouths, could suckle on Miss Pinky, and the nourishment they took from her sustained them far longer than any of Holly's earlier attempts, which had withered and died in weeks.

It was a constant challenge, and many of the new things had to be put down. But in time, Holly got better. Some she made with many legs, others with no bones but flexible tentacle-like limbs that could cross from one end of the basement to the other in a blur. It was always a surprise what kinds of unique features she could put together. Like the set of test tubes and liquids her mother used to teach her chemistry, endless combinations could result from limited ingredients.

In time, she taught Miss Pinky to communicate, and by Holly's eleventh birthday she could almost form sentences, in a childish sort of way. She became Holly's closest friend and confidante, and as much a mother to the Babies as Holly was. Holly would lie with her head on Miss Pinky's soft belly, feeling the doughy hand stroke her hair while she related all that was on her mind. She told her about her father's scary moods and her mother's desperate attempts to make everything happy and nice when it wasn't. Miss Pinky told her that one day Holly would be a grown up and she'd be able to live just how she wanted, with no one the boss of her and all her Nobodies – as many as she wanted – to be her friend.

Holly told her secrets, too – things she'd never said aloud. About how the house was alive, and how it had saved her and her mother from her father many times. It distracted him, and sometimes when she pressed her ears to the walls, she swore she could hear words of comfort and love whispering through the pipes or creaking through the floorboards. Miss Pinky said she heard the same voices, and she thought that the house belonged to Holly, too, and that she would own it instead of her father.

"I hope you're right," Holly said one night, curling up with her and listening to the rain pattering on the small window.

"Just think of all the things I could do, you and I and the house together. We could make paradise, don't you think? Perhaps I could even make something real – a human being, even. Don't you think?"

She'd been making a lot, lately, and she was certain her abilities were improving. But it was becoming more and more difficult to keep everything hidden. She couldn't let the mask of perfection fall, or her father would… would do something. Her frustration manifested in her new babies: things with sharp teeth and nasty tempers, ugly beasts with claws and fur; mixtures of insects and animals – their bodies becoming less human as Holly took out her impotent rage on them, the way an artist might throw paint on a canvas with aggressive passion. Some could see in the dark. Some needed drops of blood mixed in with the milk to live. Some were blind; some were murderous and hard to kill. All of them, though, loved Holly. She made them that way.

Others she made only for pain – soft things with no mouths with which to scream. These she would make when her mother was sharp with her, or when her father turned his bitter rage on her for one reason or another. Then she would rip and tear and slice and twist until the life seeped from the helpless beings in drips of agony, and then she would throw them to the others. Miss Pinky didn't like to see that at all, and she did her best to comfort Holly.

"He's mad tonight, isn't he?" Pinky said one night, when the sounds from above were particularly miserable. The lights were off, because the babies liked it that way, and Holly didn't want her parents to know she was in here and not up in her bedroom.

"I think so," Holly said. She worried for her mother – she worried a lot, but for some reason this night was different. Lying there in the dark, Pinky's comforting warmth beside her and the presence of the babies all around, Holly got to thinking. She got to thinking about beady red eyes that could see in the dark, and about little hands that gripped and didn't let go. And she got to thinking about how her father loved the bottle, sometimes it seemed more than Holly herself.

She got to thinking, and pretty soon she got to smiling, and when Miss Pinky asked her what was wrong, Holly said, "Oh, nothing's wrong, Miss Pinky. Nothing's wrong at all, only…" There was a brief silence in which a soft rain began to fall, and thunder rolled far away like the crashing of a great wave.

"Only what?"

"I think I know just what to do. But I'll need your help."

And Miss Pinky, sensing the emotion in Holly's voice, slipped a pudgy hand into hers and squeezed tightly and said, "Anything for you, Miss Holly."

24
Labyrinthine Halls and Creeping Doors

James could feel a part of himself letting go of the reality he'd once taken for granted. The process had begun when he'd first seen his Doppelganger, and once he'd slid the knife into that creature's heart everything had begun to unravel rapidly. Now, creeping around corners and up crooked flights of stairs and through rooms of all kinds, he felt he had truly left the tenuous thread of the 'real world' behind and entered the land of dreams.

Crossing a hallway as wide as a main road, he slipped through a round door and into a room as large as a car with no furniture of any kind. From there he entered a lavish dining room, the table laid out with shining silverware that didn't appear to have ever been used. Then a ballroom full of rich curtains and carpets and a bar packed with fine gins and absinth.

He was about to move on when he spotted the figure standing behind the bar.

"Hello, Mister James."

It was the odd thin man who'd covered for him the night before. James had to admit, he looked no less bizarre in the ballroom's dim light, the golden orbs in the ceiling barely glowing bright enough to illuminate him at all. His whole body seemed crooked and elongated, and as James cautiously approached, an alarming smile leapt across his face. "Sorry to frighten you. But if I'd let you wander any longer, I'd have never found you at all, maybe." He lifted two glasses from behind the bar and set them up in front of him, lowering a silver spoon with a sugar cube into each. "A short sip might do you well, now I think of it." He filled the glasses with luminous green absinth, dissolving the sugar. James watched, hypnotised.

"Who…? What are you?" he said at last.

"Mr. Stretch is my name," the man said, cocking his head to one side. "I'm Miss Holly's friend."

"Not last night, though," James ventured. "Last night you helped me, didn't you?"

He sighed, head drooping on his rubber neck almost comically, and took a sip from his glass. He leaned on the bar and James sat down on one of the tall stools opposite, though did not yet touch his own drink. "Holly dearest is a very lonely girl," Stretch said. "She wants only a friend, but she doesn't know that friends can't be… can't be made from nothing, like Nobodies. They have to love you back, like Miss Pinky did."

"Nobodies… is that what you are?"

He nodded sadly. "She has power born of the house itself. A power to create, to make things like me, and…" he snapped his multi-jointed fingers, "to take away. It's been a long time; I've been her friend. I was so grateful, all those years, that she let me have love, just like real people." His eyes glistened. James said nothing, knowing that the strange man was talking for his own benefit as much as James's but listening keenly all the same, trying to piece together the nightmarish world into something that made sense.

"Holly had everything she wanted, everything the house could provide. But girls who get everything never have enough. Soon she grew lost in the fairy books from the library, full of white nights and dragons and tales of adventure. Happy endings. And they made her long for those people – real living people; ones that didn't belong to her. Miss Alex, and you. Lovers."

"We're not –"

"But she'd use you like toys, like playthings to act out her fantasies. Even now, Mister James, you're stuck in this dollhouse of hers like all the rest of us. Plunge that knife into her heart if you like – it will do no good. Her soul belongs to the house, and the house belongs to her."

He swirled his glass and took a deep drink, eyes spinning in his head. James couldn't tell if he was really loopy or just drunk.

"But if you help me, there'd be nothing to stop –"

"Ssssshhh!" He whipped a finger up to James's lips. "Not so loud – the walls have ears. I can't help you, or she'll make me gone in a wink." And then, he leaned in closer, his liquorice breath hot on James's face. "Listen close. I can help you stay free and meet with your friend. If Holly finds out, I'll be all over, but I have to do it. Your friend is so good – good like Pinky! But there is only one way out, and that's to put an end to the whole place. Her soul is in the house, but it is split in three, do you understand?"

James didn't quite, but when he whispered the first thing that came into his mind, "You mean like Horcruxes?" Stretch nodded vigorously. "Yes, The Potter Books – she loved them dearly!"

"Holly did?"

"No, Pinky. Pinky would read to me, you know." Tears leaked unbidden from his eyes and rolled down his cheeks, but he paid them no mind. He tapped James's glass with a sharp fingernail and James took a sip, barely holding back a cough as the syrupy liquid scorched his throat.

"Three pieces," Stretch went on, and then, pointing straight down: "The father…" And up, toward the attic: "The Mother…" And then his face clouded over with uncertainty and he shook his head. "Stretch doesn't know the last. Perhaps the house itself… But all three must be ended, or you're to be her toys forever. Like me and Greeny and all the rest."

James took another tentative sip, and this time it went down a little easier. A small fire kindled in the pit of his belly, and for the first time he felt something like hope. "When can you take me to Alex?" he said.

Stretch stood up, wiping his tears away with the back of one spidery hand. "Tonight," he said. "But first we must hide you."

James looked around the dark, empty ballroom, and thought of the convoluted network of hallways he'd traversed to get here. "Can't I hide from her in here?"

And Stretch's bulging eyes swivelled to meet his. "It's not Miss Holly you must hide from, young James," he said. "It is the House."

25
Playdate

A lex stepped out of the garden shed, squinting in the late morning sun, to find Holly waiting for her out on the green, beaming and dressed in her Sunday best: a pretty white dress and schoolgirl shoes with long socks. When she saw Alex emerge, she waved and then made a waving motion to Greeny, who was standing in the doorway behind her. "The swords please, Greeny!"

Alex walked over to the girl, standing closer to her than she would have liked and wondering what kind of fresh nightmare Holly had in store for her. 'The Monster Game' was all too fresh in her mind, and she wasn't sure she could bear another experience like that. At least her participation in this one would be limited by her bandaged hands. Remember what Greeny said. Play nice. "Morning, Holly," she said.

"Good morning, Alex! Did you sleep well?" Holly said.

"Oh yes, thank you."

Greeny emerged from the shed, carrying with him two short swords. At a distance they looked like the kind of shiny toys that came in plastic boxes for boys who wanted to play at being knights, but up close they were sharp, gleaming steel. Greeny bowed and handed one to Holly and then one to Alex, who held up her bandaged hands. "Sorry."

"You can just cradle it under one arm, like this," Holly said, demonstrating. "It doesn't matter if you can't use it properly – I'm here, after all." Alex complied, manoeuvring her arms until she ended up with her arms folded tightly and the hilt of the sword tucked in her armpit, so that the blade pointed out at an odd angle. "Like this?" she said.

"Good enough. Was she a good worker, Greeny?"

Greeny bowed again and gave a twiggy smile. "Very much, Miss Holly. Worked off her punishment, I think."

"Oh, good, good, good! See, that wasn't so bad! Now we can be friends again and play."

Alex had more than a few words to say about that, but before she could say any of them Holly was already moving, heading across the lush green grass to the deeper part of the summer garden as she explained the day's activities. "I've planned out an adventure for us, and everything! Just wait until you see – just wait. I wanted to have something fun, to show you what we can do if you're – if you want to be my friend. So, today's game we'll play is called 'Rescue the Princess'. Just like – you know, just like in the fairy tales!"

"Oh. Okay. That sounds… fun."

"It does, doesn't it! And I've hidden a picnic basket for us along the way, and things to hunt for food in the jungle, and lots more. It's going to be grand. But first, there's one more thing to add."

They had come to the edge of the trimmed and well-maintained garden. Beyond this point, all Alex could see was a jungle of vines and elephant leaves and mossy trees.

The sun beat down, the air as hot and humid as the amazon jungle. When Alex peered through the dense foliage, searching for the far wall, she couldn't see it. Her belly gave a sour twist when she saw the look of fanatic glee on Holly's face. She waited patiently for Holly to elaborate. Just play along.

Holly took a step back from the tree line and gestured for Alex to do the same. Then, sword clutched in both hands, she opened her eyes wide and stared at an empty patch of shaded grass beneath a towering network of roots and branches that Alex remembered from geography was called a 'strangler fig'.

They stood that way for a long time, and in the silence, it occurred to Alex that something important was missing from the scene. It occurred to her a second later: there were no animal noises. No cicadas buzzing, no birds, no nothing. She turned to Holly to comment on this, but the words choked her before they could leave her mouth.

Holly's eyes had changed. No, not changed – they'd vanished – to be replaced by perfectly round holes in her expressionless face; holes through which a blinding white light shone onto the patch of grass, causing smoke to rise from the ground. Alex dropped the sword, arms rising to shield herself from the stunning glow as she staggered backward.

The smell of singed hair filled the air, accompanied by a sharp Bang! And when Alex opened her eyes again, she saw something that immediately brought to mind the Troll from the three billy goats gruff – some hybrid between a gorilla and a bull. It stood hunchbacked, only a head or so taller than Holly herself, with a deep Neanderthal brow and a trail of drool stringing from its mouth. Big brown eyes shot left and right, confused, finally settling on the neatly dressed girl standing a few feet away.

Holly blinked, her baby blue eyes returning, and let out a delighted chuckle. The beast took an uncertain step, surprised, and then Holly raised her sword and shouted at the top of her lungs, "Back, beast! Back into the jungle to guard your princess! Beware of us, for we intend to smite you and rescue her this day!"

And, incredibly, the beast reared back, affronted, and then turned and lumbered off into the jungle, glancing once over its shoulder with panicked eyes. Holly looked over at Alex with an expression of mingled triumph and nervousness, like a small child showing a picture she'd done to her mother, or perhaps a boy doing dangerous stunts and then checking to see if the girls were suitably impressed.

Impressed was not quite the word; Alex was dumbfounded. "H… how is this possible?" she said. The idea that she was in a dream returned to her and then departed. The pain in her hands had thoroughly done away with that comforting fantasy.

"Don't worry," Holly said. "I can make them as dumb as I want. And I can put ideas in their head when I make them, too. They can't hurt me – not really… Are you all right?" She cocked her head and Alex nodded. Oh, God, what are we doing today. What kind of sick game is this going to be? "Sure. Fine. Yep."

"And guess what else?"

"What?"

"The jungle?" She gestured at the dense greenery before them. "It can go as deep as I want. Neat, huh?"

Alex forced an indulgent smile on her face as she answered. "That's super cool, Holly. I didn't realise you could do so much."

Holly blushed and looked away, pretending as though it was nothing. "Oh, it's not me, really," she said. "I can only make things. It's the house that makes places and keeps everything safe. Maybe tonight…" She leaned closer, letting her in on the big secret. "Maybe tonight you can meet it."

Hot fear took hold of Alex's heart, making her false smile falter just slightly before she pasted it back into place. "Oh… yeah, if I'm not too tired," she said. "That would be awesome."

Holly nodded eagerly, apparently fooled by Alex's transparent acting, and aimed her sword at the jungle. Her voice transformed once more into an odd parody of the knight in shining armour: "Well then, dear lady, let us advance into this mighty jungle! For our princess is captured by that troll, and we must save her. Forward!"

Alex cast one final glance behind her and saw Greeny standing beside his shed, one twisted arm raised in goodbye, his expression unreadable. The house loomed behind him, cottagey white walls like pale flesh. Through one of the upper windows, two blurry faces watched her go.

Oh God, help us, Alex thought, but then the trees blocked everything from view, and it was only the two of them.

And, of course, the House.

The hunt was, as expected, a nightmare.

Holly, the expert tracker: pointing out broken twigs and misshapen footprints in the mud, her face blazing with excitement, mistaking Alex's terror for the same. Then a terrifying ambush – Alex throwing herself to one side when a drooling beast charged out of the bush. It was a hideous hybrid between a pig and a pit-bull, but it had no eyes and no ears. Holly ran the thing through with her sword – bravely absorbing its (toothless) bites on her arms. "Ha ha! Got you now, you mangy thing!" She sat on it while it bled to death, breathing its last with a mournful gaze fixed on Alex all the while.

It was the most horrifying thing Alex had ever witnessed. It was alive, she thought. It was really alive. It felt pain. But she pushed the thoughts away, locked them in a dark box she hoped she'd never need to open, so that she could play nice.

At Holly's direction, Alex ventured into the jungle to collect firewood while the other girl butchered the corpse, skewering hunks of nameless meat over a campfire to roast. She found that as she moved, the bandaged right hand that was tucked into the crook of her arm was rubbing against a section of her sword. At first, she tried to re-arrange her grip on it, but then it occurred to her that maybe letting her bandage unravel wasn't that bad. Sure, her raw burns would be out in the open… but she would have a free hand. A hand that might, for example, grip the hilt of a sword.

"Hellooo?" Holly's cheerful call shook Alex from her thoughts. "It's ready!"

Holly had retrieved the hidden picnic basket, and they dined on strawberries and cream and glasses of lemonade, cooling off in the shade. Her neat outfit was completely ruined and covered in blood and dirt. She gulped her drink in a few mouthfuls and then leaned up against an enormous redwood, sighing. "Wasn't that fun?"

"I've never done anything like that," Alex said. She felt faint and lowered herself onto a mossy mound near the fire. "Never in a million years."

Holly smiled at her, wiping the sweat from her brow. "Only a little farther to the dreaded beasts cave, lady," she said in her knight voice. "And then we shall save our beloved."

They laughed together, and Alex was, not for the first or last time, amazed at Holly's failure to perceive her own sickness or, for that matter, Alex's fear. *She has no idea that she's a monster,* she thought. *Worse – she thinks she's doing a good thing. She thinks she's giving me a treat – showing me some kind of wonderful fantasy. She's insane.*

But that thought brought another, and this one was far more comforting. If Holly really was as insane – as disconnected from the reality of their situation – as she seemed… then maybe she could be fooled.

Alex smiled distantly, as though satisfied so far with the day's activities. "I guess this isn't so bad, after all," she said.

"Really?"

"Yeah, I mean, that fire thing was horrible, but. I guess I could live like this. Can I ask you something, though?"

"Of course."

"It's about my friend James. I know you're looking for him right now. He snuck in, didn't he?"

Holly nodded earnestly. "You want him to play also, don't you? So, we can all be friends together – real life friends. Don't worry – the house will get him." She said this with a tone of comforting optimism.

"Oh… great. I was just wondering, you know, when we're all together. Do you think me and him could like, have the same room together?" *Be careful, girl. You have to play this really slow.*

Holly frowned. She came over to kneel beside the fire, turning over the makeshift spit they had. "What do you mean? Is he – are you in love with him?"

Alex saw a chance and seized it. "Yes. Yes. I didn't want to admit it before…" she looked away, as if embarrassed. Inwardly, her heart was racing. The worst possible thing would be for her and James to be locked in separate rooms, away from each other like prisoners in cells. If they were together, they'd be able to gang up, or think of something – she was sure of it.

Alex guessed that Holly would react either with rage borne of jealousy – her new best friend wanting to be with someone besides her or – Alex thought more likely – shrewd manipulation. I'll let you see him, if you play nice and never disobey. What she didn't expect was for Holly to brighten suddenly and clap her hands with delight. "Oooooh, I knew it!" she said. "Just like in the stories! I know! We'll have a big wedding here and you and James can be married and live happily ever after and we'll all go on adventures together. It'll be a big party, and I'll make bridesmaids for you and Stretch can walk you up the aisle, and everything. What do you think?"

Alex had a vision of walking through rows of malformed creations, all squealing their delight and clapping their paws while she and James said their vows with cold sweats on their brow and sickening smiles pasted on their faces. "Sounds great!" she said. "Are you sure you wouldn't mind? You know, us being together?"

But Holly brushed the question off, shrugging as she used her saw to cut pieces of roasted flesh from the thing on the spit. "You belong to me now," she said. "Both of you. You're all mine."

And she smiled, closing her eyes as she chewed her juicy morsel. She handed another to Alex, who had no choice but to lean forward and take it in her teeth: a hot worm of rubbery meat that tasted vaguely of pork. She chewed it, doing her best not to think too hard about it.

Then Holly said something, a sentence so simple and plain that it might have been easy to overlook the horrific nature of its content.

"You can be my happily ever after. And you can have real live children for me to play with. Just like the stories."

Alex swallowed. The meat left an oily texture in her mouth. Her eyes watered. "Just like the stories," she said. And while Holly ate and chattered and mused on the future, the hand nestled beside the blade in the crook of Alex's arm worked and worked.

26
Brooding

Spring, 2002

Gregory began that Monday the same way he always did. Rising just after dawn and having coffee with the pristine sunrise. Showering and putting on his professional grey suit – although the school did not require that he dress formally. He had a pounding headache, and cinched his tie with unnecessary force, glaring at himself in the mirror. Every movement he made had been distilled into an unvarying routine, and no longer required thought; as he went through the motions, his mind returned, again and again, to the path his life was taking.

He was all too aware of the fact that, ten years ago, he would have killed for the life he had now. Back then, he had felt like an insect being crushed beneath the weight of a planet. He would leave for work in the dark and return home in the dark. His life was the dirty city and a job in which millions of dollars rested on his smallest decision. Mistakes cost careers, and all the while Jane waited at home for him, doing nothing but breathing in that polluted city air. How often had he dreamed about this life in Templeton?

"Just as soon as I have enough, we'll leave forever," he'd promised Jane a hundred times. "We'll build a house out in some quiet town and I'll take a relaxing teaching job. You can tend to the gardens and with that fresh country air – well it'll just be a matter of time before we have a baby. Just as soon as I have enough…"

School began at eight, and he was always on time. He began the first class of the day in the usual way; by silencing everyone, making sure backs were straight and eyes were forward, and then delivering the planned lecture. By now he was so familiar with his teaching material that he did not need to be present mentally – and he was not. His mind continued to mull, to turn over, to brood.

In the end, he'd gotten enough. The upside of working with tens of millions of dollars was that when a few thousand went missing here or there no one batted an eyelid. Even so, he was careful, converting it to cash which he parcelled neatly away in a plain brown suitcase under the bed. He liked knowing it was there – he thought of it as a parachute of sorts. Every time the work got too much, to where he felt his skull was going to implode from the pressure, he would remind himself that he could pull the ripcord at any time.

Yet now that the cord had been pulled, now that he was actually here… the sweet country air had taken on a certain sourness.

One of the boys said something and started a ripple of laughter through the class. Gregory paid no attention, using the grind of chalk on the blackboard to mask the grinding of his back teeth. Their dirty, leering faces. He could not imagine worse company for an eight-hour workday. Many of them didn't even want to learn – the rest couldn't. Some would become nothing but criminals. At least when he'd been at school there'd been a cane, but he'd learned that here there were no canes. Not only that, but he was also forbidden to touch one of the hooligans, even to grip one under the arm to remove him from the class!

So, he resorted to fantasies on the short drive home, in which he imagined a line of them laid out on the road, their heads popping under his car tires like watermelons as he left the school.

Then when he got home, he had Holly to deal with, and then Jane, and it was all he could do to not keep a flask in the car to keep him level-headed enough not to lose his temper as soon as he walked through the front door.

In this way he watched his dream of country life, so long nurtured and hoped for, wither and die. But he hung on, still he hung on because he had hope, because he was strong willed. Because, though he was rough and ill-tempered at times, he did love his family. If they would only be the way, they were supposed to be. Perhaps next year's class would be better. Or perhaps he would pull the ripcord again, one day, and this time rely on no one but himself…

And then at last, another day was over, and he lay back in the comfortable chair with a glass of that precious golden-brown liquid, the wife and child asleep, and peace enough to think, and ruminate, and brood.

Tomorrow, after all, was another big day.

27
Tick Tock

T he House, Mr. Stretch explained as he led James from one haunted room to the next, did not think the way humans thought – or Nobodies, for that matter. The latter thought with their minds, the house with its gut. All instinct and intuition and no craft. The House was driven blindly, and its will was intertwined with Holly's equally blind and volatile impulses. "It has a nose, but no eyes," he said. "It has other senses – not like ours, not better, just different. You understand?"

James didn't – but there was no time to answer in any case; he was too busy trying to keep up with Stretch's enormous strides and ease of movement. The tall butler changed courses in a split second and crossed hallways just as quickly, making choices that were as decisive as they were arbitrary. Sometimes he would glance right and then take the door to the left or knock on a trapdoor with his foot before pulling himself up through a window.

They were in the deep parts of the house, now, and none of the rooms seemed to have any real purpose or structure. Some were plain empty boxes with no furniture

– others were overwhelmingly bizarre. All of them, however, were of the old English mansion décor, in varying states of disrepair.

"But Stretch…" (A tiled bathroom with a bath the size of a child's swimming pool on golden feet in the middle.)

"Where are we…" (He paused to climb a short ladder into a polished room full of glass cabinets, each one packed with statues carved from valuable gems.)

"Going?" (A dusty music room with every kind of instrument scattered across the flaky ground.)

"She used to play, you know," Stretch said as they picked their way through the wreckage. A spider spun cobwebs through the strings of a cello. It had already caught several juicy flies, and they hung in cocoons of web over the hole in the middle. "When Miss Pinky was alive, she would play for us. It was when we fell in love." His eyes swam with emotion, but before James could think of a response, he was already pulling him onward through a crooked doorway.

They were going so quickly that when Stretch stopped abruptly on the other side it was all James could do not to crash into him. "Aha!" he cried happily, spinning to face James. "I have found it."

"Found what?"

Stretch stood back and allowed James to step out into the longest hallway he'd ever seen. It must have stretched from one end of the house to the other, and they were at the very end. A small round window let in a beam of light on the far side, and just behind them stood a varnished grandfather clock, its heavy pendulum knocking steady seconds aside in a comforting rhythm. A row of exposed lightbulbs hung from the narrow ceiling, providing just enough light to see by, and either side of the hall was lined with doors of all kinds, as many as could fit in the hall, long as it was.

"The Centre line," Stretch said, the relief evident in his voice. He lowered himself to James's height and rested his floppy hands on his shoulders, his face contorting itself into an expression of earnest concern. "This is the way from which all other ways go. The centre line of the house, the only place that never changes."

"Won't the house find me here?"

Stretch nodded vigorously. "Oh yes, very quick it will find you. But it must smell you out first. You see, if you keep moving, the house cannot catch up."

"I don't get it."

Stretch made a vague gesture down the length of the hallway. "The doors are the way," he said. "One by one, you go through each door. You wait on the other side, ear pressed up against it, and you listen." He cupped a hand to one of his elephantine lobes. "You listen to the clock. When ten minutes passes – six hundred ticks and tocks – you leave the room and return here. Then, the next doorway, and the next, and…" he pointed to each door in turn down the hallway.

"Why can't I just go back into the first room again?" James asked, but Stretch wagged his finger. "Every step you take," he whispered, "the house follows."

In the brief silence, both of them could hear the old grandfather clock ticking ominously behind them. How long had it been so far? Three minutes? Four? Just then, checking the time on the old clockface, James noticed a trapdoor at its foot, an ornate lion's-head handle carved from iron. Stretch followed his gaze.

"That is the way to the basement room," he said, and then nodded toward the far end of the hallway, where James noticed another trapdoor, this one in the ceiling instead of the floor. "That one to the attic. Do not go to these places, not yet. I must first get Holly away, or she will know."

He took hold of James' right hand – lifting the kitchen knife from his belt and pressing it into his palm – and closed his fingers around the hilt. "If Holly comes, you run away, James – run, run, run. The knife won't do any good. She is too strong, with the house. The blade is for you. There are worse fates to be had here than a knife in the heart."

James swallowed. He realised, with a jolt of terror, that Mr. Stretch – this odd stranger who had no doubt saved his life already – was about to leave him. Tick, Tock. Tick, Tock. Each second seemed to come quicker than the last.

"Stretch, promise me you won't let anything bad happen to Alex. Promise you'll help her escape."

But Stretch looked down at the floor. "I can't promise, Mr. James. I made someone else a promise too, once."

"I'm going to get her for this." James was surprised at the hardness in his voice. All he'd experienced for the last two days was fear and despair, yet the words came out strong and full of emotion. "I don't care who she is or what she wants, I'm going to get her, somehow. Even if it kills me." It sounded like bravado, like something some action hero in a movie might say, but to James's surprise he meant every word.

Stretch gave him a loopy smile and patted him on the head, as you would a dog, but his eyes sagged, and his ears drooped.

"There are worse things than death, Mr. James," he said.

And Tick, Tock, he slipped around the door through which they'd come, and was gone.

38
Beauty and the Beast

They sweated along jungle paths, Holly confidently hacking vines, leaves and branches aside like a bold adventurer; Alex following behind her as slowly as she could, working the blade of her sword against the bandage. Dampened by her sweat, the material was tearing more easily now, and a new problem emerged: how to keep the shreds from hanging loose where Holly could see them. And, of course, Alex had no idea whether or not she'd be able to grip the sword properly. Despite Greeny's ministrations a few hours earlier, her hand itched and stung as though it was covered in fire ants.

Holly, fortunately, was too lost in their journey to notice, singing off key, clearing the way with flourishing swings of her sword, and in general behaving like a bad actress in a play of some kind, or an old movie. To her, it was as though Alex was nothing but a sidekick – the Short Round to her Indiana Jones. Fine by me. The less attention Holly paid her, the better.

While they cut their way uphill to some final destination Holly was referring to as 'The Troll Cave,' she let her mind wander. It was, after all, better than living in the discomfort of the moment: beside her hands, both of the girls were covered in mud, blood and sweat. Stretch had supplied Alex with a plain white shirt and black skirt, but she still wore the same school shoes she'd been captured in, and her feet were beginning to form blisters. She just wanted the day's nightmare to be over; any escape her tortured mind could provide was welcome.

Her thoughts turned first to James. Part of her couldn't believe he'd had the balls to break into Holly's house, part of her raged at him for being stupid enough to do so, and part of her longed to pull him into a tight hug and thank him and see the perplexed look on his face he used to get when she laughed at his jokes. She wondered where he was, then – in which season of the estate, or which room of the great house. She hoped he was hidden, and that if anyone found him it would be Stretch and not Greeny. Stretch would help them, but Greeny she was not so sure about.

She wondered if James had told anyone on the outside. Perhaps he'd visited her parents' house. The thought of him trying to explain what had happened to Mr. And Mrs. Miller made Alex want to cry. They'd have burnt him for a witch. Besides, she thought, with a sudden resentment that surprised even her, they don't know I'm missing, do they? They've got their perfect pretty doppelganger. I bet they're patting themselves on the back, thinking they've finally made me into a good Christian girl.

James, she knew, would roll his eyes the way he always did when she complained about her parents. "At least your family cares about you," he'd said once. "My dad thinks of me like some kind of stray dog."

"Oh, you're being dramatic," she'd said, but he'd only looked away across Greenway Park's dingy oval and said nothing.

The memory depressed her – not so much because of what he'd said as because it meant that, most likely, no one else would come looking for them. They were alone, at Holly's supernatural mercy.

"Behold!" the girl's triumphant voice snapped Alex from her brooding thoughts, and she looked up in time to see Holly cut a swathe of hanging vines aside to let in a piercing sun in the blue sky. Alex squinted in the glare, unable to see a thing until they crested the clover-tangled slope and stepped out into the valley beyond.

It was a sight, alright. Not least because of the sheer enormity of the space in which they found themselves; The size of the clearing around them was as large as the house itself. The brick walls that bordered the property were finally visible, and Alex couldn't help but wonder what would happen if she made a run for it. Perhaps the boundaries would retreat from her, step by step, until she collapsed from exhaustion. In the middle of the clearing, a gentle hill led up to a tall rock structure, at the base of which loomed the black mouth of a cave. Orange light flickered against one of the walls, hinting at a fire deep within.

"The Cave of the Beast," Holly declared sternly. "Where our beloved princess awaits us. Squire! I order you to scout ahead and report your findings."

It took Alex a moment to realise she was referring to her. "Y… You want me to go up there, alone?"

"Yes. Go on, now. Signal to me when the time is right for attack!"

Alex shifted her grip on the sword and felt the steel tear through some more of the bandages. The friction was killing her, and sticky fluid from her burns were leaking through with a smell like bad meat. She tried to wiggle her fingers and was rewarded with a line of skin splitting at the joint like a papercut. She nodded at Holly stiffly, barely suppressing a scream. "At your service, Madam Knight."

She started to go when Holly leaned forward, her eyes lit up like Christmas morning, and said, "Alex? This is fun, isn't it?"

Alex would have gladly given up on freeing her hands and kicked Holly to death. "The best," she said. "You're my best friend. I can't wait for James to join us."

Holly beamed. "Me neither."

A cloud came over the sun as Alex ascended the rocky slope toward the mouth of the cave, giving the impression that darkness was spilling out of the open mouth. Alex's sweat chilled in the shade. She stopped on one side of the opening, gathering herself for what she would find. Calm down. You look in, see the nasty troll, scream like Olive Oyl from Popeye, and then let Holly come charging in to the rescue. Easy.

A thin film of smoke crept along the ceiling from a crackling fire, and as she ventured further the sound of boiling water reached her along with a sour smell, tangy and slick like stale sweat.

Alex kept to the wall, pulling her sword in as close to her body as she could, and edged around the bend.

It was worse than she'd imagined.

The troll that Holly had created hunched over a simmering pot. On the far side of the cave, a girl was trussed up with rope, squirming and gasping around a cloth gag. Alex recognized her immediately. It wasn't hard – they were the same person, after all, only Sister was looking considerably worse for wear. Her face was drawn and pale, her hair a matted mess, and there was a strip of flesh missing from her shoulder.

Only then did Alex see what the troll was doing. Lower jaw jutting out in concentration, revealing his tusk-like canines, he had one hand inside the boiling pot. When he removed it, his fist was as boiled as the strip of Sister's shoulder. He tilted his head back and dropped the strip into his mouth, chewing with some relish and apparently not realising until he tried to swallow that he'd chomped half of his index finger along with it. He sucked the tip of it down, revealing bone. Holly, it seemed, had forgotten to supply him with a capacity for pain.

Alex leaned back into the shadows, feeling sick. She meant to tiptoe backward to the opening of the cave, but while she'd been taking in the horrific scene some of the bandages had unravelled, and now they caught on a rocky protrusion. The tear was audible, and the troll looked around, eyes blazing red in the fire's glow.

In that moment, Alex understood that Holly had made a mistake. They were not safe. The Troll was not playing their game. It was a giant, confused, drooling animal, and it wanted meat.

And Alex's bandages were tangled on the rock.

"HOLLLYYYYY! HELLLLLP!"

She yanked at the bandages, nearly dropping the sword, and a spool unravelled, exposing her raw flesh to the hot air. The Troll let out a gurgly grunt and came thumping toward her, flexing his thick hands. He was barely taller than Alex herself, but he had the dense musculature of a gorilla.

She gave another tug and this time the bandage ripped all the way off. The troll made a lazy snatch for her throat but missed as she fell backward. Instinctively, Alex stuck out her free hand to brace, only to have it slip out from beneath her when her loose skin scraped the gravel. White pain flashed across her vision.

Somehow, she rolled to her feet and turned to sprint for the opening. The Troll stomped on her instep, not quite breaking it but bending it – and forcing a heavy landing onto the rock, the breath whooshing out of her lungs. She tried to scream but couldn't, and a moment later the dirty hand was gripping a handful of her hair and pulling her head back. One long fingernail – Sister's skin still stuck under the nails – curled around her exposed neck. He was going to slit her throat, there and then, and she would watch her blood gushing across the stone floor, each pump of her heart emptying her body until there was nothing left.

"DIE TROLL!" And there she was, at the crucial moment – no doubt having waited for just the right time. "YAAAH!" Holly rammed the point of her sword, two handed, through the Troll's head. In the chaotic seconds that followed, all Alex could see was the hem of Holly's skirt and her stained schoolgirl socks and shoes pushing in the dirt against the weight of the Troll. Then the great paw let go of her hair and hot blood cascaded over her head and face, temporarily blinding her.

The weight on her back vanished as Holly pushed harder, forcing the Troll backward, grunting and gargling.

"Release my squire, vile animal! We are here for the princess!"

Alex rolled over onto all fours and turned in time to see Holly thrusting the Troll up against the cave wall just a few feet away from Sister, who was curled up in the corner, weeping. Holly wrenched her blade back and then, resting her entire bodyweight on the hilt, pushed the point through the Troll's heart. It let out a sickeningly human cry and then slid back against the wall, its eyes dimming and then snuffing out altogether, thick blood pooling in the dust.

Alex, numb with shock, looked down at her free hand. She flexed the fingers and found that the ripping of her fresh burns, while painful, had freed up the motion in her tendons. Gritting her teeth, she took hold of the sword. The moist sores caused her palm to stick to the metal hilt.

"Phew." Holly stood back to admire her handiwork, breathing hard. She let go of her weapon, not bothering to pull it out of the dead Troll, and came toward Alex, who was pretending to use her sword as a crutch to push herself back to her feet. "Are you alright, Alex? That was a harder fight than I thought."

Alex smiled through the streaks of blood. She must have looked like Carrie on prom night, but Holly didn't seem to see anything wrong with the situation. They had been on an adventure – that was all; just a couple of brave knights rescuing the princess.

"Oh, Holly, I don't know what would have happened without you. Thanks so much. And hey, look!" She stood up a bit straighter, lifting her sword and turning it this way and that, as if to admire it. "My hand is getting better."

Then her eyes moved from the sword to Holly, who was standing directly before her, hands on hips and a satisfied smile on her face. She had her back to the fire and the boiling pot.

"We did it!" she said. "Smote the beast and rescued the princess. Now it's time to take the journey back and be on our way." She spoke with an oddly loud voice, almost as if she was addressing someone outside the cave, but in the moment, Alex paid no attention; all she could think about was that the psycho bitch who burned her hands was standing in front of her, and now she had a goddamn sword.

Only then did Holly see something in Alex's face, and something like dismay crossed her countenance. "Alex? what –"

But she never finished her question. Alex lunged, swinging the blade at Holly's neck with everything she had.

Holly threw herself backward into the fire.

If the pot were larger, she might have fallen into it and that would have been that. Instead, her lower back slammed the rim and the pot collapsed, tipping gallons of boiling water over the cavern floor. Holly went down screaming in an explosion of fire and ash and might still have burned to death if it weren't for the wave of hot water rebounding from the cave wall.

Alex was already moving forward to deal the killing blow when the quenched fire belched black clouds of hissing smoke, simultaneously blinding and choking her. One hand up over her watering eyes, she swung for the spot Holly had been, but the blade struck hard ground.

Twig-like fingers closed around Alex's wrists, pulling them roughly behind her back and nearly dislocating her shoulder in the process. Her cry of pain was cut short as her lungs filled with smoke and doubled her over in a coughing fit.

Greeny dragged her to the cave opening and flipped her on her stomach so that he could secure her wrists with a length of leathery rope. He left her there for the moment to recover his creator, who was still screaming – though it was hard to tell how much from pain and how much from anger.

"Don't let her get away! Bitch! Evil bitch! Get your hands off me and grab her. You! I can't – I can't…"

Alex staggered to her feet, meaning to make a run for it, as hopeless as that would have been, but Greeny was there in an instant. He snatched her collar and twisted it, thrusting her up against the wall. He leaned in close to her, his wooden mouth a twisted snarl.

"You've done it now," he said, his breath like moss and swamp water in her face. "Damn you, girl, you've ruined any chance you had for a life."

"I don't care," Alex said, and now the tears she spilled were not from the smoke. "I'd rather die than live like that psycho's plaything."

"Fool! That's not the choice you had. She's not going to kill you." And when he stepped back, she saw pain in his eyes. He shook his head and looked away for a minute, though his hand remained on her collar.

"You've left her no choice,' he said. 'Now she has to break you."

When Greeny pushed Alex back into the cavern, Holly was in the process of untying Sister. When Alex entered, her doppelganger locked eyes with her, the corner of her mouth twitching in the hint of a smirk.

Holly was not so smug. She was no longer screaming, but her mouth was drawn in a tight white line, her rage restrained beneath the thinnest of veneers. She was horrendously burnt – raw flesh and blisters just as bad as they were on Alex's hands, only they covered large patches of her body. She had to be in shock, and Alex felt savage satisfaction at the sight of her hands shaking. Get it now, bitch?

It was a short-lived victory. When Holly turned to her a moment later, the prim and proper schoolgirl mask had well and truly slipped, and what Alex saw in her expression was nothing short of monstrous. Alex expected her to scream and yell and berate her, but when she spoke next, she didn't address Alex at all, and her voice was deadly soft.

"Greeny? I'm going to visit Mother now. You're to help Sister tie Alex up nice and tightly, and then go back to the house and tell Mr. Stretch to dig a grave. But not the sort of grave for dead people, do you understand?"

"Aye, Miss Holly."

"Good. And Sister? You're to escort Alex up to her bedroom and make sure she's properly locked up. And when that's done…"

She stepped up closer to Alex, and now there was a touch of smugness to her tone, the nasty relish of a gossip sharing a juicy secret about someone else. "And then you're going to help Stretch find Alex's sneaky little boyfriend and lock him up somewhere else, and then I want you to break him, too. I want Alex to know, while she's down there in her grave, that her knight in shining armour is screaming because of her. Because she… Because she didn't know how to play nice!"

Without warning, Holly slapped Alex with a cold white hand hard enough to make coloured dots flash across her vision. "WHY COULDN'T YOU JUST BE MY FRIEND?"

Everyone stood frozen in the dripping cave, the words echoing in the terrible silence. Alex opened her mouth, wanting something defiant and cutting to come out, but she was weak with fear (tell Mr. Stretch to dig a grave) and what came out instead was a pathetic "Please, Holly…" but before she could finish Holly was pushing past her, wiping her eyes with the back of a blistering hand.

"Show her what I do with lying fakes, Sister."

And with that, she stormed out of the cave.

"Greeny?" Alex said, but the groundskeeper pushed her toward Sister, who was sneering openly, twirling a loop of rope.

"Yer barking up the wrong tree, Miss Alex," he said. "You don't understand yet, but you will soon enough. I'm as helpless as you. We all dance to her tune, and it's she who decides when the play is over, not us."

Sister cinched Alex's wrists together tight enough to break skin. "I think she's safe with me, Greeny," she said. "Why don't you run along? I think you've got a grave to dig."

"Right you are." He said, and a moment later Alex heard his big feet slapping the water as he left the cavern.

"Hm, look at that," Sister said. "All alone."

29
Under the House

Spring, 2002

All alone, at last. Only, it never felt that way. It wasn't Jane's whimpering – Gregory had put a stop to that an hour before. He picked up his scotch, the cool glass a blessing on his bruised hands, and strode back and forth around the study, trying to make sense of it – this niggling, biting, crawling feeling all over him. It was worse when Holly was yelling and jumping around and distracting him, and it was worse still with Jane fussing and running errands for the little tyrant and being so damned weak. But even when they were gone it was still there, a sense of someone watching him all the time and worse, someone laughing at him. It was intolerable.

Everything seemed intolerable, lately. Coming home to a house of mess and chaos and trying to put it into order as best he could. Searching endlessly for a minute alone to soothe his mind with some scotch and never quite finding it. Being laughed at behind his back. Being watched.

He closed his eyes and took a long sip, listening to the sounds of the night. The grandfather clock ticked steadily from the second floor. It would be two or three by now, and the only sounds should have been the natural creaks and groans of the house itself. But there was a layer beneath that: a wall of silence that hid something more sinister.

An imposter.

He suspected that Holly had been talking to the neighbour children over the walls, or as they passed the front gate in the hours after school ended and he had yet to arrive home. He heard her talking when she was alone, and he wondered if she wasn't sneaking others into the house. Boys, maybe – like the weaselly little beasts he dealt with at the school.

The thought made his guts twist in rage. That was the problem with that damn girl – and it was all her mother's fault. This tendency to sneak, to hide around corners and dark places, to be deceptive. She lied, and her mother lied to cover it up. He couldn't help but think they were conspiring against him, concealing some secret from him.

He took another deep sip and was on the point of letting his thoughts carry him away, as he often did on these long nights, brooding and pacing with glass in hand and teeth clenched – when he heard something over the clink of ice blocks. He paused with a mouthful of scotch and opened his eyes.

Holly stood in her pink pyjamas at the entrance to the kitchen, curly haired brown teddy dangling from one hand. "Daddy?" She said, her voice full of terror – knowing that to be awake at this hour and disturb him was two crimes in one. He gulped down the mouthful, the burning fuelling the fire inside him. Perhaps he could shake it out of her now that her mother wasn't around to get in the way –

what this great secret of theirs was. Who was she talking to when she should be alone and studying? "Yes?" he said.

"I'm scared… There's monsters in the basement." That whining pitch made him want to twist her damn shoulder off. "Speak, don't cry like a rusty hinge, girl. Just what in the hell are you talking about?"

She stepped back, tears springing to her eyes. "I keep hearing sounds, daddy. When I'm trying to sleep. I hear them moving in the basement. Don't you hear them, too?"

That gave him pause. He did hear them, didn't he? He certainly heard something. But there was more to it than that – she knew more than she was telling him. She and Jane together, with all their lies and deception, thinking they had him fooled all the time. Well, tonight he was going to find out. He was going to get to the bottom of this, one way or another.

He set his glass down on the coffee table and stepped over to his daughter, crouching down so that they were at eye level. He put a warm hand on her shoulder, ignoring the way she flinched and clutched her teddy closer. "Now, Holly. I'll get rid of the monsters for you. I'll find out. But I want you to tell me something. Are you bringing friends home to the house while Daddy's away? Is Mommy hiding them for you, hmm?"

She shook her head, and he gripped harder. "Are you bringing boys back here?"

"Nooooo. Daddy, it hurts."

"If I find out you're lying to me," he said, his voice as pleasant as he could make it, "I will put your little friends in hospital. And your mother, too. D'you understand?"

She nodded, sniffing. "Good. Now." He stood up, patting her on the head. "Take daddy to the basement and I'll chase away the monsters. See, if you're nice to me, I take care of you. You understand that don't you, Holly Dolly?"

She gave him a teary, but grateful smile. "Yes, daddy," and then, taking his big hand with her small one, she led him eagerly through the kitchen and out into the hallway, where the door to the basement stood beside the laundry.

He followed along, riding the heavy buzz of the last swig of scotch and feeling suddenly more at ease. It occurred to him that this was the first time Holly had ever actually come to him for help, needing his authority instead of fearing it for once. He wanted to march upstairs into the bedroom and slap his wife's face one more time. You see? I'm the man of the house and I'm required. I'm needed. I'm not to be deceived and lied to and cheated on.

That last was not something he ever thought consciously about – it was an implicit accusation, an idea that lived in the back of his mind without his knowledge. A seed.

While these thoughts rushed through his mind on the wave of alcohol, Gregory noticed something odd about the teddy bear that Holly had slung over her shoulder. Its curly head wasn't hanging limp and bouncing with her steps down the hall but perked up as though it were alert. The eyes were not sewed buttons like her other stuffed animals but glass – or at least that's what they must have been to look so real, to shine with such intelligence.

Holly came to an abrupt stop in front of the basement door, and as she turned to face him, spinning the bear away, the bear winked. It was too quick to be sure, and Gregory was too tired and drunk to trust himself, but in the moment, it was like someone tipped a glass of ice water down his collar, and it was accompanied by a terrible idea. What if there really was something down in the basement?

"Daddy? I think the light's not working."

He grunted, pulling open the basement door to the pitch darkness beyond and, sure enough, when he slipped his hand inside and felt the switch, the light didn't come on. They stood at the threshold for a moment, listening; but whatever sounds either of them might have heard earlier, the basement was as quiet as outer space.

"See? No monsters," he said, gesturing at the concrete steps that seemed to descend into nothing. But they both knew that wasn't good enough, didn't they? She blinked up at him, and then came that whiny voice again. "But dadddyyyy, pleeeeease."

"Alright, you silly girl. But if I go down there and it's empty – the next time you come bothering me at three in the morning you'll have to sleep down there, understand?"

The threat should have brought on a tearful nod or a shaky sob, but Holly smiled instead, a mischievous smile that struck him as out of place as the wink he'd (hadn't) seen. "Okay, Daddy."

The idea that she'd set up a tripwire or something of the like popped into his mind, and as he started down the stairs, Holly watching anxiously from the hall, he kept an eye out. It would be just like her to play some prank on him. Maybe then she could run off and giggle about it to her mother. Well…

The thought never quite completed in his mind. It trailed off instead, like a small boat drifting away on a strong current. It was consumed by the darkness of the basement, the darkness that seemed to encroach on him like a solid thing as he descended into it.

A warm, mammalian smell stung his nostrils: the smell of dirty animals at a zoo. Maybe she was keeping a dog down here, and that was the big surprise. He'd reached the bottom of the stairs now, and it occurred to him that he should have brought a flashlight so that he could show her there wasn't anything. Damn scotch was making him fuzzy around the edges. "Holly!" he called up to her. "Get my torch from the cupboard over the stove, will you?"

"Yes, Daddy!" And before he could stop her, she shut the basement door and went clomping up the hall.

"Bitch!" Now it was so dark he couldn't even see the stairs, let alone the rest of the basement. The only light came in the form of a pale blue rectangle from the small window near the ceiling.

Scccrreeeeeeeee. The sound, so shocking in the quiet basement, was a familiar one. It was what he used to get his students' attention in class, a terrible squeal achieved by scraping long fingernails down his chalkboard. In a flash he understood. She'd snuck in one of his students. Wes Rogers, probably, the smart aleck who couldn't add. They were here to play some trick on him. Well, he was going to just...

A low snorting sound came from the opposite end of the basement – something no human child could have made – and it was accompanied by what sounded like a stack of books or newspapers toppling over and a shuffling of pages as something dragged itself over the top of the pile.

Fear and rage boiled up inside him. How dare these – these bunch of illiterate children make him feel this way. If they thought they were just going to get a detention for coming to his house and playing a trick like this, they were sorely mistaken. I thought they were intruders, officer, he imagined explaining to the police as the ambulance carted half-conscious bodies beneath blood-soaked blankets. How was I to know?

He balled his hands into fists, flinching as he heard someone else hiss behind him, quick slaps as whoever it was came crawling on all fours.

He waited until the last minute, until he could feel them all around him in the dark, gurgling and giggling and thinking they had him frozen in terror. And then, letting out his famous silence-in-the-classroom bellow he spun around and booted the thing crawling up behind him with everything he had.

His shoe connected with something soft and small – too small to be even a primary school boy – and sent it sliding to the back wall. He must have winded the lad because he didn't hear a scream.

Someone bit him on the ankle.

"Bastard!" He tried to grab a collar and felt hair, grabbed that instead and reigned hard punches down on the back of the head. Instead of a hard skull, his fist sunk into what felt like the soft layered skin of a bear cub.

Then, just as a hot mouthful of flesh tore away from his ankle, a bookshelf rattled against the wall as something leapt from the top of it and landed on his back before he could get fully upright. That was when he understood that he was not in the basement with children. These were things; hungry, deformed things with claws and teeth.

In seconds he was overwhelmed, several of the beasts clinging to him at once, pulling at his legs and arms with dense weight like little monkeys, taking nips with wet mouths and removing strips with jagged fingers. Hissing and chuckling and bark-laughing like hyenas. He was being eaten alive.

But Gregory Anderson was, whatever his failings might be, not a weak man. He had a secret power, a power that had saved him from his own insane father, and from the hard men on the railroads, and again later from the criminals and Neanderthals he'd met in the military. That power was an animalistic, untempered rage – a superhuman force not unlike that which allowed toddlers to lift cars off their mothers. A deep redness descended over everything, and for a minute as he fought his way back to the staircase, flinging bodies, cracking bones, tearing limbs, he was the monster.

He wasn't completely conscious of what he was doing until twenty or thirty seconds later, the basement door slammed and locked shut, stumbling into the kitchen for a new bottle – not scotch this time but harsh, unfiltered bourbon, the kind he drank when the mission was oblivion.

Bites and lacerations covered areas of his exposed skin, but they were minor – the worst being the chunk taken out of his ankle, which he cured by slipping his belt between his teeth and pouring bourbon into the wound.

He ranted and raged through the house, drinking deadly amounts of liquor and turning half the place over, searching for Holly. At one point he found himself standing at the basement door with a gallon of gasoline and a lighter, thinking he just might light the whole house up with him in it, and then the hallway seemed to tilt up sideways and it was all he could do after that to drag himself back to the living room.

When he woke up twelve or so hours later, he started vomiting and didn't stop for a full day and a night, alternating between the arms of his concerned wife and the colder embrace of the toilet seat.

The day after that, he dragged himself out of his semi-coma and tried to remember what had happened to make him get so drunk, but the past forty-eight hours were nothing but a blur of delirious hallucinations, nightmares, and violence. He had torn apart half of the first floor in a rage, Holly said, her big brown eyes making him feel something like shame amid his confusion.

He was covered in bumps and cuts and a brutal looking laceration around his Achilles.

"You were so angry and wild," Jane said, clasping his hand in hers, eyes full of concern. "You almost did yourself in, Gregory. I was so worried."

He allowed her a tight smile and found he couldn't quite look her in the eyes.

"Think I'll give the harder stuff a rest for a while. I'm sorry, it's just…" Just what? What had it been? What of those mad nightmares, and those things that felt like memories but couldn't be? He shook his head.

"I'll go clean… for a while. I've been wanting to get my fitness back for a long time after all."

And she hugged him, head nestled against his shoulder, wetting his shirt with her tears. "Thank you, Gregory. It'll do us all good, I think. I only want us all to be happy, you know."

"I know, dear." He patted her on the head, smiling as Holly ran to the edge of the bed to hug his leg. She was sucking her thumb the way she did when she was little, and her other hand gripped her curly brown teddy, its limbs torn and loose and barely held together.

30
The Green-Eyed Monster

It didn't take long for Alex to become very aware of two things. One, there was no way she was going to escape the ropes. The knots on her wrists had no give at all, and Sister had tied her ankles together with barely a few inches of slack. Two, for all Greeny's talk about them being puppets on strings, her doppelganger gave no sign that she intended to follow orders. At least, not immediately.

There was something feverish about her – sweating and shaking, perhaps from the pain of her wound but Alex suspected rage had more to do with it. Holly almost got her killed. You can use it. It was a slender hope, but the words escaped Alex's mouth before she could stop herself. "We could get her if we work together. You and me. We could take her by surprise and –"

Sister took hold of Alex's collar with both hands and thrust her up against the cave wall. "Shut up. And stay put."

Leaving Alex to blink away the stars, she retrieved the sword from beside the Troll's deflated corpse, which was already beginning to smell like soil. Sister poked it with the point of the sword and then spat on it. "Who's crying now?" Fierce though the words might have been, Alex heard a dangerous fragility in her tone. Even in the darkness of the cave, no longer lit by firelight, Alex could see cold malevolence in her expression.

"What happened to you?" Alex asked her. The evil hadn't been there in all those long hours they'd spent together in the room. Back then she really had been like an innocent child, eager to learn, and unselfconscious.

Instead of answering, Sister began to cut Alex's clothes off with the sword, removing pieces of fabric and letting the rest fall away from her naked body. "Hey! What are you doing? Holly said to take me back."

Sister sneered. "Holly almost got me eaten by a troll for one of her insane games. You think I care what she wants? I hope those burns get infected and she dies, but she won't. The House will take care of her. Now shut up."

Her brow furrowed with concentration as she worked to expose more and more of Alex's skin – goose pimpled despite the cave's tropical heat. She was muttering to herself, things that disturbed Alex, though she didn't quite know what they meant. "What do you have that I don't? What's so good about you, hmm? Why do you get to be real?"

When Alex was completely naked, Sister stood back, glaring at her as though she was an affront to nature, and then began to undress herself, too. Alex cringed from her gaze, though there was nothing sexual about it. That made it worse, somehow, giving Alex the impression that Sister was detached from her body – even from the idea of a body. Clinical was the word for it. Cold and clinical. Like a surgeon.

It wasn't long before Alex discovered the cause of Sister's curiosity. When she stood, finally naked, she looked like a store mannequin made flesh: the basic form was there – the shape that made her appear normal in clothes, but she lacked the defining features. She had no nipples, no genitals, no bellybutton. Her skin was smooth white and free of freckles or blemishes of any kind. It was like someone had cut a uniform suit for her to slip into out of some stretchy material – only there was no zipper up the back.

Sister's glare darkened, no doubt making the same comparison and finding herself wanting. She stepped closer to Alex, inspecting those parts of her with a strange intensity. "What's so good about any of that?" she said finally.

"Nothing. If anything, Holly made you better than a real person…" She broke off, aware too late that she'd made a mistake. Sister's face twisted into a mixture of rage and derision. "I don't want to be better than a real person."

And then she turned away and headed back to the pile of clothes – Alex's clothes – she'd dropped beside her sword. Alex thought for a wild, hopeful second that she was going to dress herself in a huff and then drag Alex back to the house, but when Sister bent down it was not the rose-patterned dress she reached for, but the sword.

"S-Sister hold on a second. Just hang on. You can't change anything, okay? I can't help the way I am, and neither can you. Do you understand? No one can. You just have to…" She swallowed; her mouth dried out from the adrenaline coursing through her blood. Sister marched towards her with deadly purpose, the light splashes of her small feet echoing through the cave. "Sister, Holly will kill you for this."

But Sister wasn't listening. She held the sword up in front of Alex's face. "My name isn't Sister,' she said. 'It's Alex."

31
Hide and Seek

The day crawled by in tense minutes, and pretty soon James was starting to run out of doors. Each room had an unnerving sense of vacancy about it – a feeling that someone or something alive had been in it only a minute ago and would return a minute hence. It reminded him of the story of the Mary Celeste, the ghost ship that had come drifting to shore with no one aboard, yet plates of half-eaten food were still steaming in the mess hall and personal belongings of the crew remained undisturbed in their quarters. It was all James could do to stay in each new room for the nine and a half minutes, made slower by the need to count every tick and tock of the grandfather clock.

Then he would step back out into the central hall, feeling twice as exposed, expecting Holly to burst through one of the doors at any second, and then he'd open the next door and start the count again.

There were eight doors to go before he reached the end of the hall. The light from the small window grew darker

as the day changed quickly from late afternoon to dusk –
though that meant little in a universe which was dictated
by the moods and desires of a capricious young girl. Six
doors, now. Then four. Where the hell was Stretch? There
had to be another way to keep hidden from the house.

And then he found the playroom.

It was third from the end – a narrow blue painted door
with a wooden knob designed to look like a laughing face.
When James slid inside and closed the door behind him, he
was struck with a sense of significance. Each room of the
house had felt alive in its own way, but this one was
electric, somehow. Something happened in here, a long
time ago. It was a mad thought, but as he looked around
the innocent, colourful playroom – A rumpus room, wasn't
that what they were supposed to be called? – he had no
doubt that it was true.

Everything about the room seemed emphatically
childish, but it was as obscene as clown makeup on a serial
killer – a thin mask that did little to conceal what was
underneath. The light blue carpet was covered here and
there in mysterious stains and littered with toys. In one
corner a heap of barbie dolls had been dismembered and
scattered amidst Lego blogs. In another a beanbag was half
buried under hand sewn dolls and stuffed animals. One in
particular, a curly brown bear, had eyes that seemed to
watch James with ungodly light. Against the opposite wall
was a wooden chest, padlocked, and high above it, most
curious of all; a small hole about the size of a twenty-cent
coin in the wall.

Tick, tock, tick, tock. Three minutes had passed. There
was time. James tip-toed across the carpet to the chest and,
wincing at the creak it made as he stepped up on top of it,
brought his eye up the little hole.

It was a peephole, but one in an odd place. The room
on the other side was raised above this one, so that he was

looking in from somewhere at the bottom corner. It looked like any guest bedroom one could expect to find in a house like this, except for two things: the bed had been recently slept in, the covers tossed half off the mattress, and a lamp lay broken on the floor. Someone had put up a fight. Alex.

James's heart leapt into the back of his throat, but his excitement was short lived, closely followed by a bleak *now what?* He couldn't afford to wait for her, after all – and even if he did how would he break her out from here? He was just as reliant on Stretch as before – more so now because – tick, tock – in two more minutes he would have to leave this room and he'd have one less place to go.

It was then, with his eye pressed against the hole in the hopes that she would return to her room in this last minute, that he became aware that he was not the only one doing the spying. The all too familiar tickle of another's gaze on the back of his neck set his nerves on end, but when he turned around there was no one there.

Or so he thought, until his gaze returned inevitably to the raggly brown bear in the heap of stuffed animals, the one with the keen brown eyes and the wide stitched smile. It wasn't smiling before. On the tail of this realisation came another; he could no longer hear the ticking of the great grandfather clock. The whole house, in fact, had become deathly quiet.

He padded across the blue carpet, knowing he was too late but rushing anyway, and pulled the playroom door. He hadn't expected it to budge, but it swung open with ease, on oiled hinges.

Right onto a solid brick wall.

32
Hanging by a Thread

Stretch knew something bad had happened long before he saw Greeny emerge from the jungle, cradling Holly's small form in his arms. He'd been in the garden shed, rooting through the groundskeeper's tools for something – anything – to help James when he heard a black peal of thunder and looked out of the window to see that the day had taken a decidedly dark turn. He snatched a half litre tin of lighter fluid from the work bench and jammed it into his jacket pocket and then stepped out of the shed just in time.

Greeny glanced at him as he broke out into the open, but where he'd have been suspicious before now, he was too preoccupied with Holly. She had both arms latched around his neck and even from where he was across the open field Stretch could hear her cries of agony. Her once neat dress was in tatters of blood, mud and who knew what and Stretch's heart sank; Alex was nowhere to be seen.

"Mr. Green! What has happened?" he rushed over to lend a hand, but Greeny brushed past him, intent on getting to the house. Stretch followed, wringing his hands and reaching up to tentatively stroke Holly's head. She didn't notice him at all. Her eyes were squeezed tightly shut and she hissed and gasped through gritted teeth, barely holding back screams. Only then did Stretch see the flowers of red skin blooming all the way up her right arm and note the charred holes in her once white dress.

"Alex tried to kill her," Greeny said, but he wouldn't say a word more until later, when he had delivered Holly to the attic and the safety of Mother. Then he took hold of Stretch's arm and pulled him back through the house and back outside. Stretch waited while Greeny rummaged through the shed, trying and failing to come up with a lie if he noticed the lighter fluid missing – and then he returned carrying a shovel.

Stretch's heart sank, and he followed Greeny across to the autumn graveyard with shoulders hunched and ears drooping. He had done this before.

By the time they arrived, Stretch could practically feel the pain in the air. The cold whipped at his skin like steel wool on a raw wound and a flash of lightning cut through the clouds high above. The sun was long gone.

Greeny pressed the spade into Stretch's hands. "You know what to do. I have to get inside and make sure the house got the other one."

'B…. But Greeny, you know you're not supposed to. You're the groundskeeper – I'm the house Nobody. It's my job to get the…'

"She might be no more'n a little girl, Stretch, but I'm no idiot." He jammed a twig finger at Stretch's chest. "You're soft inside. You tried to help the girl escape, didn't you? Think I believe she'd have escaped the cottage like that if you hadn't let her? This is your fault more than anyone's – only right you should dig the grave."

"We can't let her – Greeny, we can't." He looked down at the heavy shovel in his hands, tears springing to his eyes. He remembered Alex's spontaneous kiss before she'd tried to scale the wall.

Greeny's mossy face looked as pained as Stretch felt, but when he spoke his voice was hard as rock. "You don't understand, Stretch, we have to. The sooner we break these kids the better, or they'll bring the whole world down around us and we'll all die. Don't you understand that the only reason any of us can keep on living is that mad girl up there?" He pointed a knobby finger at the attic's round window, shining like a lighthouse beam in the dark.

"If they'd go along with what she wanted, none of this would have happened. All they have to do is play her fairy tale games and pretend to be her friends and everything would be like before, when your little Miss Pinky was alive. Don't you want that again, Mr. Stretch?"

Stretch nodded miserably, sniffing. Those had been bright days, hadn't they – when Holly had been sunshiny bright and summery all year long and they'd built the winter cottage together and drunk hot chocolate with marshmallows and climbed trees the height of mountains to see the view. There were the babies, though – but Stretch didn't like to think about them. Those were Holly's own business. Her damned creations, they'd existed only to satisfy her mean streak, and all the better, too, or it'd be the Nobodies she'd take it out on. His eyes darted to the basement window, then, and he shook his head.

"Why must she hurt them so much?" he said sadly.

Greeny sighed and looked away, frustrated as usual with Stretch's sentimentality. "Holly doesn't want them dead – she just wants them to be her friends. The quicker we break them, the better for all of us, because there's no getting out of it, otherwise. If we let them push her over the edge, there's no telling what she'll do. So," He slapped Stretch on his sloped shoulder. "Dig the grave. And mind she's enough air to breathe. There's no telling how long she'll be down there."

33
Dead Girl Walking

Greeny saw her before he knew what she was, on the way back to way to grab his axe. Chances were, the house had James locked up in a neat little box, but why take chances? He had his head bowed under the rough wind blowing out from the jungle, and it was there that he first caught a flash of red amidst the dark green. He knew that shade of red well, had seen it gushing out and drying on the skin of many a sentenced Nobody, Stretch's chubby girlfriend among them. Tonight, it merely made his dry lip curl as he watched Alex emerge from the tree line, Sister pushing her from behind like a soldier with a POW.

The poor girl was naked in the icy air – the summer humidity having vanished along with the last rays of sunlight. She had her hands and ankles tied with short lengths of rope so that she was forced to move with small, hunched oversteps, and her straggled hair hung over her face. Blood stained her chest; her burnt hands were once more exposed to the elements, and Sister had carved a strip of flesh from her left shoulder to match her own injury. Strangest of all, Greeny noticed that Alex wasn't the only one who'd suffered under the knife.

Blood streamed down Sister's inner thighs, as if she'd hopped on the sharp side of that sword she was carrying and ridden it around like a horse. Not only that, but her blue top was similarly drenched over her breasts and bellybutton. She had an obscenely satisfied smirk on her face, in stark contrast to the expression of absolute misery etched across Alex's otherwise identical features.

"What the hell did you do?" Greeny growled, heading her off halfway across the summer field. She drew to a stop, pulling back on Alex's ropes as though she were reigning in a horse. A faint drizzle flurried in with the wind, the first of many tears the house would no doubt shed for Holly.

"We're both the same, now," Sister said. Without warning, she raised her bloodied shirt to show him the pair of severed nipples she'd stuck onto her own breasts, the blood drying on her skin.

Greeny spat a wad of green mulch at her feet. "You're mad." He snatched the ropes out of Sister's hands and pushed her firmly away, making her slide in the wet grass and almost topple. "Hey! I have to take her back."

"I'll do it. Don't you have a family to get to?"

"I was promised the boy! Holly promised me I could do whatever I wanted with him!"

"We don't even know where he is yet. Tomorrow night, when her grave is dug. Last thing anyone needs is for you to get reported missing by the family you're supposed to be fooling."

"But Holly –"

He loomed over her, breathing his rank air over her face and showing her his rotted teeth. "You best get moving, doll face. Or I'll fetch my shears from that there shed and when I'm done with you, well… it'll take an awful lot longer to make the two of you look the same again."

She reared back, disgusted. "If you hurt me, Holly would know." But her voice held no conviction and when she saw the look in his eyes, she couldn't maintain her defiance any longer. "I'll be back tomorrow," she said. She started off toward the front gates, but Greeny whistled her back.

"What?"

"The sword."

"Oh."

She tossed it at his feet, but before she could turn, he pointed at her blood-stained outfit. "Get changed before you leave here, or you'll have a question or two to answer when you get home, won't you?"

"Huh? Right." And then, incredibly, she laughed.

Greeny shook his head as she walked away. "Didn't think it was possible Holly could make anything as mad as herself," he muttered.

Alex said nothing. She hadn't said a word or looked up for the entire conversation, though he could hear her teeth chattering a little in the cold.

"Well. Come on then. Let's get you inside and find out if your boyfriends fared any better."

It didn't take long to find out. The house let Greeny know as he led Alex, still silent and unresponsive, back to her room. He took a flight down, then through the dining hall to get to the centre line, and there he found that one of the doors near the end of that long hall – which normally led to the playroom – had been left open. A wall of bricks filled the frame, but even more interesting than that was the little doll that had been shut out. It was a crudely made sock puppet made of felt, but the proportions were unmistakeable, Mr. Stretch. The doll's chest cavity was torn and some of the stuffing missing; the poor things heart ripped right out of its chest – or at least that was what Greeny believed he was supposed to see. He chuckled to himself, as much from relief as genuine amusement.

He'd been worried for a while there, but it looked like things were going to turn out alright. Holly would be upset, of course – inconsolable… for a few weeks. But the integrity of the house, the safety of her universe was intact, and soon they would be one droopy-eyed bastard less.

Holly would make a new bunch of Nobodies, and maybe they'd be better, next time. Maybe then she'd see; there was no outside world – not really. It was just them and the house.

Yes, everything would return to normal. He thought he'd head down to the ballroom bar – he was sure the house would have a drink or two waiting for him there. Stretch could dig the grave and weep over his buried Pinky – Greeny would allow him that, at least.

As he passed the attic trapdoor on his way, he cocked his head to one side, listening to Holly's agonised weeping and her Mother's crooning. The sounds comforted him in a strange way, as if he were wrapped in the warm embrace himself.

He hoped there would be some milk waiting for him downstairs, too.

34
Lonely Heart

Stretch's long arms made short work of the digging, but he had to stop often to wipe the tears and sweat from his brow, and the job from start to finish ended up taking much of the night. When it was done, he dug the shovel into the pile of earthbeside the hole and went to flop down beside Miss Pinky's grave, arms aching.

"Any more grave digging and my noodles are like to fall off!" he said, trying to make light of it, only to burst into tears a minute later. He hugged her cold headstone, imagining her comforting arms encircling his narrow waist and giving him a playful squeeze like she used to, but that only set him off even harder and he could hardly take a breath for crying.

When he was too exhausted to do even that he pulled himself together cross legged in front of her tombstone, eyes skimming over the words engraved there without really reading them. Miss Pinky forgot she owed her life to Miss Holly, and now she's just Miss-ing. Rot in Pieces

"Oh, Pinky. What am I going to do now? Both of them are caught now, and who knows what awful things Holly will do to make them hers. Perhaps Greeny was right, and they made it happen. Perhaps if we just get them to play nicely it'll all be alright, in the end…"

And Pinky's warm voice floated to him from the grave, from beneath the weight of all those years ago in space and time. "You've got a good heart, Stretchy. Follow it and you'll never fly wrong." It was a silly thing to say in some sense. As Holly was never shy to remind him, Nobodies weren't real people, and they didn't have hearts. But Pinky's words struck home all the same.

He knew, deep down, that the right thing to do was to stay true to Holly. She'd created him, after all, and loved him and nurtured him. She might have taken Pinky away from him, but if it weren't for Holly, Pinky would never have existed in the first place.

Stretch looked up at the starless sky and let his mind drift for the moment, absent-mindedly stroking Pinky's tombstone with one hand.

He recalled one hot day in the summer garden when they'd all gone for a picnic by a river in the summer jungle – Stretch, Greeny, Miss Pinky, Sarah Stiltskin and even Tiny too – a goblin of a Nobody no larger than a puppy. There was a tombstone for him here, but there had been no need to dig him a grave. Just a month after the picnic Tiny and Holly had tried to cross that same river on a log and Tiny had fallen in. That wouldn't have been a problem, usually, but Holly had read a story just the week before all about explorers in the amazon jungle and learned about piranha fish. It wasn't her fault – Stretch knew she couldn't always control how the house made things for her; it was only trying to make her happy. She'd liked Tiny, hadn't she?

But the picnic was before that, and Tiny was jumping up and down and juggling coconuts while the rest of them applauded from the side lines and munched on fruit from the trees and drank iced milk. It had been a happy day, that, and even glum Greeny had been grinning ear to ear. How lucky they all were, Stretch remembered thinking, to have such a perfect princess as their maker, someone who could give them days like these? It had seemed like a golden dreamland, then, and it was still new to Stretch – the joy of living, the sights and smells and tastes of happiness. He'd fallen asleep with his head in Miss Pinky's lap, her soft hand massaging his bony skull while he listened to Holly's delighted laughter.

Then his thoughts turned to Alex, the poor girl, and her brave friend who had by now almost certainly been caught. Stretch had done what he could, but when Alex attacked Holly, she'd committed the unforgivable sin and set things in motion that were far beyond Stretch's control. This was Holly's world, after all, and he was part of it.

"Why, oh why did she need the real people?" he wondered aloud. "Why couldn't we be good enough for her?"

But for this Pinky had no answer.

35
Dinner with the Millers

"How was school today, Alex?"

Their happy faces made her want to cry – the love in their eyes was almost too much to bear. It was agony to live so close to a world that didn't belong to her, in a life that wasn't hers… yet. Agony, but also paradise.

"It was okay," she said, picking at her food. She knew that they were asking because of her downcast expression, and likewise she knew that this was where she was meant to furrow her brow in deep concern. "Have you heard about James, yet?"

Her father set his knife and fork down with a clink and steepled his hands in front of his face. "James? The boy who came by just the other day. Your – ahem – your friend?"

Alex nodded. "His Dad reported him missing this morning. Everyone at school was talking about it."

"Oh dear," Mrs. Miller raised a manicured hand to her mouth. "Did he run away?"

Alex shrugged and then sighed, setting aside her own cutlery. She would be sad at first, but in talking about James she would let slip that he'd mentioned to her he was going to walk home through Greenway Park. Then, when they found the body, she would be devastated, and receive all the love and comfort her family (and they were her family now, weren't they?) could bestow upon her.

"I don't know," she said. "But I'm worried. He said he was going to walk through Greenway Park on the way home and, you know, it's a really dangerous area. I hope nothing happened to him."

"Honey… that's very important information." Her father said. "Did you tell the police that?"

She shook her head, as though it hadn't occurred to her. "Oh, no – I didn't even think. Should we call them now?"

Five minutes later her father was hanging up the phone and her mother was chewing her nails to the beds, her own dinner forgotten. "Terrible, just terrible," she kept repeating, and then "I'm sure it'll be fine, dear. He seemed like a nice boy."

"Well, the police are going to come by and get an official statement," Mr. Miller said, returning to sit beside Alex. He placed a comforting hand on her shoulder and squeezed. "Luckily, since the park is a public place, they can start searching right away. Most likely he just had an argument with his father and decided to sleep there for a night. It happens in these broken families now and again."

Alex wiped her eyes and nodded gratefully. "Thanks, Dad. I'm glad we're not a broken family. We're all together."

Yesterday, she had cleaned out her room and put everything in order – the way a normal girl should be. All her horror movie posters were taken down, her curtains drawn so light could enter the room, and her piles of clothes and Stephen King books filed away and organized. It had almost brought her mother to tears, and she'd pulled Alex into a warm embrace and declared that she was so glad she was over with that 'Horrible Dark Phase.'

Now, she saw a similar look in her father's eyes as she extended a hand toward him and her mother and suggested that they pray for James. "That he should be found and returned to safety."

And their dinners still cold and partially eaten, they clasped hands and prayed, and Alex had to keep the smile from touching her lips. She had never felt so at home, so real, and so loved. Once they found the body, the real James would belong to her, and with the Other Alex out of the picture, she could begin life anew. Alex Miller: Human Being.

She couldn't wait.

36
Witching Hour Whispers

James tore the little brown bear's head from its body, slicing through the stitches with his knife and then, last of all, pulling those creepy glass eyes and jamming them in his pocket where they couldn't see anything anymore. He doubted it would do any good at this point, but it made him feel better, that was for sure. It had been a long time since his drinks with Stretch in the ballroom and he realised his bladder was full. He emptied it on the pile of soft toys, thinking that would make him feel good too, but instead he was overwhelmed by a sense of pathetic helplessness. It was like spitting at an oncoming train. He was done for, and he knew it.

That was the state of his mind, anyway, crouched up in the corner of the darkening space, when he heard something in the next room. A door opening and a gruff voice he didn't recognize, saying, "best recover your strength now, girl. You'll need it… if she decides to let you live, that is." And then a slam and the click of the metal lock. A minute or so of silence followed, and then the gut-wrenching sob of someone completely broken.

James had never heard Alex cry before – but then he'd never heard anyone cry like that before. He hesitated halfway between the door and the peephole, listening to her cry, suddenly not sure if heshould even try to talk to her. What was he going to say, after all? Hey, guess what, I came to rescue you! Oh, no, I don't have any way out. In fact, I'm just as trapped as you are. Now we can both die together. Cool, huh?

But he knew she wouldn't take it that way, and besides, he needed to see her, to hear her voice again, so badly it was almost physical. He needed to find out what had happened to her, and what she knew about this mad dream world in which they had lost themselves. Most of all, though, he just needed another voice, a human voice, to stop him from losing his mind completely. He pressed his eye up against the peephole.

For a second, the breath caught in his throat. It was Alex, alright, but it was not a version of her he was familiar with – not the sunny, cheerful girl with a biting wit and easy laugh; this was someone who'd been dragged to hell and left there. She was naked, curled up on the floor beside her bed, less than five feet from the peephole. He could only see the top of her head and her back, but she was hugging herself and her ruined hands were visible against the bare skin of her back. It looked as though someone had boiled them and then scraped at the blisters with a cheese grater.

"A… Alex?"

She stopped shaking, her body frozen mid-sob.

"James?" She moved her head up slowly. It took her a moment to find the peephole, tucked away in the far corner of the room, and then she reeled, backing up against the far wall and pulling a blanket over her. Not quickly enough, however; for a heartbeat before he looked away, horrified, James saw what they'd done to her. He couldn't bring himself to look back up until he heard her say his name again.

"James? Was that you?"

She was looking right at him, now, over the folds of blankets pulled up over her knees. Her eyes were red from crying and her hair was a matted with blood and dirt, but it was her, alright – not some creepy doppelganger – it was Alex.

"It's me!" he said. "Alex, I came to get you."

"What is this, some kind of messed up trick? How do I know you're really him?"

There was a question. The answer came to him in a flash of memory, and he smiled as he answered. "The first thing you ever said to me was you look like Edward Scissorhands." It was their first year of high school and he'd been growing his hair long and greasy, wearing leather jackets and silver rings, trying to cultivate a cool outsider look. It hadn't lasted long, after that comment.

She straightened, surprised, and the corner of her mouth twitched up. She sniffed and rubbed her nose with the back of her hand, the tears no longer flowing. "Is it really you? James, is it really you?"

"Yeah, I… Yeah, it's me," he said, and before he knew what was happening, she stood up, moving forward with the blanket still clutched around her, and then lay down right in front of the peephole, resting her head on her folded hands so she could be eye level with him. She stared at him intensely, for a minute her green eye locked on his blue one. Then she said in a low voice, "James… did you actually break in here to come and get me? Do you have a way out?"

The hope in her voice made him look away from the peephole again. "Uh… The thing is…"

"Oh, no."

"I'm kind of trapped in here as well."

"Fuck."

"Yeah." There was a long silence, and he forced himself to look back up, though he immediately wished he hadn't. She was staring at the ground, biting her lower lip, eyes squeezed shut.

He wanted to say something nice, like it's going to be alright, or we'll find a way, but those just felt like lies so instead he just said, "What did they do to you?"

She told him everything, in fits and bursts, now and then her voice growing stronger or shaking with rage, other times cracking under the strain, but she didn't miss anything or shy away from the truth, and in fact it was James who cringed when she told him, quite matter of factly, about how her doppelganger had cut her nipples off barely an hour ago and sewed them clumsily onto her own smooth breasts.

"And that's not even the most twisted thing," she said. "She cut herself, you know, down there."

"What?"

"Deep. Gushing blood everywhere – but she was smiling like she was happy about it. I think she's trying to become human."

James thought about this for a second, and then said: "Well, she's batshit crazy, so that's a good start." And, to his amazement, Alex let out a strange kind of snort that might have been mistaken for a laugh.

"James, this isn't funny," she said. "You have to understand, Holly's the worst kind of spoiled brat – the kind with actual power. She can control all of them – the Nobodies. Even Stretch was crying when he had to shove my hands in the fire. He knew that if he disobeyed her, it would have been over for him. Everyone lives in fear of her."

"Yeah, well, it's not just her, is it?"

"What do you mean?"

"It's the House, too."

And James told her his own story, about his own doppelganger's dying words and then his conversation with Stretch in the ballroom. He told her about the things in the basement, and the limbless man, and running through the ever-changing house, knowing it was chasing him, sniffing him out all the while. It sounded mad, even to him, as though he was trying to describe to her some kind of surreal nightmare that he'd had the night before, but she took it all in with hardly a question, brow furrowed in concentration.

She believed him, but this did not come as a relief. If only he'd just lost his mind, if only, if only.

"What does she want?" he asked her. "Why did she do all this? Catch us and torture you like that and make all these things?"

Alex didn't answer immediately. He couldn't see her because with his eye up to the peephole it had been too hard to hear what she was saying, so he was standing with his head beside it and listening instead, whispering into it when it was his turn to speak. He heard her sigh and ruffle her blankets as she changed position. Eventually, she said, "I think she's lonely."

"That's it? Can't she, you know, just make friends whenever she wants?"

"I don't know about that. I mean, I don't think she sees the Nobodies as real people. They're more like… toys, to her."

That was an unsettling thought. Stretch had seemed as alive to James as anyone could be, if somewhat odd. He thought of all those gravestones in the autumn garden. How many had she so carelessly killed? How many had she pulled apart, limb by limb, the way a child might pull the wings and legs off a fly? What if he and Alex weren't the first 'friends' Holly had invited into her estate?

"James?"

"Yeah?"

"Did Stretch really tell you she's got horcruxes? Like, as in Harry Potter?"

"Yeah, but he didn't know where they all were. The guy in the basement – he's one. I think he's, her father. And her mother is supposed to be locked up in the attic."

"Oh my God. No wonder she's always up there. Who knows what she's doing to that poor woman."

"But he didn't know what the last one was, or where it would be."

"Not that we could do anything about it, anyway."

"We've still got Stretch, right?"

A bitter laugh was all the response he got to that, and he supposed it was fair enough. Now that the house had them both, Stretch was about as useless as the knife James still had in his belt. The thought sparked an idea. "They're going to try to take you away tomorrow, for some kind of punishment, right?"

"Yeah, so?"

"And they think you're unarmed, don't they?"

"Yes?"

He balanced the knife in his hands for a minute, savouring the comforting weight of the sharpened metal that had already saved his life once, and then passed it, handle first, through the peephole. Alex said nothing, and he imagined her looking down at it, uncertain.

"Maybe you can take one of them out along the way. Your Doppel – or Greeny. Stretch said it couldn't hurt Holly, but I dunno. What if you cut her head off or something?"

"James, no, it won't work. You're better off using it to defend yourself when they come for – when they try to do whatever it is, they're going to do to you."

"I'll be fine," James said, though the words almost choked him. He felt naked without the knife, but he couldn't bring himself to take it back from her. She needed it more than he did. At least, that was what he was thinking until she spoke her next words.

"If they bury me alive," she said. "I'll use it to slit my wrists."

He found out, then, that she had overheard Holly ordering Greeny to have a grave dug for her. "I think she only meant a temporary grave, one where they can feed through air and milk to me for as long as it takes for me to, you know, break. But I won't do it, James. I'll kill myself first."

"Alex, listen to me. The longer you hold out, the longer I'll have to be able to get to you."

"James, you won't… Don't you get it? We can't get out of this place! Even if Holly and the Nobodies were dead, there's no way we'd be able to get over the walls – the house wouldn't let us."

He remembered his close call with the vines the night before, the way their prying tendrils had bound him so quickly. "We'll just have to burn down the house, then."

"How? James, how? I can't take any more of this, okay? I can't. I just…"

He hung his head, heart breaking at the sound of her hopeless sobs. So much for your great rescue.

"I'm sorry," he said. "I thought I could come in here and kill the monsters and be some kind of hero, but I just screwed us both. I should have done something on the outside. Got help or set the building on fire or…" He felt something tickle the side of his head and turned, surprised, to see her small finger protruding from the peephole. He reached up with his own hand and folded her index finger into his palm, the closest they could get to holding hands. It wasn't much, but it was something.

"It's not your fault, James," she said. "You came for me. I mean, do you have any idea how insane that is? Like, are you stupid or something?"

He laughed, and then for the first time ever the voice he'd denied for so long found words and he said, "Nah. I just love you, that's all."

She said nothing for a few heartbeats – thunderous, adrenaline fuelled heartbeats – and then, so quietly he nearly didn't hear, "I love you too, James."

He let go of her finger and put his head next to the peephole. "We're going to get out," he said. "Just hang in there and I'll find a way. I promise."

"Okay. Okay, James, I will. But James?"

"Yeah?"

"If it's a choice between helping me, or killing that crazy bitch?"

"Yeah?"

"Kill the bitch."

He waited with her, talking in low voices about other things, about school and movies and stupid jokes and their dysfunctional families and all the things they would have talked about on a typical day on the sunny school oval at lunchtime, or walking home after a long day. Eventually, as he knew she would, her voice grew thin and faint and then gave way to soft snoring. When he looked through the peephole, he saw only a mop of black hair and a heap of blankets, from which one hand reached toward him, finger outstretched.

He turned to face the dark playroom. Alright, Houdini. What the hell are you gonna do now? Piles of scattered toys, dolls and cushions littered the room, and he sifted through them in search of something – anything – he might use. Among the things he slipped into his pockets were a hairpin, a handful of marbles, a sewing needle (from the pile of stuffed animals) and a metal sharpener. Actually, he did not take the whole sharpener, but used the hairpin to remove the screw holding the tiny blade in place. What on earth he could use it for he didn't know – it was certainly too small to be a weapon – but he figured if prisoners could kill each other with newspapers and toothbrushes, surely, he could do something with a blade and some marbles.

When he'd completed his circuit of the room, however, he had discovered something besides his little treasures, there was absolutely no way out of here. Unless that was, you considered escape in the figurative sense; when he opened the toy box beneath the peephole he found piles of blank papers and hundreds of art supplies in varying states of depletion: crayons, paints and, his favourite, pastels.

He was alone, a captive in a strange universe, and he had hours to go before daylight. So, James did what he always did, when he felt lost, he drew.

With the slow passing of the dawn hours, James's fear, depression, and worry melted away along with the frantic thoughts that had occupied him for every one of the last nightmare-fuelled hours. He descended into that indefinable state of being that was nowhere and everywhere at the same time, a spot deeper than the deepest sleep in which his hand flew across the page and images appeared unbidden from his subconscious and onto the page. Anyone watching him would have thought him possessed, and perhaps he was.

As usual, the images told stories, but this time there were many, each one different from the next, and all of them disturbing in one way or another.

In one, his and Alex's graves stood side by side in the autumn garden, while in the background Holly and Stretch played with two new living residents of the estate, their faces contorted into fake smiles that barely hid their terror. In another, Alex stood alone on the smoking wreck of the house, knife in hand, her face lined with sadness. In yet another, it was Holly who stood triumphant, and James and Alex were the broken ones, their eyes hollow and their postures hunched and obedient, waiting their next orders. In that one, he'd drawn the other Nobody – the one he only knew about from Alex's description, standing behind them with a pair of shears and a grim scowl.

He had never seen Greeny, yet he knew the disjointed bark-like limbs and knotty root fingers and watery eyes were all accurate, and when he sniffed the green pastel he'd used, it smelt like moss. Just as he knew, also, that all of the images he'd drawn were real in some sense, all of them possible.

When the first hint of morning light crept into the playroom through the peephole, James laid out the pictures on the blue carpet and rested his back against the door, exhausted and miserable. Of all the pictures he'd drawn, not one seemed happy or hopeful. Nothing but tragedy seemed to await them no matter what. There was, however, one picture to which his gaze inevitably returned, no matter how much it scared him. It was the one in which Alex stood alone on the burnt house.

It scared him because he couldn't see himself in that picture, but it scared him even more because it was the only one in which Holly and the house had both been destroyed, and in which Alex had survived. And because it meant that these things were possible; the house could be burned. Alex could survive.

But the only one he'd drawn himself alive in was the one in which he was visibly broken, staring dumbly at his feet while Holly barked at him with an accusing finger and Greeny observed impartially.

He was still considering this when he became suddenly aware of the sound of the grandfather clock ticking loudly in the hall outside, as though it had sprung into existence with the rising sun. The brick wall, he was sure, had vanished – but it would do him no good, for even then he could hear the gardener's heavy steps clomping up the hall.

It was time.

37
Infanticide

Summer, 2002

Holly wept. She ran down to the bottom of the garden, away from everything and everyone – even Pinky and the babies – and bawled and screamed until her throat was like gravel. Why did everything have to be like this? Even her powers hadn't been enough, and since that night her father had been worse than ever, rampaging through the house, watching them through keyholes and around corners, searching the house endlessly and muttering things to himself at all hours, growing more and more paranoid. It would only be a matter of time until he found something that pushed him over the edge for good.

But it was not him Holly need've worried about, since even in his drunkest rages he didn't dare go down to the basement. The basement had taken up a black spot in his mind that was like a hole in his thoughts, a place where he didn't venture except in the pits of his deepest nightmares.

"It's done."

Holly whirled around, her face stained with dirt and swollen with tears. Her mother stood just up the hill beneath one of the towering pines that would later be part of the winter pine forest, but in those days was no more than a lone tree bristling in the summer breeze. Jane Anderson had deep bags under her eyes – though it was hard to tell them apart from the bruises – and her arms were folded tightly across her breast. Hollowed out, but fierce at the same time; a mother bear guarding her cub.

"What's done?" Holly said.

Her mother shook her head slowly, puffy face trembling. She'd been gaining weight for months now, as though hoping the excess fat would cushion her husband's nightly blows. "I told you. I warned you to stop. To keep them hidden. You left me no choice."

Holly froze. "No."

But her mother was already marching forward, grabbing hold of her underarm in a pincer grip and pulling her away from the wall and up the hill toward the house. Holly had never seen her so enraged, and she was so shocked she almost didn't notice that her mother's arms were muddy and drenched to the shoulder.

"What did you do? Mother, please tell me you didn't, oh please!"

Instead of answering, Jane dragged her daughter mercilessly on up the hill, up to the western side of the house where the basement window looked out over the soft ground where she kept the vegetable gardens, the rich sour smell of fertilizer reaching Holly long before they rounded the corner.

"We had a deal. You were going to be nice. You were going to be a good girl, and you were going to do as he said. We were going to be a happy family, and then you were going to leave this house and become a normal, brilliant woman. A midwife or a biologist or a surgeon, even – something where you could use your… your talents. Not this – this evil."

And at the word evil they rounded the corner and Holly saw what she'd done.

The babies lay like rotten fruit among the neat rows of lettuce and carrots and potatoes, their soft bodies somehow bloated and deflated at the same time, empty of life yet full of something else – rot and water – some of which leaked from their mouths and eyes into the ground. Their misshapen limbs flopped at odd angles, pitiful and limp.

Holly collapsed to her knees and let out a wail of despair.

They slept during the day. Her mother had gone down into the basement, she told Holly, and seen the abominations she'd created. She'd seen, too, the things Holly had done to them, and remembered the far parts of the garden that had been dug up by what she'd previously thought to be rabbits. She'd found the old corpses.

"How could you do this, you horrible girl! It's sick! Don't you see it's sick? These monsters should never have been allowed to live, and from now on, they shan't. You will dig graves for them before your father gets home, and we'll grow the garden over the top, and you will never permit such creations again, do you understand me?"

Holly bowed her head and bit her mother's hand. Jane let out a startled cry and pulled away, and Holly shot away through the garden at top speed, sprinting around the house to the open front door. She hadn't seen Pinky there – that was the thing – and she wasn't in the kitchen, either, where Mother had drowned them one by one in the big washing tub and, by the looks of it, stuck them with the long tines of the roasting fork to keep them under.

She almost slipped on the wet tiles, but then she hit the rougher wood of the hallway and righted herself, swinging round into the open basement and hurtling down the stairs at breakneck speed.

Her mother had rearranged everything, making neat stacks of the old boxes and cages and suitcases in which the babies had once slept, tidying the bed and straightening the bookcase. Sunlight streamed in through the basement window, illuminating the horribly, sickeningly empty room. Holly threw cushions and blankets aside, toppled towers of boxes, opened cupboards, but there wasn't a single living thing to be found.

At last, she dropped to her knees with her face in her hands and wept for them all, cursing everyone, her mother, her father, the uncaring universe – even the house, who she thought should have saved them somehow, done something. She heard the clack of her mother's shoes on the kitchen tiles and screamed at the top of her lungs, "I HATE YOU!" The clicking stopped and then retreated. She could bury the bodies herself, Holly thought bitterly. Let her sweat in the sun to hide what she'd done before father came home. Maybe she'll lose a few pounds.

The thought brought a mean smile to her lips, and she sniggered wickedly. She never would have believed she could have hated her own mother so much – not after all the beatings she'd taken for Holly, all the sacrifices. But she hated her then, and it was the heat of that rage that put a stop to her crying at last. She sniffed and wiped her nose, watching the last of her tears drip to the cold floor.

"Holly? I… Is that you?" Holly froze, holding her breath. The voice had seemed to come from the floor in the far corner of the basement, but it had an echoey quality, as though emanating from a drain. Was it the house? No, it had sounded too female, somehow, too girlish.

"Holly?" This time she located the source of the voice – and it was indeed a drain. A tiny grating in the corner that she was certain hadn't been there before. She glanced at the half open basement door and then crawled over to the grating, pressing her ear to it. "Miss Pinky?" she whispered.

"Yes, Holly it's me! Down here!"

"How did you get down there?" But before Pinky answered Holly saw it. Partially hidden behind her bookcase in the opposite corner, a small trapdoor with a metal ring. Like the grating, it had never existed before – Holly was sure of it. "I see it!" she whispered, and then jumped to her feet, rushing up the basement stairs. She pulled the door shut, bolted it, and then ran back down to the trapdoor, muttering her gratitude with each quick breath – thankyou house, thankyou house, thankyou…

Miss Pinky was huddling in the tiny concrete room beneath the trapdoor, and Holly dropped down without a second thought, though the fall was longer than she'd anticipated, and she had to roll on the hard floor, bruising her knees and elbows. She didn't care no sooner had she landed than she and Pinky were embracing, Pinky's fleshy shoulders jerking with her sobs. "I was so scared, Miss Holly, so scared."

"Me too. I thought you were dead."

"I hid in the back. I watched her take them one by one, so sneaky – you know how they sleep – so cute and snorey – and I knew I was too small to fight back. Then I heard a strange sound, a creaking hinge, and I saw the trapdoor open for me. I couldn't save any, Holly. I just had to hide…"

Pinky didn't see the blank look that crossed briefly over Holly's face just then. Holly didn't like being lied to, and she was pretty sure Pinky could have saved one or two of the babies, if she'd wanted to. Holly thought maybe Miss Pinky had been too much of a baby herself to save any skin but her own fat pink stuff.

But Holly still loved her, and she hugged her tightly and patted her on the back and told her that she could always make more. She would make more.

"And they'll be better," she said. "They'll be like you. Maybe even bigger and stronger than you, too. Big enough to fight back, next time."

She looked around the little room they were in and smiled. There were no candles or bulbs, yet the room was bathed in a warm red light, and it seemed to beat with the life of the house itself. A room created just for her, a secret place that even her parents couldn't take away from her. She could conduct her experiments here, on a scale that had never been possible before. And if they didn't work out? No one would hear or find them, down here.

Pinky interrupted her thoughts. "Do you think you could make me a friend, Miss Pinky? Another Nobody just like me?"

Ah, so there it was – Pinky didn't care about the babies because they weren't like her. She'd let them die so that Holly could make something new and better.

Holly sighed. She supposed she understood, in a way. Wasn't she, after all, trying so hard herself to make the Nobodies more and more human, more like herself and like the children she saw when she looked up from the attic's window, playing all the way down there in Templeton's school grounds and parks?

"One day there won't be anyone else," she said, smiling into Pinky's glistening eyes. "One day we'll be in control, and it'll only be Nobodies and we'll do as we like and play forever here, protected by the House."

"Oh, I hope so, Holly, I hope so."

"Don't worry, Miss Pinky," Holly said. "No one can stop me, now. Not even Mother."

38
Dawn

Of all the Nobodies Holly had ever made, Greeny was the only one forbidden sleep. Even Stretch, exhausted from his hours of digging and weeping at his beloved's gravestone, had curled up around a dusty bottle of brandy in the Ballroom and passed out. Sister would be sleeping in Alex's house, no doubt dreaming of being one of the outsiders in their mad world, and Holly herself was in the attic, snoring in the mother's embrace while her fresh wounds healed.

But not Greeny.

Holly had made him to be the watchman of the house, always vigilant, always ready. He was the preserver of the fort, Holly's protector… yet at the same time, her prisoner. She could end him in the space of a few seconds with a flash of those full-moon eyes of hers, turn him to ash in the wind. He'd seen it done.

So, the idea of contradicting her worried him. How easy would it be for her, he wondered, to concoct a new Greeny, one who smiled and said yes to her every order, as he had for so long? But if he said nothing, it could mean the ruin of their whole world, the destruction of everything as they knew it and everything it could have been.

He sighed, scratched his barky scalp, ground his wooden teeth, and paced the centre line of the house for hours, matching his paces to the steady ticks and tocks of the grandfather clock. Holly, Holly, Holly. Goddess, Tyrant, Innocent, all rolled into one. Sometimes he felt like her father, other times her slave, others her loyal and trusted subject. What to do, what to do…

When he could take it no longer, he opened the playroom door and regarded the stonework that filled the frame, the words that had been there previously now vanished.

"If I kill Stretch," he said, "She'll know. Why don't you do it?"

A minute or so passed, but sure enough, the cracks between the stones began to bleed, and the trickling red formed clear words. Greeny smirked as he read them. HOLLY WOULD KNOW.

"Heh. So rather me than you, is that it? I'm to sacrifice myself for Holly's sake, and let her kill me?"

The letters dribbled away, replaced by fresh ones. THERE ARE WAYS. LIE TO HER.

Greeny shook his head. "She'd never believe me. She loves him." He spat the word love, as though it were poisonous.

This time, only the words THERE ARE WAYS disappeared, leaving only LIE TO HER. The house, Greeny supposed, had spoken. He was on the point of shutting the door – perhaps harder than he needed to – when two more words appeared beneath the remaining three, OR DIE.

Greeny resisted the urge to snap the door from its hinges and instead closed it gently and stood in front of it for a minute. Perhaps he should go to the ballroom right that minute, slit Stretch's throat and let the House hide the body. But who was to say the house wouldn't reveal it to Holly later and point the finger at him? He muttered a curse to himself. This was all getting too cloak and dagger for his liking. It would all be fine if the two kids were dead and gone.

He looked up at the attic trapdoor. Just the sight of it made him want to get out of the house and hide away in his shed – the only place he really felt secure, anymore. If he went up there now, there was a good chance he wouldn't return. Perhaps his remains would be the first shovelful of soil tossed over Alex's grave.

Nothing for it. He reached up and grabbed the heavy ring. The trapdoor came down with a groan that sounded like a cautionary grunt – the house telling him to be careful. That wasn't a good sign.

"Damn you to hell," Greeny said. He pulled himself up.

The attic was hot. The attic was always hot. Greeny wasn't bothered by that – he was used to the humidity of the summer jungle, after all – no, what disturbed him the most was the Mother. He had seen her once, and it was enough. Since then, he refused to look at her, instead standing in the far corner of the room and keeping his head down like a chastised schoolboy.

The room smelled of sourness and yeast and the stingy tang of stale sweat. "H… Holly?" he said.

Something enormous shifted in the giant bed, blankets and linen moving, skin sliding against skin, and someone whispered something Greeny couldn't hear. Holly moaned and took in a sleepy breath. "Hmmm?"

"Miss Holly? It's me, Greeny?"

More whispering, and then a creak as Holly sat up. Greeny glanced up and then back down again. Luckily, the attic was lit only by a pair of slow burning candles, and he'd only seen a fuzzy mess of shadows and light at the back of the room. For a split second, a flare of candlelight had crossed Holly's face, illuminating the burns there. They were healing, knitting together well, nourished by Mother's milk, though the scars would never leave her – of that Greeny was sure.

"Greeny?" she said. Her voice pathetically weak. None of the tyrant here, only a hurt little girl. Greeny allowed himself to relax a little.

"Ahem. Sorry to disturb you, I just needed to talk to you about what's happened."

"That's alright Greeny. Why don't you come closer?"

Something in Greeny's chest tightened, but he obliged, keeping his head down as he approached the bed. He felt eyes on him, but he was sure they didn't belong only to Holly. There was more whispering.

"What is it?" Holly said.

"I… Miss, I think what the girl did to you today was unforgivable. And the boy… he's dangerous. The House agrees. I think we should get rid of them and try again another day. We have all the time in the world, after all, and –"

"No, Greeny."

"What? But Holly –"

"Miss Holly."

"But Miss Holly, she tried to murder you. I'm worried about you, is all."

More whispering. A thick, breathless voice. Then Holly said, "I want them, and I'll have them. No one's going to take my friends away from me. Do you understand that, Greeny? I want them, and Mother says I deserve them. I can have all the friends I want, and if they don't want to play along then we'll just have to make them play." By the end, her voice had grown painfully shrill. Frantic.

It would be dangerous to keep pushing her. Greeny was under no illusions – however highly he might rank in Holly's estimation, however well he'd served her in the past – it would do nothing to save him if he made her feel for a moment that she wasn't completely in control.

He pushed anyway. "Miss Holly," he said, lowering his head so as to appear as obsequious as possible. "I beg you. Please consider that it might be far better to start this, uh, project from scratch, and seek out friends who perhaps aren't so… troublesome? Perhaps we could snatch a pair of babies, and raise them here on the estate? They could learn from a young age and –"

"I will consider it." She said, but her voice betrayed her. She'd always been a stubborn bitch.

Greeny bowed as low as he could, feeling both sets of eyes on him like two pairs of spiders running all over his rough skin. "Thank you, Miss Holly. I'll leave you to your rest and wish you a speedy recovery."

And with that he backed away, keeping his head low, and descended the ladder, letting out a hefty sigh of relief only when the trapdoor was firmly shut, and he was alone in the centre line of the house. He swore under his breath.

Well, I tried. But the thought gave him no comfort. He could obey her, of course, and hope all turned out for the better. Perhaps she'd get so frustrated she'd kill them herself. Perhaps Stretch would expose himself as a traitor and she'd get rid of him and be forced to see that Greeny was right all along.

But then he recalled the look in the girl's eyes as he'd pushed her back into her room, torn and bloody. The hate he'd seen there. Not to mention the suspicious circumstances under which she'd made her first escape – somehow – from right under Stretch's long nose. Maybe not this night, or the next, or the next, but it would only be a matter of time before one of the three, the girl or her boyfriend or Stretch himself, snapped. And Greeny would be the first to feel the hard edge of a blade dragging across his throat, with or without Holly's protection.

No way around it. They have to die.

He nodded to himself and started along down the hall, the beginnings of a plan already forming in his mind.

39
Unravelling

Summer, 2002

T he house had always been a benevolent force in Holly's life, but in the days and weeks following Miss Pinky's narrow escape she became more aware of its presence, of its helping hand and keen eye. She noticed that whenever her father flew into a rage, there was always a door nearby through which she could slip and disappear, and her father somehow always failed to follow. His crystal bar was always full, though he seemed hardly ever to restock it, and its contents never failed to knock him out cold when he was at his worst.

The house hid Holly, but most importantly, it hid her experiments and her creations. That was for the best, because the vision of those poor helpless bodies lying in the vegetable patch remained clear in Holly's mind, and it drove her to create stronger, to create better. She began to push herself, to stretch her strange power to its limits, no matter the cost. The complexity meant that she was utterly exhausted after every effort, and ninety nine of every hundred living things she created were such horrific abominations she had to eliminate them immediately.

More than a few of them, in their moments of agonised existence, tried to rip her apart with their deformed bodies and mouths, but Holly always made sure to keep some of her power back so that she could twist them into knots and end them before they succeeded. It was, in short, a dark time.

No matter what went on down there, the screams never escaped the confines of the basement, and Holly suspected the House had more to do with that than the thickness of the walls. She could feel its presence as she worked, willing her to succeed, encouraging her with bright sunny days whenever she made progress. She grew attuned to the small signs; a door left half open, a light winking at her from another room, a carpet embroidered with arrows all pointing in a certain direction. Then one hot day, she discovered a chilled lemonade sitting on her bedroom windowsill.

And, at last, in the late summer of 2002, she succeeded.

The Nobody was born of hatred. Her mother, in tears of rage, sent her to the basement when she stomped her feet and broke a plate on the dining room floor.

"You killed my babies! I'll never do what you tell me again!" This had become their daily argument. While Gregory was home, Holly was the picture of courteous obedience, all smiles and curtseys. When he was gone, she spat fire at her mother, kicked over bins and emptied cooking oil on the kitchen table. Nothing her mother couldn't clean up before He got home, of course, but enough to keep her busy. Jane would never catch her – not with the House watching – and Holly suspected her mother was just as aware of its intelligence as she was. So instead, she pleaded with Holly and Holly retreated to the basement to create.

This particular day was worse than the others. Her mother had broken down in tears in the lounge room, begging Holly to be a good girl and help her clean, and Holly had discovered an unpleasant feeling welling up inside her. She wanted the rage back – the hot rage that felt so good and righteous, but instead she'd run away from the potted plant she'd broken in the lounge and her mother's pathetic cries and wept herself breathless.

But down in the dark room beneath the basement, Miss Pinky looking on with frightened eyes, Holly's guilt turned to resentment, and then to hate. How dare her mother make her feel this way, after what she'd done? How dare she guilt Holly, and pretend to be her mother now, when she'd done nothing but try to control her all this time? She wasn't her real mother – the House was – it was her mother and her father and her best friend. Jane Anderson was just some… some bitch.

Holly turned these thoughts over in her mind, sitting in the corner of the bare compartment and staring at the empty floor, and as she grew more furious, she felt the heat begin to build behind her eyes. It was always hot – but never like this – and she used the hatred for fuel, screaming as her head filled up with an intense red madness she'd never felt before. Her fingernails bit into her palms and her heart broke. Her soul split in two, and poured out through her eyeballs and into the Thing that was even then twisting into existence in front of her, sprouting arms and legs from a ball of flesh that squirmed on the concrete ground…

The last thing she heard was the sound of Miss Pinky's terrified shriek, and then the white light shorted a circuit in her brain, and everything blinked out as though someone had pulled the plug on a television screen. That was it;

she'd finally gone too far and blown a blood vessel in her brain. She was going to die, but she found, in those last moments, that it wasn't sadness she felt but savage glee. That will show them! That will show them! And then she was out.

When she awoke, Stretch's long face was looming over hers, his puppy dog eyes full of concern. "Miss Holly?" he said. "Are you okay?"

The House, once again, came to the rescue. Late at night it woke her with a tree branch tapping on her bedroom window, and when she opened it, still lost half in a dream, the branch snaked around her waist and lifted her out into the warm night, lowering her gently to the ground outside her window. A narrow path parted through the grass toward the corner of the garden that would later grow into a lush Amazonian jungle, and in a thick circle of trees in the corner she found the treehouse, complete with a sturdy roof, three levels cleverly designed around the hefty oak, and a rope ladder dangling from the door.

Holly, sighing with gratitude, opened her arms and fell against the great tree, hugging it as tightly as she could. 'Thank you, house, thank you so much.'

The leaves shifted in the wind, and she giggled when a couple of slender branches closed around her shoulders and hugged her back. "I just wish it could just be us," she said softly. "Just you and me and the Nobodies. Wouldn't that be nice?"

Gregory woke up in some no-where part of the night, his mouth dry as desert sand and his head heavy and thick as a wooden stump on his shoulders. His only thought was need more. Sometimes a combination of dehydration and too much sugar from the alcohol did this to him, made him come springing wide awake at some ungodly hour.

That, and the dreams. Dreams in which he blundered through endless dark passages, small leechy mouths latched on to him with every turn. His strength left him in slow drips as they drained his blood, their weight dragging him down, worm tongues lapping at his flesh.

Oblivion was the only answer to such horrors.

He found, however, once he'd poured himself a vodka soda as tall as the empire state and taken a good sip, that he didn't want to go back to sleep.

The house was rarely so quiet. Perhaps it, too, was sleeping. The thought gave him comfort. Gregory had never quite admitted to himself that the house was a living thing, but he felt it in his bones. And not the way Holly or Jane did, either. He felt it in a way that made him itch when he turned his back on an open door. The house was a predatory force; it had a hungry laugh that you heard in your mind instead of with your ears.

He left the kitchen and crossed the lounge – his favourite drinking spot – but instead of turning on the television or even the light he stood in the middle of the room, drink in hand, a comforting buzz returning to chase away the hangover, and listened.

This was the first time he had listened – since in order to listen one had first to admit that there might be something to hear.

Blessed silence.

As his eyes grew accustomed to the dark, and his tall vodka became a short one, he felt a surge of confidence – or perhaps rage; sometimes he confused the two. His father had always taught him that the best way to face your fears was to get angry, to be the aggressor instead of the victim. Yet here he was, hiding away in his own house, letting his wife and daughter creep around and whisper behind his back. Are you not the man of the house? His father demanded – and on such a still night Gregory almost believed he'd heard the voice out loud. Of course, I am, he thought back, upending his glass as though in an act of defiance. Dr. Terrence Anderson had always been a teetotaller. Then why, boy, are you letting them treat you like an ignorant child?

The words had seemed to come from the light fixture, and Gregory even glanced up at it before shaking his head and chuckling to himself. He ventured back to the kitchen and managed to fill his glass in the dark. Why indeed? He thought as he dropped in a couple of fresh ice cubes. Just why indeed should I allow them to treat me that way?

This time, instead of returning to the lounge room he took the left passageway down the hall toward the library and the music room. The music room was a recent addition, an extra project he'd pursued for a while to have something to do in the evenings when Jane was giving Holly her lessons. Conspiring, you mean. Up to something. Since he'd completed it, he'd found that whenever he opened his whiskey cabinet, it was well stocked. He assumed it was Jane, trying to keep him happy, though she must have been taking the money out of his own wallet since she had none of her own. She got funny brands, too, the bottles of sour-mash bearing labels like Nobody's Home, Goodnight Neighbour and even a powerfully strong Absinth called Down the Hatch. They were all, quite surprisingly, delicious.

As he passed the music room something tugged at him, an urge to play on the grand piano. He'd served a brutal apprenticeship as a child, back when there was a piano in every house and playing well was a sign of class and nobility. He gave in, ducking inside and breathing deep the nostalgic smell of varnish and sawdust. When he sat, straight-backed, on the little stool and looked down at the ivory keys shining blue-white with the moonlight streaming in from the window it was almost as though he'd travelled back in time. He could practically feel his music teacher standing just behind his right shoulder, hawk-eyes piercing the back of his hands and his metal ruler ready for the moment Gregory made a mistake.

He sighed, rested his glass on the cherry wood top, and began to play.

The notes and bars formed slowly at first, stopping and starting, but soon enough the floodgates were open, and it was all coming back to him, his fingers dancing nimbly over the keys as though he'd had his last lesson that morning. Fur Elise first, then Midnight Sonata, and then he felt himself fall into that magical place where the world no longer existed and the only things were his fingers and the keys and the notes, and he dropped into Hall of the Mountain King, playing as though he were in concert before a thousand – no, a hundred thousand people!

And there at the peak of that masterpiece, when the crowd was rising from their seats, screaming his name with tears in their eyes, he stood up and spread his arms, bowing low before them, his expression a professional deadpan while inside he roared with exhilaration – his dream come true! And he had played it well, hadn't he? He bowed left and then right, and the vodka must have taken more of a toll than he thought because he stumbled, knocking his glass across the top of the piano and causing vodka and flat soda to cascade across the keyboard.

"Shit! Bastard bastard bastard..." He pulled a cleaning rag from the broom closet in the hall and then returned, cursing as he did his best to get all of it, already embarrassed at the intensity of his own fantasy. It wasn't like him to play such childish games after a–

What's this?

He had opened the top of the piano, meaning to reach in and wipe the places the vodka had seeped through before it got too sticky, but the liquid had dripped onto something else – something that didn't belong inside a grand piano. Something, furthermore, that certainly hadn't been there when he'd bought the piano in the first place. A notebook.

He lifted it, a stained brown square no larger than his palm, and took it back with him to the lounge room, taking his empty glass with him for refilling. A minute later he sunk into the couch with a fresh drink (now considerably more vodka than soda) and pried open the pages.

He recognized his wife's handwriting in an instant; she had written most of the textbooks that Holly left scattered throughout the library. It would be easy to check, but he didn't bother. It was just like her to keep a diary; her mind was a beehive of pointless frets and fears. It was the secret part that bothered him. Had she kept the stupid thing on her bedside table and written in it every night, it never would have crossed his mind to glance at it. But in the piano? Which, as she well knew, he hadn't touched in almost a decade and in all likelihood never would again…

The first entry began:

Dear Nobody,

What an awful place this has become. Oh, how I longed for just such a house as this for all those years before Holly was born. A nice peaceful estate with a large garden, neither too far nor too near to the city. A happy little home to raise my princess… I thought it would mellow Gregory out, let him see that things needn't be so… Rigid all the time. Now, I see that –

He hissed, a curious habit he had adopted whenever he was growing impatient and flipped several pages ahead. This was just more of her whining. She never stopped. He paused as he caught sight of an unfamiliar name on an entry dated one year prior. As he read, he lifted his heavy glass and brought it to his lips, eyes flying across the page – but the glass never quite reached his lips. It stopped halfway; his arm frozen along with the rest of him. Impossible.

Dear Nobody,

Mad bliss today when I saw him. Oh, yes, I think I'd completely lost hope until he arrived, but now hope is all there is. Joseph, Joseph, Joseph, my saviour. He was inconsolable when he saw the bruises Gregory laid on me this past Monday, though by now they're yellow and nearly fading. He wanted to rush in and sweep Holly and I away, but I persuaded him not to. He'd have to kill Gregory. It would be the only way, or my dear husband would spend his last breath hunting us down – across the whole world, if he had to. He has a strange love for us, Gregory. A strange love that allowed me to forgive him for so long.

Better that he never sees it coming at all. Better that he wakes up one day, alone in this great house he built for himself in his lonely life he made his and his alone. Better he never sees us again and stews in his rage, a bitter old man. Perhaps then he'll find it in himself to regret what he's done to me and poor, poor Holly.

He remembered his drink at last, nearly cracking a tooth with the edge of his glass in his rush to swallow the burning liquid. He got up and took a step toward the staircase, meaning to pull that damned woman kicking and screaming and push her nose into the book, the way you pushed a puppy's nose into its own business. Didn't think I'd find it did you?

But a breeze drifting in from the entrance hall chilled his rage for a moment and he hesitated. For once, the cold voice of reason cut through the heat of the alcohol. This is not a thing to be acted on rashly now. We don't want them to know, do we? No, this is something to be planned and executed with a clear mind.

He nodded to himself, muttering as he poured another drink to quell his anger. He returned to the couch, glancing briefly at the clock above the fireplace (twelve past three, plenty of time), and once more opened the little diary. There would be no secrets in this house, he thought. Not ever again, not ever.

And he was so immersed in the loopy scrawl on the small, lined pages, swimming before his eyes, that he never heard "The Hall of the Mountain King" continuing to play merrily on the piano down the hall, the notes floating along the breeze and out of the cracks beneath doors and windows, lost to the night.

40
A Dark Fate

When the door to the playroom had opened early next morning, James was too stunned by what he saw to attempt an escape: not that it would have been possible in any case, with the hulking tree of a man blocking the doorway. Greeny.

As for Holly, gone was the sweet little girl who'd struck a conversation with him at the front gates so long ago. In her place was a glaring, wide-eyed lunatic with burnt hair and terrible scars visible all over her arms and neck. She stared at James with psychotic intensity, and when she spoke her voice was shrill, a temper barely held in check.

"You came for her, didn't you?"

He nodded, not trusting himself to speak.

"Well, you can't have her. She's my friend. And you can't leave, either. You belong to me."

"Wh… What are you going to do?" he said. He was fully aware that he was no match for the groundskeeper – even if he'd still had the knife. He searched the big brown eyes for a sign, hoping that he was of the same ilk as

Stretch, no more than a reluctant follower – but didn't find one.

"I could make you disappear if I wanted," Holly said, eyes shining with an unnatural light. "I could put you in the middle of the house, and never let you out. The house would eat you, and then you really couldn't leave. But Alex loves you, doesn't she?"

He wasn't sure how to answer that, but before he could try, Holly continued. "And I want her to be my friend forever. So, you can be my hostage. If she won't listen when I punish her, maybe she'll listen when I punish you. I'll let Sister take care of that, because I promised her. But afterwards, if you both play nicely, I won't have to."

She shrugged one shoulder and then folded her arms as if to say so there. After a few tense seconds, James realised she was waiting for him to say something.

"What if... What if I agree to play nicely? Like, if I promise to be your friend and everything? Would you let Alex go? If you let her go, I'd do anything you want. We could be friends forever and you'd never have to be lonely again. That's what you wanted, isn't it? I'd never leave, and we could play games and go on adventures and everything."

He held his breath. To his amazement, Holly's expression softened, and she came running towards him, tears streaming down her face. She hugged him, burying her face in his chest, and James patted her awkwardly, all too aware of the Greeny's glare. Touch her and die, the look said, and he believed it.

At last, Holly pulled back, beaming at him through her tears. "That's all I wanted!" She said. "Oh, I'm so happy. Alex will listen to you, I'm sure she will. You'll tell her. You can even have your own home – the winter cottage or the treehouse in the summer jungle! I'll have the House make it nice for you both. And I can make Nobodies for you, too, to do whatever you like."

She was chattering, her eyes bright and eager, once again the innocent little girl James had taken her for when they'd first met.

"So, you won't punish her? Let me talk to her and I'll make it alright."

But no sooner had he spoken the words than he knew he'd made a mistake. She stepped away from him as though he'd said something unforgivably horrendous. "Not punish her? Look what she did to me!" And she pulled up the sleeve on her right arm so that James could see the tenuous white and pink scars running up to her shoulder.

"She must be broken. She has to know that I'm the one in charge. ME."

Then she caught sight of something just over his shoulder and her jaw dropped in indignant horror. "MY BEAR!" James felt something die inside, and he turned to see her running over to the torn body of her beloved stuffed toy – him with the beady, watching eyes who'd been reduced to a torn rag in the toy box.

"This was mine! My mother sewed it for me for my fifth birthday. It had the house's eyes." Her voice sounded hollow. James didn't know whether she was going to fly into a rage or break down in tears. When she next spoke, however, it was not to James at all but to the groundskeeper standing in the doorway behind him.

"Greeny?"

"Yes, Miss Holly?"

"When Sister arrives, I want you to tell her that she'll get her wish, and more. Tell her that she may do anything she wants to James, as long as she keeps his head intact. I want it sewn onto the bear. Alive. He is to become part of the house, just like father."

"An excellent idea, Miss Holly."

"Wait – I thought you said you'd leave me alive," James said, his mouth suddenly very dry. "I thought you said you'd let me talk to Alex – that you'd let us have a cottage and everything."

Holly stood up slowly, lips drawn into a tight line. "And I will. Once you're a part of the house, you won't be able to get away, and nor will you be able to die. Alex will have to stay, then, if she knows you can't leave. And she'll have to do what I say, too, or I'll have your lips sewn shut, or perhaps your eyes – or I'll ruin your face, so she doesn't recognize it. The house will keep you for me."

And only then did the words just like father truly strike home, and James understood what she was saying. He recalled the hideous limbless man he'd seen in the basement, half buried in the very foundation of the house, a part of it, fed by it, kept alive by its supernatural energy… for how long? If that was possible, then was it so hard to imagine his own head, sewn onto the limp body of the curly haired bear? Forever joined to the house, and kept as a hostage and threat to enslave Alex?

The tiniest smile, smug and triumphant, crossed Holly's face. "There, Greeny. I think he understands, now."

She tried to brush past him – but in an impulse born more of panic than pre-meditation James seized her neck with both hands and squeezed with every ounce of strength he had in his body for one second… two… and then the thick knotted arms of the groundskeeper tore him away and slammed him face first against the blue carpeted floor, stunning him.

Holly staggered, coughing, and for a minute he thought he might have crushed her windpipe after all – but then she recovered herself and uttered a bitter, rough laugh.

"Make sure you tie him up nice and tightly for Sister, Greeny," she said, her injured voice barely a whisper.

"And make sure she understands that as long as his head lives… I don't care what happens to the rest of him."

41
Burial Day

Alex vomited for the third time that morning and then crawled onto the bed, curling into a ball. She didn't feel any better.

Two hours ago, Greeny had stuck his leafy head in and, in a bland voice that nevertheless woke her as quickly as a glass of ice water to the face, told her that she would be buried alive before lunchtime. He had closed the door without waiting for a response.

James hadn't answered her urgent whispers at the peephole, and when she stuck her eye to it, she found the adjacent room empty. She had the knife, now tucked inside her right shoe, the blade stuck in the heel and the handle concealed by her jeans. She had no idea what good it would do, but it was all she had.

Forget butterflies – it was as if someone had unloaded a ball of snakes into her belly. She imagined this was what people felt like on death row the day they had to go to the chair; paralysing, all-consuming dread. Her lips were cold. She ached all over from the wounds of the day before, and her hands were as bad as ever; they wept, and the raw skin had developed a plastic film of moisture that made the pink skin shine.

If only she could stop time and just for a moment think, but the grandfather clock marched relentlessly onward, each tock slamming home like a hammer on the head of a nail, reminding her that she had moved, against her will, one step closer to her fate.

Holly's 'lunchtime' was a tea party at noon; ornate floral teacups and generous servings of that sour but oddly filling milk to go with the peppermint or earl grey or Russian caravan. The last time the clock had chimed, Alex had counted eleven bells. It wouldn't be long now.

She touched the knife for reassurance. The blade had grown warm against her skin. Maybe the right thing to do would be to start slashing as soon as anyone opened the door. Then she remembered how easily Greeny had carried her. And how the vines had curled around her feet the first time she'd tried to make a run for it.

But what else could she do? Let them bury her? The thought alone was terrifying enough. What had Greeny said about it? Now she's got no choice but to break you. Break, not murder. Holly just wanted to subdue Alex, that was all. She wanted to turn her into some kind of zombie that would play nice. A broken person. A Nobody.

Alex began to formulate a plan. A dangerous, unlikely plan that would probably not work. What if she emerged from the grave just the way Holly wanted her? Subdued, obedient, vacant – all the qualities the little psychopath apparently wanted in a friend. What if she played the part so well that Holly began to take her harmlessness for granted? If even the house itself turned a blind eye? What if Holly let her get close to her – close enough, perhaps, for Alex to take that knife and gouge out those pretty blue eyes, and then saw at that dainty neck until Holly's head separated from her body?

Stretch had told James that he couldn't hurt Holly with the knife, but maybe he'd just been protecting Holly. The more Alex thought about it, the less certain she became. How could a little girl like that be immortal? She had supernatural powers, but at the end of the day she was still a living, breathing thing, wasn't she?

And anything that lived could die.

In the darkness beneath the thick blanket, Alex thought. It wouldn't be hard, kneeling beside Holly during one of their tea parties, to slip the knife out of her shoe unnoticed. Then, as Holly leaned forward to pour a fresh cup, Alex could grab a handful of hair and slip the knife around her neck. A few seconds is all it would take, not enough time for the house or Stretch to come to her rescue, or for those eyes of hers to go to work…

So, when the grandfather clock at last chimed twelve and she heard Greeny's rough steps clunking down the hall towards her door, Alex wiped the tears from her eyes, took a deep breath, and got out of bed.

She stepped into the pristine bathroom where only an hour ago she'd been vomiting with terror and faced her reflection in the mirror. She had changed a lot over the last few days. The girl that looked back at her now was deathly pale, eyes red, expression drawn, and serious, black hair matted with cold sweat.

"Okay," she said, her voice shaking. Clunk, clunk, clunk. Greeny would knock and enter in less than a minute.

"Here's how it is. You're in a horror movie. You love horror movies, right? Well, you're in one now, and if you don't act like Ripley in Alien, you're gonna end up like 'The Babysitter' at the start of Scream.

"When they take you, you're gonna be weak. Shaken up, in pain. You're gonna beg them not to do it, but it'll all be an act, okay? Just like in a movie. And you'll let them bury you in…" She swallowed, closing her eyes to steady herself for a second. Greeny stopped outside her door.

"When they let you out, you'll be broken. Not all there anymore. But you'll do everything she says, no question, no hesitation, no matter what. You'll play the part so good they'll give you an Oscar. And when the time comes…"

Her bedroom door creaked open. "Come on, girl. It's time. Don't make it any harder for yourself."

The last part she whispered to herself, so that he couldn't hear. Don't let me down.

She took small steps, staring at her feet and hunching her shoulders – the picture of vulnerability, though it didn't feel like an act. Greeny walked beside her with one hand gently gripping her arm above the elbow, leading her on. They left via the front door and rounded the house.

Stretch and Holly stood beside the open grave, and when Alex saw the plastic piping and the circular hole in the coffin, she almost fainted with relief; it wasn't a death sentence after all. There was still hope.

Holly had healed quickly – far more quickly than any normal human being would have, but the mottled scars visible on her pale arms weren't going to disappear anytime soon, and the pink-white scar tissue extended even up one side of her neck. The hair on that side was singed short. Alex looked down, suddenly afraid that Holly would see the triumph in her expression, but not before she saw Holly's face.

To her surprise, Holly wasn't looking at her with hate or indignant rage, as she'd expected. Instead, there was something like hurt in her eyes. It was the kind of look you might expect from a loyal puppy that had been kicked by its owner.

It was afternoon, but the clouds were dark enough to blot out the sun and cast the graveyard in an evening light.

The smell in the air was rich soil, dead leaves, and rain that had yet to fall. As they arrived at the empty grave, Stretch put a hand on Alex's shoulder. She looked up into his watery eyes.

"It's alright, Miss Alex. Just think of it as a taking of medicine. When you come out, we can all be together – like a family."

"Be quiet, Stretch," Holly said. He backed away, bowing, and now Alex was face to face with Holly and there was rage in her eyes, after all. Her irises clouded, as though she were summoning some of that strange creative energy, but nothing came of it. Instead, she pointed to the plain pinewood coffin set beside the hole.

"You'll go in there and think about what you've done. I'll let you out when I think you're ready to behave, but this is your last warning. If you can't be my friend, well… Well then that's all. I can always get another one." Her voice hovered on the edge of collapse but didn't break.

Alex lowered her head; a child being chastised by her mother. She didn't trust herself to say anything.

Greeny took hold of her arm once more and took her over to the coffin. "Go on," he said.

She stepped into it and lowered herself gingerly, conscious of the knife in her shoe. She lay down on her back, the hardwood sides allowing just enough room to shift an inch here or there, no more. Her heart slammed in her chest, but when she opened her eyes and took in the view above – the heavy clouds shot through with streaks of sun and misty light, all she could think was beautiful.

And then Greeny reached over and swung the coffin lid shut.

Once the pipe was in place, Stretch reached for the shovel, his face a comically miserable frown so elaborate that it did in fact look like a smile turned upside down.

Greeny put a hand on his shoulder. "Let me take care of that, eh?"

Stretch turned, surprised, and Greeny gave him a friendly nod. "I'm the one in charge of punishments, ain't that right, Miss Holly?"

"I don't care," Holly said. "I just want to be alone." And without another word she turned her back on them both and headed for the front of the house.

Stretch relinquished the shovel and watched her go, his brow furrowed, and his face lined with stress. "It's all so backwards, Greeny," he said. "Why does she have to be like this?"

"Don't bother about it," Greeny said, scraping the first mound of dirt into the grave. "Why don't you go and watch over the boy? Holly's got a mind to break him too, I think, only she's putting Sister in charge."

"Sister?" His droopy ears pricked up like a dog. "But she's not right – she's mad!"

Greeny snorted, remembering the state of Alex when he'd come to get her the day before. "You think? If you ask me, I hope she kills him. One less problem to worry about. Don't think Holly would like that, though. Might be useful to have someone watch her."

Might be useful for you not to see what I'm about to do. Might be useful for me to know where you are, too. Me and the house. Greeny smiled a twiggy grin, and Stretch smiled back, mistaking his scheming for compassion, as Greeny had known he would. Ah, poor Stretch. How such a mad girl as Holly could have created a soft heart as you is beyond me.

"Thanks Greeny. It'll be alright in the end, won't it?"

"Sure, it will, Stretch. Holly's just in one of her tantrums, that's all. It'll pass. It always does."

Stretch nodded, tipped his tall hat, and headed off in Holly's wake, leaving Greeny to fill in the grave by himself.

Just the way he wanted it.

He took his time, making sure the dirt was packed nice and even, and the pipe stuck up beside the tombstone, open just wide enough for a bare minimum of fresh air to get down to Alex.

Then he stuck the shovel in the soft ground and searched the graveyard until he found a rock that was just the right size and shape. He knelt beside the mouth of the pipe and leant over it, knowing his voice would sound loud and clear on the other end.

"Sorry about this, girl. But I did warn you. I can't risk you bringing this place to an end. No matter how much Holly wants a real friend. It's for her own good. Hope you've a better time in the next life."

Without listening for a reply, he jammed the heavy rock down the pipe's opening, forcing it as far along as he could get it so that Holly wouldn't be able to see the blockage. It wasn't a perfect fit – some air might still get around the sides, but it would do the job.

She'd have a few hours at most before she fainted, and perhaps a few more after that of life, experienced as a dreamless sleep. As deaths go, it wasn't the worst thing, really.

The boy, after all, wouldn't be so lucky.

Everything Has A Price

42
Bloodletting

Holly did not visit any of her usual haunts – the library or the treehouse in the sunny summer or the cosy winter cottage or even the attic. She found herself instead descending from room to room, via stairways and trapdoors, until she was in the hallway on the ground floor, standing in front of the door to the basement.

Everything had, once more been restored to order. Once James was imprisoned on the body of her favourite bear, he would be more open to getting to know her, to becoming her friend and – above all – to making sure Alex no longer wanted to leave. Alex herself would be resigned at first, no doubt bitter. But as time went on, she would grow comfortable with her new place, and when Holly showed her how generous she (and the house) could be to obedient friends – friends who played nicely – everything would be better.

Today, however, would be a quiet day of reflection and waiting. Sister was busy being Alex on the outside, and so could only come later. Holly resented her demands, but she was doing an important job. Perhaps in the future she would even be able to deliver more living things to Holly. Despite all the trouble Alex and James had caused already, there was something so madly exciting about real life. Not like the Nobodies. They held no mystery for Holly; she knew all their moving parts and had control over everyone. They were no more interesting than wind-up toys.

And Alex would have to stay below ground for quite some time, Holly thought, one hand absently tracing the itchy burns on her right arm. She shivered, though not from fear. Such a terrible, scary thing to happen. But also, so… exhilarating. Holly couldn't wait to do more experiments. There were so many games to play with alive people, weren't there? You never knew what they might do.

She sighed, dreamily, and then shook herself awake and pulled open the basement door descending fearlessly into the pitch blackness beneath the house.

For her, it was a happy dark, a benevolent blanket of night deep in the house's embrace. Almost immediately her babies crawled from their boxes and crates, nipping at her and rubbing against her legs like playful pets. She laughed and swatted them away good naturedly. They never failed to cheer her up, but she was not here to cuddle or read fairy tales by lamplight, as she often liked.

No, she had come to the basement because the events of the past few days had left her with a boiling hate inside her that she knew, if left unattended, would grow like cancer. That, and the babies were due for a feeding, and they had no appetite for Mother's milk: only blood.

She had come to see Father.

The lowest room in the house was always lit by the same heavy red light. Red was Holly's favourite colour; it reminded her of red lips and blood and roses and hot fire. After so long in its monotone glare, her father had gone blind, and he blinked with unseeing black eyes as she dropped down beside him.

He must have been sleeping. "H… Hello? Please…" His voice was croaky and weak. Long gone were his days of bellowing violence and intimidation. She liked him so much better this way.

"Hello, father," she said.

"No, please, no…" But even his fear held no conviction. He had been through this process too many times to believe it could go any other way. Perhaps, she thought, he understood that he deserved it all. Maybe he felt remorse, in the end, and took his punishment willingly.

In any case, Holly paid him no mind for the minute, rummaging through the rusty toolbox Greeny had so kindly donated from his garden shed. The implements she removed were deceptively harmless; a fettling knife and a potter's needle – two of the expert sculptor's most essential items. Holly's mother had, against her father's will, bought her a pottery set so that she could learn to sculpt. Gregory had near lost his mind when he found out. A bloody waste of time! Art? Huh!

But he had stopped short of confiscating them and had even nodded his approval when Holly had presented him with a set of clay plates and cups she'd made. At least it's something useful. Now she bet he wished he had taken them away, after all.

When she cut into him and saw the thick blood oozing from the wound, she felt as though the pent-up frustration and madness was oozing out of her, too. It was like having the world's worst poison sucked from a snakebite. Or like finding relief after having a bladder full to bursting for hours. She pushed the potter's needle into his eye and sighed as it burst.

He was screaming – or as close to screaming as he could get, which was something between a frog's croak and the slow gurgle of a shallow stream. It was calming music to Holly's ears. It was revenge and justice and peace. If she'd ever seen the possessed, faraway look on James's face as he drew his pictures, she would have understood it – because it was the same expression she had now. Drifting, floating away as if in a warm bath, finding bliss as the pain of life was exorcised onto a canvas of her own.

She had plenty of time, and she let her thoughts wander as she traced red lines of idle complexity in her father's doughy flesh. They turned, inevitably, to the past. The dark days when Gregory Anderson had still been the tyrant of her life and her own mother had betrayed her, and when thoughts of fleeing or suicide were never far from her young mind. When the house had come to her rescue, in this black period of her life, and told her that there was a way…

43
Secret Room

Summer, 2002

But it wasn't what she'd expected. In her most vengeful moods, Holly imagined creating an army of Nobodies at the bottom of the garden and then marching up to the house like Joan of Arc at the head of it, to take the house for herself.

It was Stretch and Pinky who convinced her otherwise, in their cautious way. They were good friends even then, less than a month into Stretch's life. She saw the way they smiled at each other and even sometimes held hands when she wasn't looking. They knew she didn't like it, though she'd never admit that she was jealous that any of her creations should adore anything besides herself. Don't risk it, Holly! They told her. What if your father finds the Nobodies before the right time? What if they hurt you? Maybe you're not ready. Best to trust the house.

They had a point, she supposed. She'd conducted a few experiments but eliminated one after the other in fits of frustration and disappointment. None of them were as good as Stretch himself – or even the duller minded Pinky. And the ones that were smart had other things wrong with them, sometimes so badly wrong she'd barely managed to vanish them before they'd got their teeth into her. No, it was going to take a lot more practice before she could make a Nobody better than Stretch.

And the House was on her side. The House told her there was a way. The House had a plan…

There was a room.

Deep, deep down; far, far into the middle of the house, there was a room. The House told her about it, sometimes with cryptic messages found scratched on floorboards, sometimes in her dreams. The room was pitch black and went on forever, and all she had to do for the plan to work was to get her father to enter it.

After that, the house would take care of everything.

Holly could have the whole world to herself. Just her and the house and the Nobodies; anything and anyone she could create, or that the house could create for her. Paradise.

And one night, as Holly tossed and turned in her bed, half in a dream and half out, something fluttered gently in the dark and brushed against her cheek. She sat up in bed, thinking of spiders, but when she reached out to pull the blankets up, her hand touched something smooth and square, a piece of paper.

It was a map.

Dear Nobody.

Less than a month, and then we'll be gone forever – just Holly and I and freedom. Everything we need is hidden away, but I am so afraid that Gregory will see something in my face and get it out of me that I don't know where! Imagine that? I gave it all to Holly and had her hide it in one of her secret places, a flaw in the building plans that left a crawlspace that only she knows about. Sweet, brilliant Holly. I can't wait until it's only the two of us. With everything I've saved and stolen, we'll be able to live for a year or more anywhere on earth while I find a job, at a coffee shop or a fine wine restaurant in France. Perhaps we'll spend some time on a beach somewhere, drinking out of coconuts and watching the waves. How dreamy.

With every day that goes by I grow more afraid Gregory will find it all. But Holly knows just how to keep a secret, even from him. One more month, please Lord, let us last another month.

By the time he reached the last entry in the diary, a week or so after he'd found the thing, he had an escape fund of his own stored up in a suitcase which he'd buried under the shed – a fresh new safety net. Almost everything he had in cash. Untraceable.

But this messed things up, didn't it? He couldn't let them get away with it, could he? No, they would have to suffer for this betrayal. They had to be left with nothing but dirt. They could have the house – Jane could try paying for the rates and taxes with a waitressing job, for god sakes. But he didn't like the sound of this escape fund. There would be no safety net for his dear wife, not if he had anything to say about it. He was going to have to find it.

Holly appeared to be asleep, but it was all she could do to keep her eyes closed and her breathing steady: it seemed as though her heart was pumping adrenaline instead of blood, and every hair on her body prickled with sensitivity. She was terrified, tonight was the night. She didn't know what would happen, but the map, torn and crumpled in the bin beside her desk, was committed to memory. Pinky and

Stretch were hiding in the room beneath the basement, safe and silent.

Tonight.

She knew something was different; her father was never this quiet. Usually, she could hear him late into the night shouting or mumbling, breaking glasses, knocking over tables. Or stumbling up to the bedroom just down the hall, and what happened then Holly didn't know, only that on those nights she would hear her mother calling out as if in the throes of a nightmare, and then sobbing quietly until dawn.

Not this night, however. True, the rain was falling steadily, it's comforting rattle and drip enough to cover the general creak and groan of the boards beneath her father's feet – but it was still unsettling to hear nothing at all. Holly had grown up in a world centred around her father's presence.

So, it should have come as no surprise, in a way, when her door swung open without so much as a warning knock and it was his silhouette instead of her mother's outlined against the hall's yellow light. He stood sideways, as though he were halfway through fainting but was somehow keeping his footing.

"Holly… Little Holly girl, wakey wakey," he said thickly, even more badly drunk than she would have expected even at this time of night. She rolled over in her bed and groaned.

He didn't say anything for a few minutes, just stood slanted in the doorway, watching her, until finally, "WAKE UP!"

She went cold all over with fear, her body drawing rigid in the bed. Then she forced herself to sit up slowly, rubbing her eyes as though she'd only just woken up. "Father? What's the matter?"

"Father, what's the matter?" He imitated her in childish falsetto. She slid up against her backboard, pulling her knees up to her chest.

"What are you afraid of, girl? You've got me tricked, haven't you? Fooled me once, fooled me twice, fooled me all the times, eh?" He strode sideways into the room, his eyes full of light and conviction, unaware of the nonsense that was spilling out of his mouth.

"Father, I don't know what –"

"The notebook, idiot!" He raised his hand and she flinched, expecting a blow, but then she saw he was holding up a small diary. A damning piece of evidence, apparently, though Holly had never seen it before in her life. When the cover flipped open in her father's hand and she saw the rigid pen strokes, however, she recognized it instantly; it was her mother's handwriting.

Before she could even begin to unravel the implications of this bizarre fact her father was pulling her out of bed one handed. He dragged her out into the hall and pushed her up against the wall. Suddenly he was nose to nose with her, his breath sickly sweet and hot in her face. "Take me to it," he whispered. "Take me to the secret room."

And then it clicked. Holly didn't know what the house had put in that notebook. Perhaps it really belonged to Jane Anderson, some private diary from years ago – but that wasn't important. What mattered was that it had brought her father right to her now, asking to be taken to the very place she needed him to go. In that moment, it was all she could do not to cheer with joy. This was it – they were finally going to get him.

"Okay, daddy."

And for the first time ever, she slipped out of the house's physical world – the world of solid beams and structures and material – and into its interior; the endless hallways, moving doors, and secret rooms through which, many years later, James and Stretch would race. Mr. Anderson's enraged mutterings fell away as they moved through rooms he'd never seen before. It was his house, alright – he'd built most of it and knew every dusty inch of its architecture - yet he was as lost as if in a hundred-acre forest in the middle of the night.

Holly pulled him along by the hand, through narrowing halls and carpeted rooms furnished with antiques they had never owned, in spaces that shouldn't have existed, decorated with paintings of people who were not quite people and were more alive than any paintings had a right to be. Only Holly recognized them for what they were, Nobodies.

The secret room stood at the end of a long hallway – the mirror image of the Centre Line that Holly would later discover on the third floor. This hallway had no windows, no lights, and no doors save one; a plain block at the very end that looked like a chopping board stood on its end. The handle was nothing more than a rusty nail jutting from the wood. "There it is, Daddy," Holly said. "The secret room."

Holly's father let go of her arm and she let out the breath she'd been holding. She'd been terrified that he would force her to go inside with him, and if there was one thing, she was absolutely certain of in that moment it was that she did not want to see what was behind that door. Just looking at it gave her a funny feeling in her belly. Something was waiting there on the other side, something worse than even she could have conjured up on her most vile day, and she didn't want to see it.

Holly didn't think her father wanted to see it either – he felt it too – but he wasn't about to let it go, either. He held the notebook loosely by his side, his attention focussed completely on the door. Holly sat down on the bottom of the staircase they'd just descended, the entrance to which had itself been a secret door at the back of a closet. When she looked back, the stairs seemed to ascend into darkness. The dim light in which she sat now seemed to have no source – it simply emanated from the walls and ceiling themselves.

Her father continued to walk in an off kilter, slanted way, leaning to the right while his head was cocked slightly to the left as if to offset his centre of gravity. When he finally reached the heavy door, reaching for the rusty nail – Holly was not at all surprised when he recoiled, swearing, having snagged his palm on the sharp point. It seemed as though it had to happen – like sleeping beauty sticking herself with the point of the spinning wheel; it was a condition of entry.

Even though she wanted it, even though she'd dreamed of little but this for weeks – if not years in a more indirect way – Holly found herself screaming inwardly; no no no no don't go in, don't go in! But she kept her mouth clamped shut and, when he finally took hold of the sharp handle and pulled the door open, she had the presence of mind to close her eyes so that she wouldn't catch even a glimpse of what might be on the other side.

Instead, there was nothing but total silence, as though all the air had been vacuum sucked from the hallway. It seemed to stretch on for so long, until she wanted to open her eyes just to make sure she hadn't dropped out of existence entirely, and then she heard her father whisper something from an impossible distance, "how can it be so dark?"

And, following this, the sound of the heavy door sliding shut and the return of the air and breath to the hall. She opened her eyes, and her father was gone. The chopping board door watched her from the end of the hall, expressionless.

Holly stood and ascended the staircase to her parent's bedroom, where she found her mother tied to the bed, beaten and crying. She loosened the knots, massaging the places where the ropes had bitten into her flesh, and they hugged each other fiercely. Holly only wishing there was more of her, more solidity to this mother who seemed even more helpless and weak than she at times. But they hugged and her mother stroked her hair and it felt so nice, and when she asked Holly what had happened it felt good to say; "He's gone, this time, mother. He's finally gone for good."

If only it were true.

44
The Skinned Boy

"He's dead, isn't he?"

The two officers on Frank Harmon's front porch stared at him in bland surprise. They had just enough time to introduce themselves; West, a clean-cut college boy who looked like he should still be living at home with his parents, and Gardner, a female sergeant with greying hair and a hardened grimace. Before the words 'bad news' had fully left her dry lips Frank had guessed – correctly, by the looks on their faces.

"Yes sir," Gardener said after a beat. "I'm deeply sorry. If you need to visit a counsellor or therapist, we have –"

"How'd it happen?"

"He was murdered." And then, when no one said anything, she added: "I'm sorry."

"Who killed him?"

"We aren't sure yet," West said. Trying to be professional but coming off robotic. "Judging by the, uh, nature of the attack, we don't believe it was personal. The profiler is convinced the murderer was a psychopath, most likely someone who will kill again, and who attacked your son most likely because he was alone at the time, walking through a park on his way home from school. Needless to say, the efforts of the entire police force currently have this as the highest priority."

They were expecting him to… what? Invite them inside? Or maybe break down and cry? But Frank had none of these emotions in him, just then. Being a parent to James hadn't been all that different to providing shelter for a stray dog. You fed it and sheltered it out of the goodness of your heart, but in the end, it came and went, and its fate was its own. He didn't feel connected, somehow. He was, however, somewhat curious.

"How'd they do it? Kill him."

The officers exchanged a look for what seemed like a long time before answering. West raised his eyebrows and Gardner nodded. Then she turned back to Frank and said, "We're not entirely sure, yet. The whole… All of the remains have not yet been recovered."

"Oh yeah? What has been recovered?"

Another pause, and then, dropping her eyes, she said quietly, "his skin, sir. Just his skin."

After they'd left, Frank cracked open another beer and went up to his son's room. He'd looked in a couple of times to check if James was around, but he hadn't touched anything. Standing on the threshold, he took out the note the boy had left him and read it over for the third time, struggling to make sense of it. Then he looked from the note to the piles of coloured pictures and paintings that filled James's bedroom, and knew that his assessment was correct; the kid had completely lost his mind.

Someone pretending to be his friend. A haunted house? Frank wasn't a doctor or a cop, but he knew a couple things for sure. One, it didn't take any genius to figure out that his son had some paranoid schizophrenia, or delusions or some kind of mental disorder. You only had to look at some of his damn pictures to see that. Two, if the cops saw the gibberish note James had left behind, they would waste who knew how many man hours chasing James's crazy fantasies, and by the time they got on the right trail it would be ice cold. Hell, the proof was right here in the letter. James said he was going to 243 Twisty Lane – so how come the cops said he'd been found in Greenway Park, nowhere near there? No, best thing he could do was burn the thing and let the cops catch the real killer, not some fantasy.

Nodding to himself, he crumpled the paper up and jammed it in his pocket for disposal later.

He shook his head at the chaotic room and felt a pang of deep sadness, and relief. Something like what people felt when their old grandfather died after a decade of suffering, he figured. Terrible thing, terrible, but maybe for the best, overall. By the looks of some of these pictures, who knew? Maybe James would have grown up to be some kind of sicko killer himself.

Frank upended the beer and then went downstairs to find something that would numb him more effectively. He closed the door to his son's room for the last time.

45
Playing the Game

For all of her short life, Sister had been concerned with nothing but the intricate game of humanity; of pulling off the right facial expressions, moving the right way, looking the right way… it was, after all, what she'd been created for. When she'd got the call to the principal's office twenty minutes before the end of last period, she was inflated by a sense of purpose and exhilaration. This was it – the big test.

The police officers greeted her with smiles and nods as she entered Mr. Radeon's office. The sergeant was a middle-aged blonde lady who would have been pretty if she wasn't so worn out, and her partner was a young man with square features and a fake smile. Sister immediately congratulated herself for spotting the deception and then made a mental note to make herself appear less well kempt in future; more world weary and real, like the lady cop.

Mr. Radeon gestured for her to sit down. "Hello, Alex – now you're not in trouble or anything but Officers West and Gardner would like to ask you a few questions about your friend James, if that's alright."

Sister dropped into the chair and immediately stared straight down at her shoes, her face contorting itself into alternating expressions of stern control and total grief. "It's true, isn't it? They're all saying he was murdered." James's disappearance had been the talk of the school for two days now, and already the news of the gruesome discovery – based on Sister's own last sighting of him – had spread across Templeton like a disease.

"I'm afraid so," West said, and all three adults took a minute of awkward concerned silence while Sister cried openly in front of them until at last, with superhuman effort, she regained control of herself and apologized, sniffing and wiping tears from her eyes.

"There's no need to apologize. You two were close, huh?"

She nodded, taking a shaky breath.

That was the easy part. The hard part came next, when West began to investigate Alex's relationship with James in her gentle but insistent way. Keeping her eyes mostly on her hands clenched in her lap, Sister occasionally glanced up at West, just long enough to let the sergeant see the genuine emotion and earnestness so expertly presented on her face, and to gauge how well she was doing. By now, she was awake to the tiniest social cues, the particular nuances of tone and body language that allowed her to tell exactly the effect she was having on other people. The younger cop was completely taken in, and she could tell by the way he glanced aside whenever she looked in his direction, more than a little attracted to her. West was too smart to whole-heartedly fall for Sister's performance, but she had no real reason to be suspicious. She was frustrated by Sister's answers only because they gave her no new information.

The interview ended fairly quickly, and Sister let her relief show. Then – taking a chance – she addressed the principal for a moment. "Mr. Radeon? Would it be okay if I stayed home for tomorrow? I just… it's really hard, you know and…"

But he stood up, nodding emphatically. "No, no, of course. It's a tragedy, an absolute tragedy."

She thanked him tearfully and left the office, the other students giving her a wide berth as she made her slow way home as though the black cloud of misery that engulfed her was poisonous. She received a text on Alex's phone from Annie Walker: *Hope you're OK. Call me when you want to talk, x o x.* In the terrible hours since James's initial disappearance, she and Annie had grown much closer than ever before, a real friendship blooming from the tragedy.

Only half an hour later, in the quiet solitude of her own bedroom, did she allow a brilliant smile to light up her face.

46
Sweet Revenge

The sound of the heavy metal gates sliding open was enough to elicit a deep excitement in Sister's gut. She slipped through the opening as soon as it was wide enough to permit her and closed her eyes to brace for the inevitable vertigo that accompanied the shift in worlds. *Soon you won't have to come back,* she thought with a secret thrill. *Soon you'll have everything you need outside.*

This desire was not one she ever intended Holly to discover. Holly would never permit one of her creations to have a life of her own, but that was only because she herself was dependent on her little bubble for survival. She didn't have any idea, like Sister did, of just how large the outside world really was, and how full it was of living, breathing, human beings. She would never understand Sister's need to be a part of all that, to have the one thing Holly took for granted – the thing Sister's new family was so intent on saving; a soul.

But she couldn't cut the cord, just yet. There were a couple of loose ends she needed to tie up, first.

Greeny opened the front door as she approached, clearly expecting her, but when she reached the threshold, he didn't step aside to let her enter.

"What?"

For a moment she was worried he was going to tell her she couldn't have what was promised to her – that James was already dead and there was no use for Sister in the outside world anymore – that she was to become just another Nobody playing puppet at the end of Holly's strings. Then Greeny handed her a folded piece of paper. "There are instructions on here. Holly wants him to become a part of the house. You can have the body, but make sure you don't let him die."

Sister's eyes narrowed sceptically as she took in the crude diagrams Holly had drawn for her. "People die when you take their heads off, Greeny," she said.

"Not in here. Not if Holly doesn't want. Once you put in the nails, he'll have the house's blood in his veins. Then you can sew the head on the bear. The body will still feel everything."

"Really?"

Greeny must have seen something of the savage glee on her expression, because he scratched his grassy head, curious. "What d'you want him for, anyway?"

Sister folded the paper into a square and slipped it into the front pocket of her pressed white shirt. With her black shoes, clean chequered skirt and neatly curled hair she looked like an A-plus student: straight backed, immaculate, perfect. She was conscious of every facet of her appearance and action. One would have to look directly into her eyes to get the hint that there was something missing inside her, some indiscernible absence of presence. She glared at Greeny, tight lipped and intense, until he stepped aside.

"What do I want him for?" she said. She recalled for the thousandth time the look of disgust and horror on his face when he'd seen her naked body. The terrible rejection of her humanity. "I want his heart, forever…" And then, as she moved briskly past him, she added, "And I want him to hurt."

James was tied up in an elaborate spread eagle in the middle of the playroom. Using coils of rope from his shed, Greeny had tied loops around his wrists and ankles and secured them in each corner of the room. The rope stretching his left arm was knotted around the heavy toy box. His right leg was raised, that rope bound to a pair of bent hooks protruding from the wall near the ceiling. With the four rope lines pulling him in all directions, he was suspended like a fly in a spider's web, just waiting for some giant black widow to come over and suck his guts out from inside.

He had no idea how close that was to reality.

The first hour, he struggled himself into a mad panic, and for several minutes pulled and twisted in his binds so violently that his hands turned blue and the skin on his wrists was rubbed raw. At last, he fell limp and took a few deep breaths, calming himself. Think of Alex. This isn't helping. You gotta think. You're the artist, right? Get creative.

So, for another hour or so, he barely moved at all. He lay, spread out on the rough carpet. He flexed his fingers to keep the blood moving. He got creative.

He tested out the range of his hands, and found that, if he pulled just so with his left leg while letting his right go limp, he could get enough slack in the rope around his right wrist that he could manipulate the knot there with his ring and middle fingers. His hand cramped every minute or so, but each time he manoeuvred himself into position he managed to loosen the knot, just a tiny tiny –

Creeeeeeaaaaaaakkkk. The sound of the playroom door opening filled him with helpless fear. His heart skipped a beat when he saw Alex standing in the doorway, but it took only a split second for him to see that it wasn't her, after all. This Alex had burn-less, nicely manicured hands.

Fuck. I was so close.

Sister closed the door and, ignoring him for the time being, opened the toy box. When he'd entered, James had found the box to be empty – yet now she drew from it a hammer and a box containing enormous iron nails, like railroad spikes. And, somehow far more terrifying, a sewing needle and a reel of string.

One of the pictures he'd drawn the night before had depicted a severed head sewn on the body of the brown teddy. It hadn't occurred to him, drawing it, that the head might belong to him.

Sister lay the items out on the floor, along with a tattered piece of paper. She knelt down, finally turning her attention to James. "Aren't you going to say hello?"

"Uh… Hello."

"I think you owe me an apology. Well. You owe me a lot more, but we can start with that."

"I'm sorry…"

She raised her eyebrows.

James took a moment to remember what Alex had told him the night before. "I'm sorry, Sister?" he said.

The next few seconds happened with shocking speed. She moved forward, planting one knee firmly on James's right elbow and pinning it to the ground. Then she took one of the spikes, stuck it firmly in the soft flesh of his forearm above his wrist, and brought the hammer down on the rusty head with more force than a girl her size had any right to have – enough to bury the point in the floorboards beneath the carpet.

James felt as if someone had dropped a stone slab on his arm. A stunning impact that made his hand completely numb and sent a storm of pins and needles up his arm. The real pain came ten or so seconds later, a deep pulsing agony that ran up his shoulder and into his neck. He gritted his teeth against a scream, for the moment unable to think of anything else…

And then she planted her knee on his left arm and he became very aware indeed. "Wait, wait! Hold on! What do you want me to say?"

She fixed him with a cold glare. "Who am I?"

"Alex! You're Alex Miller, my…" he swallowed, forced himself to lock eyes with her. "Who I love very much."

She ran a finger down the side of his right cheek, a fresh spike enclosed in her palm. He noticed the sharpness of her black-painted nail. Alex never painted her nails; they were always bitten down to the quick. Sister, he thought, knew this, but had made a conscious decision to decorate hers. She was developing her own personality, and for reasons he couldn't name, this made James feel sick to his stomach, though not as much as what she said next: 'You don't have to stay here with Holly, you know."

"What do you mean?"

"Once I sew your head onto the bear and take your heart, I'll have everything I need." She leaned forward, her mouth breathing minty air as she whispered, "I have a plan to escape. To get away from Holly and make our own life out there in the world." She kissed his cheek, and he felt her smile.

She didn't know it, but with those words she'd taken the last shred of hope James had held on to. Now he understood that there was nothing left, no chance of escaping this unharmed. In a way, it was liberating, because it also meant he didn't have to play her insane games anymore.

"I don't want to be with you. I hate you. And you know what? You're not the real Alex, and you never will be."

She reeled backward, her expression one of surprise and shock, and the next nail went into his left arm with enough force to pin it as immovably as the right. She shouted a word with each bang of the hammer: "I… AM… ALEX!"

This time, as the initial wave of pain faded, he became aware of an unfamiliar sensation; a silky liquid pumping rhythmically through the spikes and into his wrists, in time with his pulsing heartbeat. Cold streams ran through his veins and into his heart, the adrenaline fuelled drumroll kicking into a higher gear. Every physical sensation, the cold sweat icing his forehead, the tightness of his thighs and biceps pulling against the ropes, the smell of roses, blood and rust… and it felt good.

It's the house. The house is getting inside you, keeping you alive with its own power so that she can take your head off and put your heart in a jar and you won't die. Maybe she'll leave your body behind for Holly to torture whenever she's in a bad mood…

Sister straddled him, settling a fresh spike in the middle of his neck, just below his Adam's apple. She raised the hammer.

"Tell me you love me. Tell me you'll run away with me and be mine forever. Tell me it's what you want."

"It's what I want," he said, but a tear was rolling down his cheek because even though in that moment his very soul depended on it, he knew he couldn't make her believe it. He loved Alex.

"Liar," she said.

And brought the hammer down with everything she had.

47
Fire and Flight

Stretch danced alone in the empty ballroom, drunk on brandy and wine, a sweet and heady mixture he'd always favoured to cheer him up when he was especially sad. He imagined he was dancing with Pinky, the way they used to do in the golden years, when they hadn't felt like Nobodies at all but like real living humans.

The bar was full, and music played for him from an unseen source – the house lulling him to sleep, no doubt. It had always been so good to him, looking after him like a father the way it did Holly. Now he swayed and drank his worries away until eventually he collapsed, exhausted and weeping, in the middle of the ballroom.

How had it all come so low? Living people taken from out there – both of them so nice and good and friendly, and now one to be tortured to death and the other buried until she went mad. Why did good things have to turn sour? Why did happiness turn to misery?

You know why, his inside voice told him.

The inside voice was a secret he'd never confessed to anyone but Pinky, and even she'd thought him loopy. "It's like another me," he'd said. "Living inside my head. It gives me advice sometimes or tells me things that are true – and sometimes it helps me think of what to do."

"You such a funny ole man," she'd said, chuckling, and he laughed drunkenly as he remembered it. Now she'd been good, hadn't she? She'd been a… a real friend, the inside voice said. But he didn't like that because of what it implied. It implied that Holly wasn't a real friend, since she'd killed Pinky the way she had, and that was blasphemy. That wasn't right because after all hadn't Holly given Stretch everything he'd ever wanted or asked for? Except for her life.

"Shut up! Shut up and go away!" He smacked his fist on the dusty floor and the voice obliged. The ballroom was silent, the music having faded away unnoticed. Somewhere in the unknown recesses of the house a door opened and shut.

But the inside voice was relentless. Pinky was good and Holly isn't. But she's not the only one who's bad, is she, Mr. Stretch? After all, what have you done but bad, bad, bad for the sake of Holly?

"NO! Holly made me!"

Dragging weeping Nobodies to Greeny's shed to be tortured. How many did you bury over the years, Stretch?

"Holly made me, I had to!"

Putting Alex's hands in the fire. Burying her. Letting James go in the room you knew the house could find him, so you could pretend it wasn't your doing?

"It was an accident, I'm sorry, I'm sorry!" He curled up in a ball of twisted limbs, hands over his head and knees over his ears, weeping uncontrollably against the wretched truth of his being. This was who he had been all along – a traitor, a liar, a destroyer of all things good. All in the name of Holly.

Who he had been?

Who you were?

But not who you have to be.

Stretch's breath caught in his throat; his cries cut abruptly short with the clarity of the thought. It seemed to echo around the inside of his misshapen skull, an idea he'd never considered but one that held all the power of life itself; Not who you have to be.

He had a choice. Not in the past – the past actions belonged to a different Stretch, a bad Stretch, a weak Stretch. But now? Now he could be Mister Stretch. He could be good, like Pinky was. He could be strong… he could…

He stood up, heard his shaky breaths become slow and steady. As if in a dream, he moved over to the bar, the crystal glass shelves always full of the beautiful bottles – the house kept it well stocked for him, as it had for Holly's father all those years ago. It had blinded Mr. Anderson, and now perhaps it was blinding Stretch. Keeping him from seeing that he wasn't like the other Nobodies. He had an inside voice. He had a choice.

Stretch began to take bottles from the shelves, eyes wide as though he couldn't believe what he was doing and yet doing it all the same, slipping rums and vodkas into his long coat, pocketing flasks of whiskey. Finally, when he was so full of clinking bottles he could hardly move, he turned his attention to the top right-hand corner of the cabinet behind the bar where a selection of the finest pipes, cigars and tobacco paraphernalia were kept.

And, most importantly of all, the matches.

He had only just slipped the box of fifty into his front shirt pocket beside the container of lighter fluid he'd taken from the garden shed, when a hand made of tree bark settled on his shoulder.

"This would have been a lot easier if you'd been asleep like I told you, Stretch," Greeny said.

Stretch tried to pull away but Greeny clamped both hands around his neck and squeezed, yanking him around in a tight circle and then forcing him down onto the bar top. Stretch's face pressed into the counter, gagging for air while his head filled with blood and his eyes bulged as though ready to pop out of the sockets.

A human being in a similar position would have become unconscious in a minute or so. Stretch, however, was under no such obligation. He twisted his bendy neck inside Greeny's fists until the two of them were face to face, spluttering and gasping. Then, bringing his right arm around in a backward roundhouse that would have popped the elbow and shoulder joints out of their sockets (if he'd had any), he swung a litre of "Down the Hatch" whiskey into the side of Greeny's head.

Greeny tumbled sideways from the counter, hands leaving Stretch's throat for the moment to clutch the strips of torn bark hanging from his face like paper. Then, with the slippery ease of an octopus escaping from a coke bottle, Stretch slid up and over the bar, flopping clumsily over the stools on the other side. He popped up to his feet, coughing, bright black stars flashing in the corner of his vision.

"Don't let him out!" Greeny screamed.

Stretch saw it all in an instant, there was after all, only one other Greeny could have been calling to – only one entity that had the power to keep Stretch inside. They had conspired to kill him. They knew, they knew!

But Stretch knew the house. Stretch had spent every waking minute of his life inside its ever-changing universe, and he knew how it thought and worked the way a clockmaker knew every cog and wheel of a timepiece. The house was all being, but not all seeing, and it could be fooled.

Stretch did not run for the great doors that opened into the ballroom. He knew that they would lead to nothing but a brick wall, perhaps with a taunting phrase in block letters etched in the clay. Instead, he raced for the scarlet curtains that lined the small round stage – the place a band would have played if there had ever been a party here besides the ones Stretch threw for himself.

Greeny staggered after him, but he was half blinded by stinging whiskey and his heavy feet were no match for Stretch's lanky strides. Stretch hopped up onto the stage and pulled the lighter fluid from his coat, upending it and then dropping it at his feet, splashing the curtains. He drew out the matches and held one up, ready to strike.

"NO!" Greeny skidded to a halt at the foot of the stage, just a few feet away. "You'll kill us all! What are you doing?"

And Stretch hesitated, considering that if the match didn't light on the first strike it would be all for nothing, anyway. Never before had he been so tired and droopy and drained, although part of it was relief for an end to the conflict that for so long, he hadn't realised was tearing him apart.

"The right thing, I think," he said.

He struck the match.

Greeny dove forward, snarling, but Stretch was too quick once again. The only way to sneak through the house without its knowledge, he learned, was to take the road less travelled; so instead of pushing through the curtains, he climbed them. Greeny let out a roar and Stretch paused near the ceiling to look down. The old groundskeeper had rushed through the leaping flames and was climbing in Stretch's wake, hot fire licking up the curtain after him.

Stretch reached the golden rail, slinked along it like a lizard for several meters and, sure enough, found what he was looking for: a dark seam, zig-zagging through the panelled wood overhead. He hoisted himself up before the house could sense him and close it.

The next room was a kind of lounge – floors of rich Turkish carpet, leather couches and the smell of incense hanging in the air. It would light up like a hay bale, and Stretch couldn't resist dropping two whiskey bottles and a new match to get things going, before he moved on, though he knew he risked his life on a razor's edge in those precious moments.

The next seam he discovered was a trapdoor beneath the burning carpet, and he lowered himself through just as Greeny was clawing his way into the freshly created inferno. "Stretch! I'll feed your droopy head to the Babies!" he screamed, but his voice had a hint of hysteria to it. He surely knew that unless Holly arrived and put a stop to everything soon, there would be no hope for any of them.

Room to room, leaving a stream of spirits and broken glass in his wake, Stretch moved through the house, barely escaping each new area by the skin of his pasty scalp. The house was racing to close every crack and corner of each new area so that it was like a puzzle in which Stretch had to find the missing piece before it was filled in.

But he did, time and time again, leaving a furnace in his wake until he was down to his last bottle, until at last he arrived through the door beside the great grandfather clock that sat at the end of the house's Centre Line.

48
Fading Out

Everyone remembers the moment their own death became real to them for the first time. Not real in an intellectual sense, or a rational sense, but real right down to the bone. Real enough to understand. For Alex, that moment came in the minutes that followed Greeny's whispered apology and the rock jarring into place in the narrow pipe.

She'd gone on a theme park ride once, called the Deadly Drop. It was essentially a vertical track that you climbed painfully slowly, every minute bringing fresh disbelief about how high up you were. The wind had swayed the tower an alarming amount, and rain spattered from the grey clouds above. The screams and laughter from the other ride goers had sounded so far away they might as well have been in another universe. Then, at last, the ride stopped, and they all waited, and waited, and waited. And then they heard a loud, mechanical click and the seats dropped. That was how Alex felt at the beginning.

Her inner voice uttered an incredulous No, but it wasn't long before the reduced airflow began to take its toll and she understood that actually, in fact, Yes.

I'm going to die.

Panic inevitably followed, spurred on by the loudness of her own breathing in her ears. A mad fantasy popped into her mind in which she broke open the coffin lid like Beatrix Kiddo in "Kill Bill" and climbed the avalanche of collapsing dirt all the way up to the surface. Nine bleeding knuckles and six splinters later she gave up. Breathing hard now, the air in the coffin hot and stifling and nowhere to get relief. It was easy to imagine losing her mind completely now, beating and beating the wood until there was nothing left of her hands at all and even less in her lungs.

Sssssshhhhhh stop.

She squeezed her eyes shut and cried, the sobs catching in her throat as she tried and failed to restrict them. The air funnelling down from above had narrowed from a steady stream to a trickle. It was like trying to breathe through a straw as long as her body.

You have to stop.

The thought seemed to come from somewhere else. It carried with it a calmness that Alex couldn't fathom at the current moment, a certainty – but of course it belonged to her. You have to stop.

I know! She wanted to scream. I just don't want to stop right now!

The voice had nothing to say to that for the moment. Alex shifted in the coffin, jamming her head right up in the corner so as to make the most of what little air she could. There were three spots of grey light peeking out from behind the blockage in the pipe. Three air streams – but she could already tell they wouldn't be enough to last her very long, and certainly not all night. Each breath she inhaled had a distinct staleness to it.

What about the rest of my life? She demanded of the calm voice.

What about it?

I was going to… what? Like a great white shark rising from the deep, a monstrous truth became known to her. She hadn't really been going to do anything except what her parents had decided for her. She'd always entertained thoughts – of travelling, hitching up North to somewhere cold and hiking. Maybe becoming a photographer or owning a café or who knew – becoming a professional snowboarder. But they were nothing but fantasies, and never had been, because only now did she realise that the plan, the real plan, had been to go to university and study finance, just like Mother and Father said she would. The other stuff had only been a story she told herself so that she could pretend. So that she could say: I'll do all that later. First, I'll go to college because they want. Maybe I'll get a job and save up, just to keep them happy…

They would, of course, have tolerated nothing else.

Despite her efforts to focus on the three points of light (now darkening with the clouds above from white to steel grey), she found her vision fuzzy around the edges. The world had taken on a nerfed-up thickness, as though she was trying to look at everything through a foggy visor. Dark colours bloomed on the edges of her vision, but they were kept at bay for now: it was a slow process.

Just like how they're suffocating you. She'd never told anyone – not even James – about some of the things they'd done to her. She'd told her father, at the tender age of nine, that she didn't want to believe in God because He'd killed Jimmy, their black lab. Mr. Miller had set her at the dinner table and made her eat Jimmy's leftover dry dog food until she'd vomited all over the kitchen floor. It's for your own good, Alexandra, He'd said. Better you suffer at my hand than walk the path to Hell.

Then again, at least he was upfront about it. Mrs. Miller was more constant, more subtle: A comment here, a disapproving glare there. Good girls don't act like that. Straight back, now. If you think you're leaving the house looking like a slut you've got another thing coming. Oh, you worry me, Alexandra, you really do. I'd do anything for you, you know that? All I ask is that you be a good girl. She was like a corset that got tighter each day, those long-manicured nails pulling Alex into shape with each brutal knot until her lungs were squeezed up into her neck and she couldn't... Breathe.

In, out. They were coming slower, now, but in a funny way Alex found it relaxing. The calm voice echoed in the back of her mind over and over: You have to stop. It was true, after all – you did have to stop, eventually. It was just a shame Alex wouldn't have a chance to change, now that she knew. Now that she understood.

But there didn't seem to be any room for rage or bitterness anymore. The colours spiralled in from the sides of her vision, hypnotizing her with their beauty. Alex let her mind wander, disconnected memories emerging in her mind like waking dreams; a projector that was flashing scenes in a dark cinema. Oh, she thought somewhere in the back of her mind, so this shit really does happen when you kick it. Guess I'll settle in for the show.

It wasn't so bad, for the most part.

The first time James had invited her over to his house, and the sheepish looks he'd given her as they'd picked their way through a mosaic of discarded takeaway boxes, empty beer cans and dirty clothes. "Ew, no wonder you stink so much," she'd teased him, and instantly regretted it when he looked away, reddening. She'd left when his drunk father started banging on his door and asking when the hell he was going to take out the trash or if he was too busy with 'his bitch.'

Her father, snapping the director's cut of Hellraiser that her new friend James had given her for her birthday. "I raised you better than this," he said, holding up a shard of the disc in front of her face, it's jagged point just in front of her wide eye. "This… This Evil? It's for sick, sick people, Alex. Now get out of my sight."

The visions became more disjointed and fleeting, after that. Sitting miserably in class for her first day at Templeton high; lying awake for hours at night and thinking about the future – sometimes with hope and sometimes with bleak despair; trying a cigarette with Annie out of spite for her clean-cut parents, hating it and smoking it down to the filter all the same while Annie laughed at her retching sounds…

The last of these wasn't a memory but a scene from the future, though it was so vivid the difference was negligible. It was a bird's eye view of her own tombstone in a field of many others, as the first raindrops began to fall from the grey sky. But then she was rising, rising until the graveyard was no more than a brown square beside the great house and its grounds, and then that was a dull block in a field of thousands car, house, and streetlights, and then she was away and soaring through a black, black sky in which there wasn't a star at all… not a single one.

49
Transformation

It seeped into him with a power that seemed to both energize and drain him at the same time. It wasn't unlike the burning of alcohol down the oesophagus, simultaneously poisoning and infusing with life. The nail that ran directly through James's neck into the playroom floor moved with each pulse of his jugular, warm blood spilling down either side of his neck in quantities that should have run him dry long ago but hadn't.

He'd never felt so awful and so alive at the same time. In these terrible minutes he understood the suffering of the severed man he'd seen in the basement; in the same way one might peek at infinity through a keyhole just briefly enough to keep from going mad.

Through it all, Sister hummed joyfully, adding to his pain with piercings of her needles and snips with her scissors, chatting to him as though they were friends. Her tone was in a strange way forgiving, as though she thought he'd accepted this torture as much to apologise to her as to save Alex. Maybe that was what Holly told her had happened.

"I don't know if you'll be able to feel down here afterward, so I'll take your head last," she was saying. She had cut his shirt off and pulled his pants down and was kneading the flesh around his thighs and hips, pinching a tiny fold here and there and snip! With the scissors, leaving a stinging red circle. The red circles seemed to be spiralling closer toward their centre of gravity at his crotch.

"I'm learning so much about humans. About their minds and souls and bodies." Snip.

"I know the outsides and I can act like one. It's hard to know what's really going on inside, but I think as long as you get the outside right, it's as good as the same." Snip. His body shivered, a ripple of electric pain zipping over him. He didn't scream or struggle. The house saw to that, its living influence acting as a kind of circuit breaker between stimulus and response, while allowing him to experience every second.

"Once I can see what's going on inside," she said, her voice dropping to a whisper, the bloodied scissors rising for a blessed second as she leaned forward. Alex's curly black hair tickled his chest. "I'll be able to make my own. Just like Holly."

50
Hatred

Deep, deep in the night, a tiny sound echoed through every corner of the house from its very core: the creak of a door swinging open.

If Holly had been waiting at the end of the hallway, she wouldn't have recognized the thing that emerged from the house's heart room as her father. Yes, his body was the same – all of his features were still there, although they were not arranged in anything resembling an acceptable expression. Rather they hung in a random, moving mosaic, as though each had a mind of its own and no connection to the rest of his body. His eyes were the only part of him that didn't move as he came staggering from the Dark Place. Having seen what lived there, they simply stared impassively at a spot ten million miles distant, no more alive than two calm pools of water in his head.

They were the first things Holly saw when she felt his hands close around her throat five minutes later – and the last things she saw: those two ripple-less pools reflecting moonlight on their surface as he stole everything from her.

The memory – so long forgotten and imagined as a dream even when she did remember – returned with a vengeance with the old man's words. He always whispered when she came down here, but usually he only pleaded for the end, begging her to let him die at last, until she'd learned to let his desperate entreaties receded to the background, like the crackling of a fire or the patter of rain on the windows.

It was a change in tone that drew her attention to his words this time. His voice grew stronger, his words sharper and meaner. "I got you in the end, didn't I?" he'd said at first, the sly remark in stark contrast to his pathetic pleas of a moment before. "I got you and the bitch that spawned you."

Holly reeled back, shocked from her reverie. When he'd spoken the words, she'd been recalling that long, silent night, in which she'd curled up in the bed with her mother, the warm comfort of her embrace and the sweet safety provided by the house drifting her to sleep. And then… and then what? Bright, empty pools in a mad face.

He chuckled, a scornful sound that made her jerk upright. She thought she'd forgotten that sound, but it wrenched her back through the years in an instant, making her feel like a scared little girl again.

"Oh, you got us, did you?" she said, meaning the words to come out deadly cold and instead hearing her own voice just as it had been back then, small and helpless. Her hand shook as she reached for the clay scooper, but that was alright, it wasn't exactly surgery she was doing. "We'll see."

And she scooped his eyes into a raw egg soup in each socket and spooned out the contents onto the already bloody floor, watching him squirm and grind his teeth – or rather the circular stubs embedded in his gums that remained – trying to reclaim some sense of who she was.

I'm the boss, I'm the boss, I'm the BOSS. She wanted to scream it in his face, and then when his eyes were gone, she couldn't hold back, and she did. "I'm the boss! I WON so shut your dirty mouth!"

But he was laughing. He was laughing, and it was the worst sound she'd ever heard, because it was the last sound, she'd ever heard alive, and finally she understood what had really happened.

Perhaps she'd always understood and simply buried it, like one of the dozens of Nobodies in the autumn garden. She'd only ever allowed herself to remember the very end, how she'd woken up in that dark room in the middle of the house and gone to find her father and mother. Save her and destroy him had been the only thought on her mind, and she'd never once questioned how she'd gotten from her comfortable bed to the endless black room in the middle of the house. Even now she couldn't remember what had been inside it: she only remembered leaving, blinking in the sudden light of the hallway.

She'd felt power surging through her – the same creative power she felt when she made Nobodies only ten times greater. She could have created an army of Mr. Stretch's, in that moment, but she didn't need even one.

He'd found Holly's mother in the attic, and that was where Holly found him, weeping over her limp form. She'd learned then that she could do more with her eyes than she thought. Or at least she could then, when she'd seen what he'd done to her poor Mother. She still remembered the way he'd screamed that first time when her eyes had melted his legs out from underneath him. He was still screaming while she tended to Mother, fusing her to the house, transforming her with the same muscle she used to create Nobodies. Later, she would use that same thing to fuse him to the basement floor.

But now he was laughing at her! Laughing with his hideous broken teeth and his vocal cords harsh from decades of screaming until they snapped and then healed. Laughing because he had won, after all – he'd killed her and locked her in this place forever. He was the reason she couldn't leave and had to settle for her twisted, imperfect Nobodies. He was the reason nobody loved her.

"I got out of that evil place you put me in, and I strangled you! Went to get some water and I wrung your neck until you were limp as a wet sock, heh heh! Stuck you in a suitcase!"

He had no legs, no arms, no eyes, and yet he'd taken more from her than she'd ever taken from him.

With a scream of incomprehensible rage, Holly raised the pick with both hands and plunged it into his heart with everything she had.

And finally, thankfully, his terrible laughter faded to a breath of hot air that dried the tears on her cheeks. There was something that bothered her about what he'd said – about getting out of the dark room. He hadn't been supposed to get out, that was the problem. There was no reason for the House to let him out. The House loved Holly, didn't it? But perhaps... Perhaps it loved her too much?

Before the thought could complete itself in her mind, Holly became aware of blood seeping out from walls around her. It dribbled through the cracks between the bricks, forming the same four letters over and over in desperate graffiti:

HELP HELP HELP HELP HELP HELP HELP HELP HELP HELP HELP HELP HELP

51
Slipping Through the Cracks

When James opened his eyes, he couldn't quite comprehend what he was seeing; it took a few moments for the mess of tangled limbs, tailcoats and flailing legs to make sense to him. The first thing that registered was Stretch's face. The butler seemed to be hanging upside down from a crack that had opened in the playroom's ceiling and had taken hold of the hammer in Sister's hand and lifted her up with it. Her black shoes kicked in the air inches above James's face as she struggled to regain control of the weapon.

Stretch did not, unfortunately, appear to be winning. "JAMES!" he cried, arcing one arm around his head to keep Sister from sticking the spike through the side of his head. She was fighting with the light-speed ferocity of an alley cat, pulling and biting at every part of the bewildered Stretch she could reach. Any second now, James was sure the two of them would fall directly on top of him.

James stared upward, mesmerised but helpless – and not just because he was nailed to the floor. The house was draining him, mind and body, turning him into a puppet from the inside out, the way a ventriloquist might hollow out a doll before jamming a nimble hand up through the centre. Any minute now, James's mouth would start snapping open and closed, barking words that didn't belong to him; soon he would be pulling free of the ropes and spikes and closing his own hands around Stretch's slender throat.

But before any of these horrors could come to pass, Stretch and Sister detached from the ceiling, and landing on James's legs hard enough to bounce. They rolled into the stack of discarded teddy-bears, struggling for power – but here Stretch had the upper hand, with his flexible joints, and all it took was a second. Pulling the spike from her grasp, he brought it down through her palm, sinking it so deep into the carpet her hand looked like a big pink spider with its legs curled into its death rictus. Sister let out scream that sounded sickeningly like it belonged to Alex. In a flash Stretch was kneeling by James's side. He gave him a sharp slap. "Mister James? Are you alive? Are you you?"

"Yes. Ow! Yes! stop slapping me, it's me!" Stretch barely seemed to pay attention as he worked at the ropes, his head swivelling around in all directions at once, his mouth muttering frantic half-sentences that didn't make sense: "Must get Holly to… Greeny on the way… No time for anything…" James found himself drifting in a sick haze, unable to concentrate on the world around him, until at last Stretch untied the final knot and wrenched the spike from his neck.

The moment the rusty metal left his body, James was catapulted back to crystal clear reality. It was like falling through warm sunlight for a thousand miles only to land in an ocean of ice and fury. He sat bolt upright, a scream in the back of his throat that couldn't quite make it all the way out. Stretch, meanwhile, had pinned Sister's other hand down and was in the process of driving the spike through it.

James rolled over, curled up in a ball and vomited black tar.

Stretch helped him to his feet, brushing carpet fluff and splinters from his clothes and then turning him to face him. He was heaving breaths, half mad with excitement and terror. "The house is burning, Mister James. We have to get out!"

Only then did James notice the hazy smoke drifting in under the door, through the peephole, even from the carpet. The room felt hot.

"Okay," James said. He looked over at Sister, struggling against her steel bonds, and wanted to vomit again.

Stretch took his hand and pulled him, not towards the door, or the hole in the ceiling - which had miraculously closed up – but to the toy box against the wall.

"There is only one more open seam here. Go!" and he pulled it open and forced James headfirst into the compartment.

It should have been barely large enough to hold him, but to James's surprise he dropped past the floor and found himself floating, swimming through the darkness. It was infinite, here, he realised, and for a minute that's all there was: an all-consuming terror that he would spend a million years here, a billion, and never find his way back.

And then one of Stretch's hands took hold of him and they were swimming for the light.

52
Salvage Mission

Greeny barely escaped the fire with his life; bark singed half to charcoal, leafy extremities singed black around the edges, he gritted his teeth and pushed back into the inferno. No sooner had he lost Stretch than it had occurred to him that he was wasting time: it was Holly he needed to save. Even if the house burned down, even if the boy escaped – it could all be redeemed if Holly lived. She was the source of it all. She could rebuild the house, she could spawn new Nobodies, keep this world alive.

He coughed through a dining room too full of smoke to see by, blundered down a hallway that was leaning at an alarming diagonal. The library was on fire, flames climbing shelves of ten thousand books to the ceiling. In another room the piano played a hysterical tap dance.

"HOLLY! HOLL-" He paused to cough out ash and sparks. The bugs that lived inside him were flooding out in droves, lines of ants fleeing from his nostrils, and he couldn't help but worry that they were somehow crucial for his survival. His whole world was crashing down around him and the only one who could save it was…

There! "HOLLY!"

He had just come to the stop of the spiral staircase from the lobby to find her walking away from him up the hallway. She turned, bewildered, her face covered in dirt and blood, the barely healed scars reopening and blistering from the radiant heat, hair wild and straggly. "Greeny, what's happening? Where are they?"

He ran toward her, her tears driving him to feel a kind of paternal protectiveness he'd never experienced before. He had only ever seen her as the tyrant, the spoilt brat, the goddess of his destiny and livelihood. He swept her into his arms, and she cried on his shoulder as he raced back down the stairs and out of the front door. For the first time in a long while, the summer garden was under a heavy monsoon downpour.

"Save mother, Greeny," Holly said as he laid her down in the soft grass. "Save mother and don't let them get away."

He looked back over his shoulder. Smoke poured from every window and an unholy red glow emanated from within, but the rain was falling hard now, and the structure was solid. The attic window, so high up, was dark.

"Get to safety, Miss Holly," Greeny said softly. "I'll be back for you soon."

53
Goodbye for Now

Stretch got him to a bathroom on the second floor, where the pale rectangular window looked out on the autumn graveyard. James knew what was coming. "Where are you going to go?" he said.

It was cool here. The tiles smelled of mildew and moisture and rain hammered the glass. James hoped the fires didn't die out. What then? Would it all be for nothing? He sat down on the edge of the bathtub, shaking, and inspected the wounds in his wrists. He should have bled out long ago, but the wounds had closed in already, the surrounding flesh swollen and throbbing.

Stretch crouched in front of him. "We don't have long, Mister James. You must go."

"I'm not leaving without Alex," he said thickly.

"No, no! Alex is safe underground, safe until the house is destroyed. You must save yourself."

But James had not forgotten the pictures he'd drawn the night before: there was no saving himself. He forced back a wave of nausea as he got to his feet and lifted the small window above the sink. A welcome breath of icy air blew into his face along with a smattering of rain. "Don't worry about me, Stretch. Just make sure… Just make sure you finish it."

"I will…" Stretch started to say something, and then jerked upright as though seized by a sudden realisation. He grabbed James by the shoulders and shook him. "James! The suitcase. You must know because perhaps… perhaps I will not come back. In the cottage, up inside the chimney, there is a suitcase. Will you remember that? For you – just in case. I don't know what is inside, but the Father always used to say it would help him escape, one day."

"Okay, Stretch, calm down. I'll remember." Stretch nodded, still deeply unsettled, and when James extended a hand, he could only look at it, bewildered. James realised he didn't know what to do. James took hold of Stretch's own hand and gripped it, shaking twice and then letting go.

"What does that mean, Mister James?"

"It means thanks for everything, and good luck. It means thanks for being our friend."

Stretch's eyes filled with tears immediately and James couldn't help but feel immense gratitude for the lanky oddball.

"Maybe when it is all over, I can still be your friend?" Stretch said, and James nodded, wiping his eye with the back of his bruised hand. "Course you can. It'll be awesome. And you can just call me James, alright?"

Stretch nodded and reached forward to shake his hand, but James pulled him into an awkward hug, instead. "Be careful, big man."

"Be careful, James."

But then it was time to go and Stretch helped James out of the window and into the downpour, lowering him by one long arm so that he wouldn't have far to fall. Luckily, they were at the back of the house, and when he landed it was in a gentle snowdrift. By the time he'd regained his footing and brushed the wet flakes from his jacket, Stretch's head had disappeared from the window and he was once more alone.

He headed for the graveyard.

54
Last Stand

The Father would be crushed by the collapsing house, Stretch hoped – and in any case he was unreachable; it was The Mother he was more worried about. As long as she survived in her parasitic symbiosis with the house, Holly would be immortal.

The house was unbearably hot, now, and each room more difficult to navigate. More than once Stretch opened a door or climbed a ladder only to discover a raging hellfire and have to reroute. A staircase collapsed beneath him just as he reached its top. Windows were blowing out on all sides from the heat.

At last, after crawling through a collapsing hallway, sprinting across scalding hot tiles and broken glass, and evaded a falling chandelier, Stretch arrived at the trapdoor to the attic. It was open, which could only mean one thing: either Holly or Greeny had arrived before him. His heart sank with despair, but the Centre line was quickly filling with smoke and sparks – the grandfather clock chiming its last – and there was no way to go but up.

The attic had always held a deep horror for Stretch, with its dim light and yeast body reek. Perhaps some part of him had always suspected that he would die there, suffocated in Mother's warm embrace at Holly's request, or choking on the too-thick milk from one of the swollen breasts.

So, it was with some disorientation that, on hoisting himself up through the trapdoor, he took in the scene that met him. The big round window looking out over the winter garden was smashed and the coarse wind had washed the room of its sour smell and extinguished the incense candles that had burned here for so long. Greeny held Mother in a bear hug from behind and was trying to drag her immense body out of the King bed and across the room to the open window. She squealed like a hog, her sausage like legs kicking the yellow bedsheets in a flurry as she tried to separate from the mattress which had all but fused to her spongey skin.

Greeny heaved once more, pulling her halfway, and then he caught sight of Stretch and dropped her unceremoniously. She grunted on landing, putting out one thick hand to right herself as best she could, and fixed Stretch with her black spider's eyes.

Greeny stepped forward, eyeing Stretch warily, "If you help me get her out, I'll tell Holly the house caught by accident. She doesn't have to know. We can still save this. We can rebuild."

"You killed Pinky," Stretch said, eyes welling with tears. "Pinky was good and nice and kind, and you killed her."

"It was what Holly wanted," Greeny said. "I had no choice."

"You always have a choice," Stretch said. And, without waiting for a reply, he lunged forward, swinging wildly for Greeny's head.

Greeny ducked nimbly away, and in seconds Stretch was sprawled out on the floor beside the bed. He rolled over just in time to see a stumpy foot accelerating toward his face and then the world flashed white. Greeny climbed on top of him, his crushing weight bringing him back to consciousness. Stretch saw the gardener's pained expression through blurry eyes as he took hold of Stretch's neck and began to squeeze. Behind him, the room's shadows danced and leapt in the orange glow of the flames at the trapdoor. It wouldn't be long now; he could sense the floor trembling under his back, the structure beneath them little more than a house of cards in a draughty room.

"You ruined everything!" Greeny spat through gritted teeth. "Holly loved you!" He squeezed with everything he had, his splintery thumbs digging into Stretch's neck and threatening to pierce him. If there was anyone who knew how to kill Nobodies, after all, it was Greeny: he'd killed more than he could remember. Stretch could remember, though. Stretch remembered every last one.

Holly didn't love me," he said. His voice was a barely audible wheeze. His right hand, limp by his side, slipped into his coat pocket. "Holly doesn't know what love is."

And with that, he swung the railroad spike into the side of Greeny's head. It made a Thuck sound, like an axe sinking into a thick trunk. When he pulled it out again, a gout of wine dark blood poured in its wake. Greeny shook his head as if to clear it of some distraction. He kept his furious gaze on Stretch's face, but with each passing second the strength leeched from his grip and he sunk lower and lower until at last he was lying on top of Stretch as though in an embrace, breathing his last earthy breaths into his ear.

"We could have lived," Greeny whispered. "We could have…" But he never finished, and a minute later Stretch heaved him to one side and climbed to his feet, shaking.

Greeny continued to bleed out, his treelike limbs twitching, his expression faraway, the light in his brown eyes receding steadily.

Mother leaned up against the headboard of the bed. Her flabby face was flushed with the heat and her enormous rolls flowed off her like an ooze, every part of her trembling with fear. Stretch might have felt sorry for her if he hadn't known too well how corrupted by the house she'd become, how many Nobodies she'd persuaded Holly to murder in all the years. This one is too dangerous, this one is nasty to you, this one is troublesome… All the while feeding them with the sour but nourishing milk they needed to live, poisoning them as surely as she poisoned Holly with her words.

She watched Stretch raise the spike, did not bother trying to stop him. When she spoke, it was not with her own voice but the voice of the house – the deep gurgle of a drowning man. "You can't kill me, Nobody. My eggs are laid."

Stretch sunk the spike into her swollen belly, not sure it was enough to kill her at first and then realising that, of course, it didn't matter – for just then the house of cards suffered a gust it could not withstand, and, in a hurricane of fire and glass, it collapsed.

55
James Dug

He worked at a frantic pace, shovelling spadeful after spadeful of dirt out of the grave only to have rain and mud seep back in to replace it. He was certain he would be too late, that he would open the coffin only to see Alex's pale face staring up at him with unseeing eyes, her flesh swollen and blue, her mouth locked open in an eternal scream. Still, he dug, while the storm raged and the house burned inwardly like an imploding star and the babies screamed their last in the basement, he dug. James dug until his shoulders tore, his hands bled, and his lungs burned.

When the house imploded in an apocalyptic blast of fire and ash, James survived only because he was sheltered by the sides of the open grave. He didn't pay it any mind.

James dug.

56
Holly

Holly watched it go down, numb to the sun on her shoulders and the cold rain on her skin. It seemed to take an age, the pointed roof falling through the middle and the brick walls falling inward along with it, the whole structure drawing in to some invisible point at its core from which there erupted a deafening explosion. Her eyes flashed white in that moment, something within her twisting in agony, but only for an instant. The blast of heat nearly knocked her off her feet, vaporising the surrounding rain and sending an immense cloud of steam and smoke skyward.

When it was over, the house was no more than an enormous pile of rubble, tall columns of fire still burning stubbornly despite the downpour, which was already beginning to abate. As Holly looked towards the lush summer garden, she saw trees wilting, their vibrant green dulling to a pale straw, the wide fields seeming to shrink into themselves, somehow. Greeny's shed looked less like a sturdy warehouse and more like a slanted shack of rotted wood.

She moved toward the ruins of the house, parts of which still stood stubbornly against the surrounding chaos: half of a staircase leading nowhere, a cobblestone wall holding up nothing, a blackened bookshelf whose shelves were layered with ash. She navigated the hissing piles of charcoal and smoke, searching.

As she crossed a small hill made up of crushed tiles and glass from one of the bathrooms, a clearing in the heavy steam allowed her a brief window across the foundations to the autumn garden. Him.

James, head barely visible over the top of the gravesite, was too intent on his task to see Holly emerge from the wreckage.

He was almost there, had cleared enough mud away to reveal the yellow coffin wood, but in his rush to reach it he'd carved a narrow hole straight down and as a result opening the coffin by hand was impossible. Instead, measuring his force carefully, he brought the shovel down in a series of hard strikes, until at last he heard the integrity of the lid break with a satisfying crack!

After that it was just a matter of using the edge of the spade to chop sections out of the wood until he'd cleared a large enough hole at the top half of the lid. The coffin had half filled with rainwater, and Alex floated face up, her eyes closed and her lips a pale blue. James took hold of her under the arms and dragged her through the hole, heaving and gasping. She was a dead weight, and when he laid her out beside the grave her head fell back, and her eyes rolled white.

She wasn't breathing.

"Shit. Come on, wake up! Alex, Please! Please." He tried to do what he'd seen them do in the movies – CPR – with his hands in the middle of her soft and horribly unresponsive chest, but he didn't know what he was doing, and it all seemed so pointless suddenly and her face was slack and dead, so sickeningly empty. He pulled her into a hug, the tears burning his eyes along with the rain dampened smoke, and it was then, holding her and weeping, that he became aware of Holly's watchful glare.

He turned, lowering Alex gently to the soil, and came face to face with the monster herself.

She looked like a monster, too – a monster who'd taken the body of a girl to live in and treated it carelessly. Her once pristine clothes were in burnt and muddy tatters, as was her hair – the clean plait hanging in loose strands across her face and shoulders. The burn scars were visible on her bare arms and neck, as were bruises and dried blood. The bright eyes that stared out from behind the thin curtain of once-blonde hair were full of nothing but hatred.

Without looking or even being completely aware of himself, James's left hand moved down Alex's leg, sliding around her ankle until his fingers caught on the handle of the knife she'd hidden there. He pulled it out, unaware also that in doing so the blade cut a thin red line up Alex's calf and brought her, quietly blinking, back to the world of the living.

The blade shook in James's hand as he started towards Holly. Her eyes were glowing a hot white now, illuminating a spot on the smouldering ground in front of her and causing something to grow there. Another Nobody – a monstrous one, by the looks of the snarling mouth and grasping claws that twisted in the smoke – but James didn't hesitate. He didn't care what happened to him anymore. The beast could tear him apart and eat him by inches if it wanted; but it wouldn't stop him from taking the life of the evil thing in the soiled white dress.

He sprinted forward, ducking under the still-forming monster's reaching arm, and slammed the knife into Holly's heart with enough force to send her reeling back a step, several of her ribs snapping from the force. Her eyes shuttered for a minute and the growth of her latest creation halted, leaving it without legs or a fully formed face – just a hunk of muscled meat with an arm and a gaping mouth squirming in the dirt.

Such a wound should have been enough to drop a full-grown man. James was certain he'd done it right – had even felt, in the brief second, he'd kept his hand on the blades handle, the vibrations of her heartbeat travelling through the metal.

But Holly did not fall. Instead, she took hold of the knife with her right hand and pulled it effortlessly from her chest, a psychotic leer stretching obscenely across her face.

"I'm going to make you beg me to bury you," she said, taking a step forward, the knife shaking in her white-knuckled hand. "I'm going to skin you alive every day and grow you new skin every night. YOU. RUINED. EVERYTHING!"

But just then, a second before he was sure she was going to show him just how real her threats were, another voice reached them across the ruins of the house. "HOLLY!"

It seemed to come from somewhere above them, and it took James a minute to locate the source of it – but when he did a surge of hope flared up inside him. It was Stretch.

The lanky butler was standing at the top of a half-staircase, swaying precariously in the wind. The rain had softened to a drizzle now, though all the fire was extinguished and even the smoke rose up in only a few scattered pillars. Beneath him stood a series of pillars, now broken into sharp spears of oak aimed at the heavens.

"Stretch? What are you doing? Help me!" But the words sounded less like a demand from Holly's mouth and more like a plea.

"I loved Pinky!" he called to her. "But if it wasn't for you, I couldn't have loved at all. I thank you, Miss Holly. Goodbye."

And they watched, Holly and James equally shocked, as Stretch spread his arms and titled ever so gently forward, eyes closed, his expression so serene that James would not have been surprised if instead of falling he had sprouted wings and flown from his perch like a swan.

The drop was short but breathtakingly far, ending on the point of one of the splintered pillars. In that eternal moment James recalled a memory from just the night before – though it may as well have been years ago. Stretch pointing down to the basement, 'Father,' to the attic, 'Mother.' And then shrugging his shoulders. The truth clicked home in James's mind in the same moment Stretch's noble soul departed.

Stretch slid about halfway down the spike before the heavy wood halted his momentum and he sagged just a few feet off the ground, blood soaking the wood and dripping from the tips of his long fingers.

"Stretch!" Holly took a step toward her friend, faltered, and then turned back to face James, her expression twisting between agony and hatred. Her left hand pressed up against the wound in her chest, which was beginning to fill with blood, but his eyes were on her right hand, then, the one still gripping the kitchen knife.

James took a wild step back as the blade scythed through the air where his neck had been an instant before. He staggered, arms flailing for balance, and Holly advanced on him, blade held high and a scream rattling her pierced lung, blood spraying from her lips as she came for the death blow.

"Move." A low, savage voice he did not recognize spoke from behind him, but before he could obey the owner shoved him aside. He went down in black mud, the air rushing out of him on impact.

He looked up, expecting to see Greeny standing over him with a sneer across his ginger-root lips. Instead, he saw Alex, her appearance as deathly as before – except for her eyes. They burned with life.

She was holding the shovel James had used to dig her out of the grave, and now she swung it with all the force her weakened body could muster into Holly's small head. It made a sound like a raw egg dropped on a concrete floor.

James did not see what came next: the arm he'd been using to prop himself up on the wet ground slid out from under him and he allowed himself to lie on his back in the cool mud and stare up at the grey clouds above. Whatever poison the House had injected into his veins was in revolt, boiling inside him and sucking his energy at the same time. The seizure didn't last long, but it felt like death. James could no more lift his head than he could have lifted the earth itself.

It sounded as though Alex was still digging in the dirt until James heard the unmistakable cracking of bone and knew it wasn't soil the shovel was splitting.

After a minute or so, the sound ceased and Alex came to lie beside him in the mud, staring up at the swirling sky.

To Be Alive

57
Mourning

Frank Harmon opened his throat and emptied the tenth bottle of Heineken of the night. The alcohol was well and truly pumping through his veins, now. It was good, it made him want to dance – and now that there weren't any concerned friends and neighbours and officers to see – he could really let it out. He flicked the television to the music station and was delighted to find AC/DC playing – Angus Young doing his famous one-foot-jig to the tune of Back in Black.

It wasn't right to feel good about your son being dead – that was the problem.

It wasn't proper. Not even when the idiot had gone wandering around in the middle of the night and got himself skinned – skinned of all things. Bloody hoodlum probably involved in gangs and drugs and all the rest. "That'll teach you not to listen to yer old man," Robert muttered, though in truth he wasn't mad. He wasn't mad or sad or anything he was supposed to be. He just felt… free.

He tottered from the living room to the kitchen, dragging a heavy black garbage bag and singing along at the top of his lungs while he threw cutlery, pots and appliances inside. Let them hear – they'd only think he was losing it in the wake of a tragedy. Fine by him. Would make his resignation easier to swallow, as well as the sudden disappearance he intended to make as soon as the funeral was over.

He didn't know where he was going to go, yet, only that it would be somewhere new. Somewhere the sun shone, and the women were pretty and didn't care if you didn't look like Tom Cruise… Thailand, maybe. No wife, and now no kid, he was free again. Half chuckling, half hiccupping, he halted his packing for a minute to belt out the final refrain: "COS I'M BACK IN BLAAAAAAAAACCKKKKK…"

And then promptly toppled over sideways on the kitchen tiles and went to sleep.

It was no wonder that when he woke up the next day, he had no recollection of the low voices he'd heard in his son's room. No wonder that when he entered it to pack James's belongings in a box marked GOODWILL that he found nothing left to pack, except a few discarded items of clothing and books, and the reams upon reams of pastel drawings that blew across the room from the breeze through the open window.

Robert scratched his head, his thick mind struggling to make sense of it – of who would commit such a robbery in the first place and why. One of the pictures came to settle at his feet: a giant middle finger done in flesh pastel and signed JH at the bottom, with today's date beside it.

The murderer, taunting him.

He scrunched it up and put it out of his mind, deciding that the police need never know. He couldn't afford to get held back by an extended investigation.

He had a new life to live, after all.

58
Runaways

Freshly attired in James's clothes – they hadn't dared risk an appearance at Alex's house – the two of them got on a train with everything they owned in a couple of backpacks and three brown suitcases. One of these, of course, being only recently acquired. The tag on the upper right corner read: Property of Gregory Anderson.

They had scoured the wreckage for half an hour before Alex had had the bright idea to venture down into what had once been the winter garden and see if the cottage was still there. Lo and behold, it was – albeit a crumbled and mouldy representation of the cosy home Alex had seen just days ago. Sure enough, the suitcase was jammed inside the chimney, blackened with soot and filled to bursting with everything a runaway father could have wanted: A passport, old plane tickets, spare clothes, and oh, yes, thick wads of cash filling every spare inch of space.

As they'd left – none of the old brown vines reaching out this time, the gate squealing open at a nudge – the vertigo had been less pronounced. Looking back over his shoulder, James saw the mansion as he'd always seen it in the days they'd walked to school along Twisty Lane, though it was perhaps a little more run down, now, a little more abandoned. In the days and weeks following, he would draw a series of pictures of the house in which it deteriorated to eventually reveal reality: nothing left but a pile of rubble and earth.

By then they had found refuge in a small seaside village by the name of Sandton. A quiet bed and breakfast owned by an unassuming old lady, and a calm bay with a golden beach stretching for miles. James would walk its breadth for hours, insisting he go alone, and each time she wondered if he'd return.

He was not the same boy she'd made friends with in high school – in fact he wasn't even the same boy who'd comforted her that dark night in the House even though he'd been in just as terrible a position as she. This James flinched when she touched him. This one barely spoke, and spent hours away from here, walking the beach or who knew what else, brooding. It had gotten so that she was terrified that it wasn't the real James that had come for her after all, but his doppelganger, rebelling against Holly.

On the day they'd arrived in Sandton, finally able to breathe a sigh of relief, Alex took him walking down the pier. "I can't believe it's over," she told him a hundred times, never getting more than a sad smile in response. Finally, with the sunset as a romantic view at the end, she took his head in her hands and kissed him. She felt him try to pull back at first, and then he relented, until to her surprise he bit her tongue – hard – and she jumped back. "Ow! What the fuck?"

Hurrying to catch up with her as she'd stormed back down the pier, he'd tried to explain. "I don't know – I can't leave it behind. It feels like it's still in me somehow. Everything that used to feel good doesn't, and sometimes I get an urge to do mean things like that. I'm sorry, I just… I just feel sick, that's all."

She'd decided to give him as long as it took for her burned hands and her breasts to heal. It took a couple of weeks, though of course the scars would be permanent; a pair of thick spiralling scars where her nipples used to be, and the palms of her hands healed flat and pink. No lines. They reminded her of the hands the Nobodies had: smooth, with no lines and no fingerprints.

Days after they'd ceased even to itch, he was no better, and Alex began to get worried. There was a lot of money in that suitcase, stacks and stacks of it – but how long would it last, really? Not their whole lives. She thought of her family, but the idea of returning to them made her claustrophobic – a feeling that was all too familiar to her now. Free. You're free, now. She kept telling herself that, but somehow it never made it feel any truer.

Certainly, the longer she watched James, the less free he looked. He barely slept at night, ground his teeth constantly, and his eyes had taken on a paranoid darting quality she didn't like at all. His skin was always hot, in a clammy, feverish way. Every smile was forced for her benefit. But by far the worst thing of all was that he wanted nothing. When she tried to talk to him about where they would go and what they would do, he would simply stare into the middle distance and shrug, even though she could tell those darting eyes did want something. They did see a future of some kind: just not anything James would tell her.

It wasn't until the fifteenth night on the beach that she found out how bad it had gotten.

The House was not dead: it had simply moved. It had taken up its legs and relocated, switching out wooden walls for skin, its foundations for bones, and its windows for eyes. It wasn't that James had no control – in fact he felt he had every bit of control of himself he'd ever had. Will his hand to move here, to open and close in a fist, and lo and behold, the limb obeyed. No, the problem was that he wanted things he never would have wanted, before. The things he wanted now were sick, no, evil. They were things only the House could ever have wanted. And while he existed, day to day, going through the motions, all he could think about was what he really wanted to do. The journey from sunrise to midnight was nothing but a white knuckled battle of the wills to do none of it.

But there was only so long one could go, fighting an all-out battle. Even the world's best fighters started to get tired after just a few rounds in the ring. What if they had to keep fighting, hour after hour and then, after a brief respite, day after day? A human being could only take so much.

Save Alex. That was what it had all been about, right? He pondered this on one of his evening beach walks, watching the sun drop to the horizon across the ocean. Save Alex, get her out, be the knight in shining armour. Only it hadn't turned out so well for either of them. Instead of sending her a lifeboat he'd just jumped right into the ocean with her and drowned. When he stood on the beach with icy surf licking his toes, and looked out to the sinking sun, he thought back to those dark moments in the house.

All those pictures he'd drawn, and none of them had included a version in which he was alive. It was either that he was dead, and Alex had survived, or else the House won. Now, he understood that this was not a beginning for him; it was an end.

He nodded to himself, and as he turned to walk back to the hotel, he pulled his hood over his head and jammed his head in his pockets, just the way he used to stalk the school grounds not so long ago. Something sharp pricked his finger and he jumped in surprise. When he removed the offending object, he couldn't help but laugh, it was the tiny razor he'd unscrewed from the sharpener in the playroom, hoping he would find a use for it, later.

Shaking his head, grinning, slid it back into his pocket and retraced his steps down the beach. Looks like I did find a use, after all, he thought.

Alex wasn't around when he got back – probably shopping or something in town. Seeing the rooms empty bathed him in cool relief: the pain would be over, soon. He was going to beat the House at last. You like that? I'd rather kill myself then let you win. How you like that, bitch?

The House did not like that at all, and once he'd locked himself in the bathroom it was in full revolt. He was hot and cold and itchy all over. Forget the blade – get a knife and wait behind the door and kill her when she comes in. No more problem. Such thoughts were all he could think about lately – but he'd identified the voice. He could see it for what it was, now, and he wasn't listening. Instead, he was running a scalding hot bath and stripping, getting eager now, a smile spreading across his face.

It wouldn't have been easy to get a proper, sharp knife from the kitchen. Some of those stainless-steel Japanese things could have cut down to the bone in seconds. But somehow it seemed right to James to use the small, rusty sharpener blade to sever his arteries. Ironically, part of it was because of the House's blood, running through his veins: it liked pain. It was hungry for agony, even though it didn't want him to kill himself.

All the better for me to eat you with, James thought as he settled into the steaming water and drew the blade from the base of his left palm right down to the elbow. He pressed the edge in until he felt resistance from the denser muscle tissue around the bone. It was painful, in the same way that having a terrible itch scratched with steel wool is painful. Then he did the other arm, and then he drew the little shred of metal across his neck, trying as hard as he could to cut into his jugular but not completely sure if he'd succeeded or not.

When he had a smile in his neck even wider than the one on his face, he laid back in the steaming tub and closed his eyes. I got you, bastard, he thought. I fucking win. She's going to live a good life now, and you won't ever get her. Fuck. You.

It wasn't a bad feeling, either: it was a feeling of triumph and relief, and he sighed as he let the hot water close in around his face, letting the strength drain from his open veins in pleasant flow.

Someone tried the door, and found it locked.

"You better open this right now, or I'm going to break it down somehow." Alex's voice, shaking. He opened his foggy eyes but didn't move. There was no way she'd get in in time. Damn, why was she home already?

"I'm having a bath," he tried to say, but his voice was so weak the words came out barely more than a whisper.

Something heavy hit the door from the other side and it thundered against the threshold. BOOM! Then again, and again, until the frame splintered and bent, and flakes of paint fluttered to the floor like white snowflakes. The world had taken on a dreamlike quality. Even when the door broke inward and Alex came stumbling through, her face red and tear-stained, James watched her as though from far away.

When she saw him, soaking in what now appeared to be a tub filled with blood, she let out a cry that sounded halfway between a scream and a sob. She took hold of him under the arms and heaved him out of the tub, the two of them sprawling over the tiles because James no longer had the strength to support himself.

"You fucking…" She rolled him to one side and wrenched open the medicine cabinet under the sink. "Asshole! How dare you…" Throwing band aids and cough syrup aside until at last she found the obligatory half used roll of bandages. "Leave me like this you selfish…" Trying to wrap his neck without cutting off circulation. "Prick!" pulling tight a tourniquet just above his elbow on each arm.

He closed his eyes, already shivering against the cold tile, sweating ice, and tried to figure out if this was good or bad. To live on, with the House inside him, wearing his skin like this? Or to break the heart of the girl he loved? But in the end the pull of sleep was too warm, too comforting, and he decided to put off the question until later.

59
Later

The world swam into focus from an oblivion so deep James stared at the little room for an hour before he could remember where he was. Or for that matter, who he was.

It was hard to know the time – the apartment's only window was in the adjoining room. The bedroom was dim enough to be early morning or twilight. He didn't try to force the memory; just let his eyes drift from one corner to the other, taking in little details, like the pinewood desk against the far wall. It was the type of cheap thing you always saw in these places – all the drawers would be empty except for a lone bible. But it wasn't the desk so much as what was on it that caught his eye: a stack of blank pages, squared neatly away in one corner, and two packs of fresh pastels. It wasn't until he saw them that he remembered what had happened.

James sat upright in the bed, shocked all the way back to full consciousness by sheer panic. *Is it still in me? Is it still there?* Peeling the bandages off his arms as if he would be able to see a trace of the House in his dried blood, somehow. But the black lines of his aching wounds told him nothing. As it turned out, he didn't need them to; he felt the poison inside him, a rage that made him clench his jaw so tightly the gash in his neck re-opened. Doesn't she know what she's done? It was going to be so peaceful and right and now she'd set the House loose on the world. He wanted to take hold of her neck and…

There it is. There it is, alright. James rolled out of bed and went over to the door, thinking there was still time to drown himself in the ocean. All he had to do was run in a straight line until he hit that cold water and then just keep going. Easy.

The door jammed, so he pushed his shoulder against it and tried to force it. Oh. Not jammed: locked.

Alex's called out to him from the other side. "You're not coming out until you draw."

That couldn't be right. "What?"

"I said you're not coming out until you draw."

That fucking idiot bitch, ruining everything! He slammed the door with both fists. "Draw? Are you nuts? Let me out or I'll break this door down and rip the skin off your face! You think I can't?"

Shut it down, don't let it win. He closed his eyes as tightly as he could and stopped breathing. His right fist was pulled back, but he let it drop to the side. This door was heavier than the one Alex had broken. It might break his fist.

"Just one picture, James, that's all I ask. Just one for me to remember you by. You slide it under the door, and I'll open it and let you go. I promise." There was a tremble in her voice, but it was firm – he wasn't going to change her mind.

But the House's keen ear lent James an insight he wished he didn't have; as well as the fear, her voice carried with it the unmistakable flavour of honesty.

"Alright, you want a picture? I'll draw a picture of what I'm going to do to you in five minutes. Ha ha."

During James's time in oblivion, the House had done a little settling in. Apparently, his vocal cords no longer belonged to him – nor, as he discovered, did several parts of his body. The House jerked him around like a mannequin with loose joints, pulling him over to the desk and swiping the chair aside. His hands snatched the first box of pastels and tore it open, eagerly picking out the shade of blood red first.

For a long minute, he stood frozen over the blank page, the pastel half crushed in his tight grip. All of his wounds were bleeding again.

The first picture the house produced was a hideous mess of scribbled gore and stick figures. Unsurprisingly, Alex pushed it back under the door as soon as she saw it. "I said I wanted a picture from James, asshole."

James felt a smirk on his own face as he returned to the desk and produced another picture, this one a similarly messy depiction of a boy and girl standing on a beach holding hands.

This time, when Alex pushed it back under the door, the House flew into a rage, throwing James's body against the door in an effort to shatter the wood with sheer force. Three times James hit the solid wood before he regained control. The House might have had control of the wheel, but James hadn't lost everything. It was like the two of them were driving a car, the House leaning on the accelerator while James pushed the brake at the same time.

James licked his bloody lips and winced at the touch of a chipped tooth. The House relented, and in a second

James's legs were walking him back over to the desk. One arm reached out of its own accord and righted the chair.

"Fine," he muttered. "She wants you to draw?" Sat down and flexed his fingers. Flattened out the white paper in front of him.

"Draw."

Alex had not been waiting in front of the door but just to one side of it, crouching. She'd tied a string across the room at about ankle height and held in one hand the largest steak knife she could find in the kitchen. When she'd heard that voice coming from the other side of the door there'd been no doubt in her mind, she would be able to do it – if he broke through.

But after three heavy slams – the last of which had shaken one of the screws loose on the hinge – James had given up, and for three hours now there had been no signs of life from the bedroom.

Alex didn't dare move from her position for the first hour, and then only with utmost care not to make a sound. By the end of the third, she was worried he'd managed to kill himself, despite the fact that she'd removed every sharp object from the room and even the bedsheet lest he try to hang himself.

After six hours, she knocked on the door and called his name, but there was no response. When she pressed her ear to the door, she thought she heard the soft sound of pastel on paper, but it was so quiet it was impossible to be sure.

Twelve hours: the sun dropped out of sight beyond the calm bay horizon, and she was sure she was waiting for a dead body. Maybe it's just what the House wants you to think, and it's really waiting in there for you to open the door and find out. The thought was all the more terrifying because she knew that if she waited much longer and didn't receive the promised picture under the door, she would have to investigate. She decided she would give it until dawn.

It was a long night.

Only once did she leave the room, to tiptoe into the toilet, which she didn't flush in case the House chose that moment to smash through the door and come for her. She felt like she was trapped once more in the room in Holly's house. In the bleak morning hours, she cried until her chest ached, and as the dawn crept closer, she thought of pushing the moment of truth back even further. She was sure there was nothing on the other side of that door, but James's cold body and she wasn't sure she could bear to see it.

But the dawn came. Alex waited until the pale light strengthened to bright gold and filled the apartment, and at last she could put it off no longer. She hadn't slept, eaten or drank at all and the salt from her tears was sticky on her face. It was as though she'd been drained in every possible way, and now all she needed was for her fears to be realised and shatter her for good.

Alex took a moment to brace herself, redoubling the grip on the steak knife. Instead of strength, what bore her through was exhaustion: she was so sick of being scared. At least, for better or worse, it would be over once she opened the door. Nodding to herself, she stepped forward and reached for the lock.

And then looked down, because at that moment something shot through the crack beneath the door. It was a sketch paper, every inch of which filled with smeared pastel. A self portrait of James's face battered and complete with a stained bandage wrapped around his neck like a scarf and a sheepish grin on his face.

He'd signed his name in the bottom right corner, and the title of the portrait was listed in quotes beside it: 'Sorry.'

She didn't know what to expect when she pushed open the door, but it certainly wasn't this: Every inch of the room was covered in pastel drawings. On one wall, James had sticky-taped thirteen pages together to make a larger picture depicting what Alex instantly recognized as the House itself. No blank pages remained on the desk at all, and the two boxes of pastels had been reduced to a few crumbled stumps scattered here and there. The waxy colours covered everything including most of James himself, who was lying atop a pile of pages on the mattress as though he meant to make a snow angel out of them.

When he looked up at her, she almost collapsed with relief: it was him – it was definitely James, his eyes dark and clear as ever. Perhaps he wasn't the same person she'd known just a few weeks ago, but it was the same soul, and that was all that mattered.

"How did you know it would work?" he asked her.

"I didn't," she said. "I just hoped." And she rolled over on top of him, running a hand along his coloured face.

"It's okay," he said with a grin. "I won't bite."

Smiling, she kissed him, and felt for the first time in a while as though she had left the grave behind and was truly alive.

They spent a long time in that bedroom, but somehow Alex didn't get around to looking at any of the pictures James had drawn until about two days later. She saw them, of course, but she hadn't really looked.

The first one that she picked up was a portrait of Holly, standing on a neatly kempt lawn and holding her little brown bear. She seemed to stare out of the page at the viewer with a piercing frown. It took Alex's breath away, but not because of the look on the portrait Holly's face. She grabbed James, who was propped up in bed and scrolling the internet on his phone, looking for any mention of them in mainstream media.

"What?"

"James, have you seen this? Do you see this?"

He laughed. "I drew it, so yeah."

She shook him, shoving the paper in front of him. "This isn't, like. I mean, you could sell this."

He looked at her as if she was an Alien. "No, I couldn't."

"James, this is like… I've seen worse pictures than this in actual art galleries."

"Come on. I'm not that good."

"No, you're not," she said. "That's the whole point. You've never been anywhere close to this good. I mean, I like your drawings and all that, James, but this isn't even you. It's almost like someone else drew it."

He took the picture from her hands and looked at it, running a hand through his hair. "Yeah. I don't know, I was just trying to get it all out, you know? The poison."

Shaking his head, he tossed it aside. "But it's weird, creepy. No one would buy that stuff."

But he was wrong, and when she started going through some of the other pictures, she found that they were all of the same quality. Each and every one of the hundreds of pages in that room alone was a masterpiece. They were alive in the most unsettling way.

Alex sent the pieces to several art galleries across the country, and less than a week later she got a reply from an enthusiastic gallery. By then, James had created more work, and now he was working with purpose, with deliberation, they were nothing short of transcendent.

"I have to keep doing it," he said to her on the day they received the letter. "Otherwise, the poison builds up."

Alex knew just what he meant. She doubted she'd ever be free of her recurring claustrophobic nightmares, but she knew already what her own outlet would be, her own future: travel, experience, freedom life.

They headed South.

60
My Eggs Are Laid

Sister pulled herself from the wreckage of the house, clinging to life by the tips of her charred fingers. She should not have lived at all, but it wasn't until she was soaking in a warm bath in a coat of fresh skin that she recalled those last catastrophic moments before everything collapsed. She'd felt a surge of power through her body, so powerful she thought it would break her apart. The ceiling had come hurtling toward her – or had she risen to meet it? – and then everything had been soaring nothingness: roaring blood and heat and that sense of impossible power.

The pain had come later.

Her skin was charcoal: small black flakes borne away by the wind. The rain hissed when it touched her, and the air was agony on the raw patches of meat that covered her body. She struggled through the gates and down the street. It was late, somewhere between midnight and dawn, and there was no one to see her.

All she could think of, beyond the next step and the next, was the need to replace what she had lost. She needed blood. She needed skin.

Annie's father had no time to scream, so fast and deep did the blade of his prized filleting knife slide through his jugular and windpipe, choking him with a gurgle like the last drops of water swirling down a drain. The last thing he saw was a nightmare vision: his daughter's best friend with a face that was little more than a blackened hunk of meat. A single eye like boiled egg-white stared out at him and a crooked finger pressed against her lipless mouth: ssshh.

She strangled Annie and her mother in their sleep, so that the skin could be preserved. This she would keep, neatly folded and vacuum packed in the freezer, until it was time to leave.

As she lay, several hours later, in a warm bath, she and the living tissue melted together, bringing blessed relief to her burns and hydrating her at the same time. She blinked slowly and then drowsed, letting herself drift, the smell of blood and fat in the hot water as comforting as incense.

She didn't dare stay longer than a couple of days. When she left in the dead of the night with all of her most prized possessions in a couple of travel bags, she didn't quite look human. She wasn't certain she ever would, but she wore her hat with the brim low, kept her head down, and hoped. Now and then she had the opportunity to check her reflection in the windows of the buses and trains on which she travelled, and she noticed a change for the better. The scars were not setting but moving and smoothing out, accompanied by a maddening itch.

By the time the news report aired about the serial killer the police were calling the Templeton Skinner, Sister was nowhere near the town. She had pawned some of Annie's mother's jewellery and booked a hotel room in Jonesburg, a suburb just outside of the big city.

The place might have looked dingy to anyone else, but to Sister it was nothing short of magical. It was a palace, from the mouldy tub in which she lay to the stained mattress on which she slept. The first night, she didn't sleep at all but lay in the dark daydreaming about her future in the big bad city.

It had seemed impossible, but she had escaped Holly at last. The mad little dictator had taken her medicine and, incredibly, Sister had not evaporated along with her creator. She knew that partly it was because she was linked with Alex, somehow. She had taken something of her in those early days of transformation – and even now she had a lingering connection with her doppelganger. Partly, though, it was because something of the House had moved into her during the collapse, and it was this that had kept her from perishing in the heat of the fire.

When she looked in the mirror the following morning, she discovered that not only had she healed completely, but the changes she'd made to herself before the fire had now cemented into her body. She stood naked with her arms and legs spread out, admiring her handiwork. She was a human, at last – a real living human. Just because she needed flesh instead of food to live didn't make her any less real. In her eyes, it made her more, if anything.

She smiled, and the smile in the mirror was more, too, because it was no longer an imitation of Alex's smile. This one belonged to her, and in the future, it would be the one she used when she met strangers for the first time. Bright and sweet and warm.

Later that night, she took a walk along the highway, which ran quite high along the hills of Jonesburg, and found a breathtaking view of the city. The lights shone out of the dim smog like colourful stars in a galaxy. So many people, so many games to play. She breathed in the thick air and vowed to leave tomorrow.

So much to see and do.

My eggs are laid.

THE END

ABOUT THE AUTHOR

Ben Pienaar was born in South Africa and moved to Melbourne, Australia in 1999. He works in a bottle shop to finance his crippling caffeine addiction and spends his non-writing time surfing, playing chess, and training Jiu Jitsu. He has published stories in several anthologies and magazines, and more of his work can be found at www.freenightmares.me

He's currently working on his second novel *'Neighbourhood Kids'* and is set to publish his second short story collection later in 2021.

Other HellBound Books Titles
Available at: www.hellboundbookspublishing.com

ReIncarnate

Cil Franklen wasn't good. He wasn't nice, liked, or thin. Hell, he wasn't even handsome!
And soon, he wouldn't even be HIM!
Some people get the chance to do good things: Bill Gates, Al Pacino, Einstein, Mother Teresa, Martin Luther King. Given a little magic, people can be magical, but not Cil. He just wanted to kill. All life's fog built up in him to the point of leaking out... but it wasn't the pleasant puffy fog - it was dark and sickening.

Cil found a way to live again. And again, and again and again.

And he killed again. And again, and again, and, again. REINCARNATION!

The Dead Room

A week before Christmas, terrorists detonate dozens of dirty bombs throughout Britain and release a man-made contagion, leading Nicola Allen to begin a frantic hunt for her husband and daughter while a nation burns. Fleeing from a horrendous event she refuses to speak of and desperate to find shelter in a dying country, Nicola's sister-in-law, Cate, takes cover in a partly destroyed hospital. Terrorised by visions of mutilated bodies and the screams of phantom children, Cate joins a group of survivors, all of whom are under attack by ruthless scavengers and looters. If Nicola is to have any chance of finding her family and if Cate is to escape from the siege, they must reunite and then descend into the belly of the ruined hospital where the horrific truth of what truly connects the two women is waiting for them. Waiting for them down in the dead room.

The Toilet Zone
RESTROOM READING AT ITS MOST FRIGHTENING!

Compiled and edited by the grand master of 80's schlock horror, Bret McCormick, each one of this collection of 32 terrifying tales is just the perfect length for a visit to the smallest room....

At the very boundaries of human imagination dwells one single, solitary place of solitude, of peace and quiet, a place in which your regular human being spends, on average, 10 to 15 minutes - at least once every single day of their lives.

Now, consider a typical, everyday reading speed of 200 to 250 words per minute - that means your average visitor has the time to read between 2,500 to 4,000 words, which makes each and every one of these 32 tales of terror - from some of the best contemporary independent authors - within this anthology of horror the perfect, meticulously calculated length. Dare you take a walk to the small room from where inky shadows creep out to smother the light and solitude's siren call beckons you?

Dare you take a quiet, lonely walk into… The Toilet Zone

Invasive Species

A monster has come to Maldus, Arkansas, and the residents of the small mountain town are too busy to notice. With the monster comes something even more terrifying and threatening than gnashing teeth or razor-sharp claws. The monster has brought change.

The residents of the small mountain town are too busy to notice at first. Busy with things such as addiction, racism, work, or land deals. Unnoticed, the change the monster brings in its insidious wake spreads like wildfire. Unnoticed, the town of Maldus falls prey to an Invasive Species.

Tremble

Widow and single mother, Rebecca Noland, wants nothing more than to rekindle the passion with her overworked fiancé, Detective Dan Slaviche. Expecting to surprise him by slipping into his apartment before he comes home from work, her curiosity gets the best of her when she discovers the key to unlock his desktop. What she finds there is a nightmare that sends her, along with her seven-year-old son, running for their lives.

Terrified and broke, her only option is to flee to her family's estate in Tremble, Tennessee where memories of her mother's violent death still haunt her childhood home.

But bad memories aren't the only thing that await her.

As Dan abandons all morals in his attempt to locate his bride-to-be, Rebecca struggles to make the house a home for her son while growing closer to her next-door neighbors.

Her sanity comes into question when she realizes the entity responsible for her mother's murder is lying in wait, intent on destroying anyone who tries to come between it and the object of its deadly obsession… her.

**A HellBound Books LLC
Publication 2021**

www.hellboundbookspublishing.com

Printed in the United States of America

www.ingramcontent.com/pod-product-compliance
Lightning Source LLC
Chambersburg PA
CBHW061310190726
48288CB00002B/435